HOLY TERROR

"It's vitally important that we stand up and fight," said the minister. "Everyone who has the courage, join me at the altar."

People shifted, whispered, looked around. The double doors at the rear of the nave crashed open.

Everyone jumped, twisted in his seat. After an instant of silence, the screaming started.

Vasquez advanced down the center aisle. He had become so obese that he repeatedly bumped his hips against the pews. He was nude. His jaws, jutting like the muzzle of a carnivorous dinosaur, gaped impossibly wide as he snapped at the fleshy, purple hunk of meat clutched in his hand.

Vasquez gobbled the last of the meat, licked and sucked his fingers. The terrified crowd fell silent.

"Congratulations, Reverend," he said. "This is quite a turnout for a weekday."

Praise for Richard Lee Byers's previous novel:

"THE BOOK IS A WINNER, AND SO IS THE AUTHOR."

—ED BRYANT, *Locus*

"ENTERTAINING AND INTERESTING."

—*SCIENCE FICTION CHRONICLE*

DARK FORTUNE

RICHARD LEE BYERS

DIAMOND BOOKS, NEW YORK

This book is a Diamond original edition, and has never
been previously published.

DARK FORTUNE

A Diamond Book / published by arrangement with
the author

PRINTING HISTORY
Diamond edition / January 1993

ISBN: 1-55773-864-5

Diamond Books are published by The Berkley Publishing Group,
200 Madison Avenue, New York, New York 10016.
The name "DIAMOND" and its logo are trademarks
belonging to Charter Communications, Inc.

PRINTED IN THE UNITED STATES OF AMERICA

10 9 8 7 6 5 4 3 2 1

For Keith

DARK FORTUNE

1

TOM CARPENTER TRIPPED over the curb and grabbed the lamppost to keep from falling. The narrow brick street rolled upward like the picture on a defective television.

Tom's stomach squirmed; he closed his eyes. It had been years since he'd done any heavy drinking. Somehow he'd managed to forget that he didn't *like* being dizzy and clumsy.

He'd order food and a nonalcoholic drink in the next bar. Abstaining or not, he had to find a next, because all the restaurants and movies had closed hours ago, and he still wasn't ready to face what was undoubtedly waiting at home.

When he sensed that the world had stabilized, he opened his eyes and peered up and down the street. Then he blinked and looked again.

He was lost.

Considering how much he'd imbibed, maybe it wasn't too strange that he'd strayed from Martin Avenue without realizing it. But he would have sworn that he was familiar with every street in the parish, and yet he couldn't tell where he was.

It only rattled him for a second. Wherever he was, he couldn't have wandered far. Sooty two-, three-, and four-story buildings with wrought-iron balconies lined the sidewalks. Many of the street lights were broken. The overflowing garbage cans stank, and when the fitful wind gusted, litter rustled and scraped down the gutters. All in all, it looked like every other commercial street in Corona City. Dark as the night was and muddled as he felt, so what if he didn't recognize this particular block?

Grinning at his own timidity, weaving slightly, he hurried past storefronts sealed with sheets of graffiti-covered plywood and others caged in burglar bars toward the only illuminated doorway ahead.

But when he reached it, he hesitated. There was no sign and no neon beer logos, just a bare green bulb glowing above the door. Maybe it wasn't a bar.

Well, it would be easy enough to find out. He didn't know why he was standing here staring at the brass door handle as if it were going to bite him. He gripped it and pulled.

The space inside was blacker than the street. Black like a bar. He groped his way forward, ran into a curtain, pushed through.

It wasn't a bar after all.

The room smelled of dust and incense. A few solitary candles burned here and there atop sagging bookshelves. Ranks of multicolored jars and bottles gleamed in one display case, crystals, jewelry, and a glass ball on a three-footed stand in another; posters depicting the zodiac and a hand surrounded by odd symbols and pointing arrows decorated the left-hand wall.

Nope, not a bar and no place for him. He turned to leave.

Something stirred in the shadows at the back of the shop. "We're open. Please don't go." The voice was a rich, jolly baritone.

When he squinted, Tom could just barely make out a counter with a massive antique cash register and a figure seated behind it. "Sorry, I'm in the wrong place."

"Not as far as I'm concerned," the man at the counter said. "I don't care whether you buy anything. You're the first living soul I've seen since this morning and I'd be profoundly grateful for a few minutes of your society. Would you like to share my supper? I have fresh Cuban bread, and ham, salami, and cheese from the deli down the way."

"Sounds good, but—" Tom's stomach growled, a long, loud gurgle. Both men laughed. "Well, I was planning to get something to eat, and I guess you can tell I love Cubans. Okay, what the heck."

As Tom crossed the room the shopkeeper's features swam out of the murk. He was a pudgy little cherub of a man dressed in a baggy pinstriped suit. His polka-dot tie was loose, his vest and collar unbuttoned. He'd combed his few remaining strands of hair to cover as much scalp as possible.

His lucent gray eyes glittered.

When he met their gaze, Tom felt a chill. Had liquor always made him this paranoid? Shrugging off his trepidation, he opened the folding chair propped against the wall.

The shopkeeper glanced over his shoulder at a percolator seething and bubbling away on a rickety three-legged table. "We'll have espresso ready in a moment."

"Great. I wondered if you had electricity."

"Oh, certainly. I just like flame." He began pulling food, dishes, cups, silverware, and condiments out from under the counter. "I can't tell you how delighted I am that you decided to stay. I must confess, I didn't think you would. I thought you'd be afraid of what your congregation would say if they caught you consorting with the proprietor of a *botanica*."

Tom remembered he wasn't wearing his collar. "How'd you know I was a minister?"

"Your picture was in the paper."

"Oh, yeah." Once, six months ago, when the *Register* ran its first story about the Coalition. "You have a good memory."

"So aren't you afraid?" the little man prompted again.

Tom smeared mustard on his bread. "I was for just a second. But I'm sure some of the flock already spotted me boozing my way down Martin, so it's a little late to worry about scandalizing them now. I don't know, maybe I *want* to scandalize them."

The shopkeeper smiled; his apple cheeks dimpled. "Would you like to tell me about it?"

"I guess not really."

They ate in companionable silence for a while. Then the

little man said, "Actually, it would be more productive if *I* told *you* about it."

"Come again?"

"I'm a cartomancer. I tell fortunes with cards."

Of course he did; after all, he made his living pandering to people's superstitions. If Tom were sober, he would have been expecting some kind of a come-on. "I'm afraid I've drunk my wallet pretty dry."

"But you're my guest. It would be gratis, of course."

No kidding. Maybe Tom was misjudging him. "That's nice of you, but . . . no offense, but I just don't believe in this stuff."

The cartomancer sighed. "A priest who doesn't credit the supernatural. I suppose it's a sign of the times."

"Don't get me wrong. I believe in God." A little, sometimes. "But not *santeria* or root or any of that."

"If you're right, then it would just be a harmless parlor game, now wouldn't it? Please, Mr. Carpenter. I'd like to offer you some guidance, and I believe I can if you'll only permit me to try."

Well, Tom supposed, it would be rude to disappoint his host. Besides, it might give him an idea for a sermon, and at least it would delay his return home that much longer. "All right," he agreed, "if you don't mind parting the veil for a hardcore skeptic."

The cartomancer smiled. "There's no one in this world I'd rather read for."

Reaching back under the counter, he produced a worn wooden box with a five-pointed star inlaid on the lid. Inside it was a stack of foxed, musty-smelling pasteboards.

Dexterous as a cardsharp, he started riffling through them. "Are you at all familiar with the Tarot?"

"I've heard the name, that's all."

"The ancestor of our modern playing cards, a cryptogrammic key to the occult sciences, and the most acute instrument of divination ever devised. This particular pack dates from the sixteen hundreds, and the philosopher who created it gave it some extraordinary properties. Aha! Here you are, the King of Cups. A brown-haired, hazel-eyed man of divinity." He laid the card on the counter top.

Tom examined it curiously. A robed, crowned man with an outsize goblet in his hand sat on a throne that rose from the sea. Despite the crude drawing and the faded ink, the king's face actually did seem to resemble his own. Funny coincidence. Or, more likely, a trick of the alcohol and the dim, wavering candlelight.

"Shuffle, then cut the deck three times with your left hand," the little man said. "The hand closest to your heart."

"But also the *sinister* one, the hand of evil." Tom smiled to show he was kidding.

"Some say. It's an oversimplification."

"There you are. Shuffled and cut."

The cartomancer set the first card on top of the king, the second on top of that but at right angles, the next four in a cross around it, and a final four in a vertical line to the right of the cross. Then he pursed his lips, furrowed his brow, and leaned forward to study them.

He looked so grim that after a few moments Tom couldn't help chuckling. "Give it to me straight, Doc. How long have I got?"

The cartomancer managed a wan little smile in return. "It's not *that* bad, but—well, I'd better take you through it step by step. The first thing I'd like you to notice is that half the cards belong to the suit of Swords."

"Is somebody going to challenge me to a duel?"

"Not in the literal sense, but Swords are cards of strife. There are also three Cups, cards of emotion. Unfortunately, in combination with the Swords these particular three suggest distress."

"Not the thrill of victory but the agony of defeat."

The little man pointed to the first card, a faceless, black-cloaked figure brooding over five overturned chalices. "The Five of Cups defines the climate of your life; it tells me you feel bitter and disappointed. Everything you've worked for is turning into trash."

Tom was somewhat taken aback. It was general, but it was

dead-on. "I bet you'd tell the same thing to any thirty-nine-year-old drunken preacher who sat down here."

"Only if the Tarot told me first. The Five of Swords crosses you." The card depicted a victor and the vanquished, a sneering warrior with two wounded captives sprawled at his feet. The conqueror was clasping three blades; two more, no doubt trophies from some previous battle, hung from the tree behind him. "It represents your enemy."

"He looks mean."

"He's cruel, cunning, and determined, so you must keep your guard up. He'll crush you if you let him."

Next he indicated the pasteboard below the king, a peasant-type staring in slack-jawed wonder at the apparitions, a dragon, a castle, and a Medusa among them, rising from the mouths of seven floating cups. "This card represents the tendencies that made you what you are today. It denotes wild fantasy and unrealistic expectations, sometimes overt delusions."

Tom grimaced. The cards had him pegged again.

"Here behind you is the Six of Cups," the cartomancer continued. It showed a man walking away from a stack of goblets. "You recently turned away from something or someone in disgust.

"And above you is the Hermit." An old, bearded man with an upraised lantern gazed into an abyss; his card was upside down. "Someone wise will offer sound advice."

Tom wondered again whether the little man was hoping to run a scam on him. "Does this wise man have a mayonnaise stain on his lapel?"

The cartomancer snorted. "If he does, he won't try to charge a single penny for any service he provides you. Now will you please forget about protecting your pocketbook and just listen to the reading? What I'm doing isn't as easy as it looks."

"Sure. I'm sorry."

The card to the right of the king was inverted too, a thin, frowning queen with a sword in her hand. "This is your immediate future. A stern, dark woman will rebuke you."

"Why didn't you tell me you knew my wife?"

The cartomancer pointed to the seventh card, at the base of the vertical line. Once again it was upside down. This one depicted the Grim Reaper slashing down human wheat with his bloody scythe; there were severed heads and limbs heaped around his feet. "Here's what you fear."

"Who doesn't?"

"The trump doesn't signify death when it's reversed. It represents stagnation and inertia. You suspect that you're going to spend the next twenty years living exactly the life you're living now, and the notion is nearly enough to make you scream."

Just above Death was a gagged and blindfolded maiden chained to a torture rack fashioned out of eight swords. "Here are your friends and family," the cartomancer said.

"I didn't know any of them were into bondage," Tom joked. Maybe he should suggest it. Becky certainly wasn't very interested in normal sex anymore.

"I'm afraid you're the one in bondage. You feel trapped by everyone's demands and expectations.

"The Knight of Swords reveals that you dream of being a hero." The knight was a mounted cavalier charging full tilt into battle, his plate armor flashing in the sunlight and his scarlet plume streaming backward in the wind.

But Tom *didn't* want to be a hero, not anymore. He was tired of trying to change the world. If he ever got loose from the eight-bladed torture machine, he'd go someplace where nobody knew him and spend the rest of his days blissfully minding his own business.

The last card showed a woman weeping. Nine swords hung on the ebon wall behind her. "And this card represents your final destiny," the little man said. "Misery, probably the loss of a loved one."

"Do you do this professionally? I can't imagine that you'd get any repeat business."

The cartomancer shook his head. "Your cards are so bleak, but you're so flippant. Is it because nothing I saw seems at all relevant to your life in any way, shape, or form?"

Tom opened his mouth to make still another joke, but for some reason the truth tumbled out instead.

"No," he said. "I don't know whether somebody told you all about me or you're just a whiz at sizing people up, but except for that nonsense about an implacable enemy, you were right on target.

"But your lousy cards didn't really offer me any help or hope at all. Why should I let myself take them seriously when it would only—" Suddenly he realized he was about to cry. Blinking furiously, he averted his face.

The little man affected not to notice. "I quite understand your dismay and I apologize for subjecting you to an unpleasant experience."

Tom brought his tear glands under control, then pushed his chair back. "That's all right. It was an interesting experience. But it's gotten very late and I'm turning maudlin. I'd better go."

"Wait. I told you, I want to help you."

"Believe me, you've done more than enough already."

"I thought the divination would tell us how you could improve your life, but apparently your destiny is fixed and can't be improved by conventional means. Fortunately, we're not limited to conventional means."

"You lost me."

"As I mentioned, this Tarot is special. It can do more than reflect a man's fate; it can reshape it."

Tom chuckled. "What do you mean, it will grant me three wishes or something?"

"No. These seventy-eight cards can be used to predict the future because they correspond to seventy-eight forces that together comprise the universe. If you want to personify them, you could think of them as seventy-eight angels who keep the world working the way God designed it to, with stars emitting light and gravity drawing matter together and so on.

"Not even an adept as advanced as the one who fashioned this deck could devise a tool that would coerce such entities into doing his bidding, granting wishes, as you put it. It would have been sacrilege to try. What he could and did do was design a way to petition them.

"It works quite simply. All you do is shuffle, then draw a card. The power represented by the one you choose will somehow manifest itself in your affairs."

"Why didn't we have miracles going off right and left when you told my fortune?" Tom asked.

"Because the deck only performs this particular function when someone wills it to.

"So," the little man prompted. "Would you care to pick a card?"

Tom grinned. "Nah, I don't think so. What if somebody up there doesn't like me? I could get turned into a frog or something."

"It doesn't matter that you don't believe. The cards will answer anyway."

He was right, Tom didn't believe.

But so much of the Tarot reading had seemed so accurate. What if he was wrong and it really would work?

If there was nothing to it, then it couldn't hurt, and if there was, then it could be the only chance he'd ever have to get his life back on track.

Bemused at his gullibility, Tom started gathering up the cards, then hesitated. "You did say this is free?"

The cartomancer rolled his eyes. "Yes, yes, a thousand times, yes! If you get it done before sunrise, I'll give *you* a shiny new dime."

"Just double-checking."

As he shuffled, the room darkened; two of the nearer candles guttered out. For some reason the cards now felt clammy, and as he fumbled them apart and slipped them back together their grave-mold odor intensified until he could almost imagine he was kneading rotten meat.

When he raised his head, the cartomancer was staring at him.

Tom shivered. He spread the deck across the counter and plucked a card from the middle, then set it down and wiped his hands on his pant legs.

"The High Priest," the cartomancer said.

The man on the pasteboard wore a pope's tiara and vestments, but he was standing in front of a menhir with a scourge and a long flint dagger in his hands. A female angel and a bat-winged succubus knelt before him, each offering a golden key.

Like the King of Cups, he had Tom's face.

2

THE OLD MAN propped up in the canopy bed looked like a deflated balloon. Inside the blotched gray folds of skin his body was as skinny as a pencil. Price was sure that some nurse must bathe him every day, but even from the doorway he could smell his sour odor. A dozen pill bottles and an untouched steak-and-egg breakfast sat on the table beside him.

"Terminal cancer," the old man said. "Take a good, long look. Everyone wants to, and it's better when they stare than when they peep."

The stooped, lanky kid in the tailored suit patted him on the shoulder. "Please, Papa, don't call it terminal. Dr. Warner—"

The old man pushed his hand away. "Idiot. Mr. Price, meet my son Steven the idiot. He's afraid I'll cut him out of my will."

Steven flushed and started to say something, then looked at his feet and swallowed instead.

Price walked to the old man's bedside, his heels clicking on the parquet floor. It took a while; the room was nearly as big as his whole apartment. "Nice to meet you, Mr. Vasquez. Sorry you're sick."

Vasquez snorted. "Don't worry about it. If I hire you, I'll pay you a lot up front. Actually, it wouldn't be so bad if I could eat. I love to eat. Three years ago I weighed two hundred and eighty pounds.

"Pull up a chair. Steven's going to tell you what I want."

Steven scuffed his foot like a shy student forced to address the class. "My family owns a lot of property," he began, "some in nearly every part of the county but most of it here in Corona City. My father thinks he has a right to manage it as he sees fit."

Price surmised that the old man screwed some people making his money. "Sounds reasonable."

"Well, a few years ago they brought a new pastor named Carpenter into the Holy Assembly church on Palm Street, and *he* doesn't think so."

"What's his problem?"

"Corona City is a depressed area. He seems to think my family is to blame for that, and that we could make it a paradise on earth if we only would."

"Specifically what does he want you to do?"

"A lot of things. We own commercial buildings that are currently standing empty. There are tax advantages, we avoid competition with our own stores, and we think we'll be able to sell to a developer at some point in the future if they aren't tied up in leases. So we don't do much maintenance and we don't rent them except at a very good rate on a month-to-month basis."

"So you wind up with no new businesses making no new jobs, and Reverend Carpenter is ticked."

"He also objects to the way we keep up our apartments, the rents we charge on those, and the prices in our groceries and drugstore."

"What does he do, preach about it?"

"At first he just came around and pleaded. Then he brought us petitions. Papa didn't mind that. But when Carpenter realized we weren't going to listen, he organized this pressure group he called the Corona Coalition.

"They go through our properties making lists of code violations, which they send to the building inspectors, the city manager, and the fire marshal. They tried to organize a boycott of our stores, bused people outside the area to do their shopping. Now they're talking about rent strikes, and lobbying the city to put up a low-income housing project. The point of it all is to make it unpleasant and unprofitable for my father to conduct business unless he does it Carpenter's way."

"Is it working?"

"No," the old man said. "Not yet. Although I suppose eventually it might. But it keeps the newspapers interested in me, and I don't want some nosy reporter uncovering the details of every private deal I ever made.

"Actually, though, I don't think that's likely to happen either." Grunting, he struggled to sit up straighter. "But my great-grandfather *built* Corona City. Since then a Vasquez has always run it and I run it now. Running it is about the only satisfaction I have left, and I'll be *damned* if I'll stand for a pissant preacher and a bunch of niggers and white trash trying to dictate what I can and cannot do with it. *That's* why I want this bastard Carpenter stopped."

Steven grinned; a hot light flared in his watery eyes. "We sent for you because you're supposed to have contacts. You can get someone beaten up, or a church burned down."

Startled, Price almost took a step backward. Who would have guessed it? Vasquez's little nebbish son was a sickie.

Price didn't like clients who had a thing about violence. They always wanted a detective to act out their daydreams, even when it wasn't the most efficient way to solve their problems. It could get you killed.

But he needed a fat job and he needed it outside Miami, where bill collectors from Vegas couldn't find him, so he guessed he was going to put up with it.

Vasquez said, "Let's not get ahead of ourselves. For the time being, I just want you to investigate him. I'd much rather solve the problem by discrediting him than get involved in anything criminal. All these modern ministers seem to steal from the offering box and sodomize the choirboys, so you ought to be able to find some dirt.

"But even if he's clean, I intend to be rid of him."

Price nodded. "Let's talk about my fee."

3

BECKY HAD INTENDED to stay awake until Tom came home, but some time after three she drifted off. When she awoke, sweaty and shaky from some unremembered nightmare, his half of the bed was still empty. Really frightened now, she raked her black curls out of her eyes, threw on her ratty flannel robe, and hurried downstairs to phone the police.

He was asleep on the living room couch.

Part of her wanted to sob and hug him and another part wanted to give him hell. When she stepped closer, she smelled the booze; the angry part won.

"Did you have fun?" she asked.

His bloodshot eyes fluttered open; he winced. He looked haggard and miserable and for a moment she felt a little flicker of guilt.

She squelched it. He was the one who should feel guilty.

"I'm sure half your congregation's already complained to the Regional Council," she continued, "so I just hope you had a glorious good time."

Tom swung his feet to the floor and sat up. "I don't suppose this could wait until I clean up?"

"I've been waiting for you since seven o'clock last night. Don't you think I've waited long enough?"

"All right, but let's cut to the chase. I humbly apologize for screwing up at the catechism class. I beg forgiveness for not coming home. I promise it'll never happen again. After I shower, I'll make some calls and smooth everybody's ruffled feathers." He started to get up.

"Is *that* all you've got to say?"

He collapsed back onto the couch. "Please, have mercy,

don't screech. I groveled to you and I said I'd grovel to the rest of my masters. What else is there?"

"I want to know just what you thought you were doing."

He smiled, not the old boyish grin she now saw so seldom but a weary twist of the lips that was almost a sneer. "No you don't. You haven't wanted to know what I think in a long time."

"Bullshit. The truth is, you care so little about me that you don't even think I deserve to know."

"That's *not* true! I—Look, you want an explanation, I'll give you one."

She sat down on the ripped red fake-leather recliner they'd bought at the church rummage sale two years ago. "Thank you so much."

"My day started swell, with hookers back working the corner in front of the church. In the morning, can you believe it? So I called the cops to shoo them away. One patrol car cruised by two hours later. It didn't stop and it didn't come back again."

"Well, they're busy. And there's not a lot they can do if they don't actually see people breaking the law."

"So they keep telling me. Anyway, the working girls were still outside to proposition the elders when they showed up for our board meeting. I wouldn't be surprised if some of them accepted."

"I really hope you didn't do anything stupid at the meeting."

"No, my love. I maintained my clerical dignity, even though it wasn't easy. They spent over an hour griping because I recommended we sell that land to fund a comprehensive social services program, but then the church needed a new roof, the mortgage payment went up, revenues dropped, and now somehow there still isn't any money. You would have thought I embezzled it."

He sounded so resentful that she couldn't help feeling a twinge of sympathy. He wasn't supposed to be solely responsible for church administration and finances, but everyone always acted as if he were.

Tom began pulling off his loafers and socks. "After the

meeting broke up, I heard from Johnny Langone. He's talked to a bunch of Vasquez's tenants and it's no go on the rent strike; a lot of them don't even want to record violations anymore. They said they don't know where they'd live if Vasquez evicted them or their buildings got condemned. I had to admit, I didn't know either. It made me feel like a real cloistered, arrogant, bleeding-heart idiot. What right have I got to gamble with *their* lives?

"Then Mrs. Donovan showed up to whine about her husband's incontinence. I tried to be sympathetic, but how many times am I going to have to listen to it? What am I supposed to tell her that I haven't said a hundred times already? If she insists on keeping the old vegetable at home, she's going to have to mop up his pee.

"It took me until six to get rid of her," he continued. "Since it was already time for catechism class, I'd missed dinner.

"After the day I'd had, I was pretty down, but I brightened myself up by sheer willpower. I wanted to be good with the kids."

He was crazy about children. Becky often wondered if he'd still love her the way he used to if she'd been able to give him some.

He crossed his legs, idly scratched the top of his foot. "But the kids weren't interested in being good with me. I don't know what got into them, but I've never seen them behave so badly. They fidgeted, whispered, giggled. Threw paper wads and passed notes. When I tried to calm them down, they sassed me. Even Willie Harper! I don't know how many hours I've spent trying to bring him out of his shell, and there he sat giving me lip!

"I'd thought it was going to be the one pleasant part of my day and it was awful. I wound up screaming and kicking over a chair, and that finally shut them up.

"And as I stood there in front of their sullen little faces, droning away about the Apostle's Creed, I suddenly realized that it was the first time that day that I'd thought about God.

"Actually, I was reciting by rote and barely even thinking

about Him then. I was concentrating on forcing the kids to obey me.

"I wondered why I expected them to act interested and respectful when I talked about religion, when obviously it didn't mean anything to me.

"And then I walked out. I just couldn't bear to stay there any longer."

Becky found that much of her anger had drained away; in its place was a wary tenderness. "Sounds like it was all pretty awful."

"I never pray anymore, except when some parishioner expects me to."

She didn't know what to say. He was the one who was supposed to know how to rekindle people's faith. "Didn't you tell me that even Jesus and the disciples doubted?"

"Sure, but they could always perform a few miracles to reassure themselves. I can't even control a roomful of kids without throwing furniture and foaming at the mouth.

"When I was little, I thought I could *feel* God out there somewhere. But I don't feel Him now and I don't suppose I ever really did."

"Whatever you feel inside," Becky said soothingly, "you're good at your job. You provide comfort and support for a lot of people."

"What's the matter with you?" he snapped. "I'm a minister, not a salesman. It's not okay for me to convince people to buy into the Bible if I don't believe in it myself."

When he lost his temper, so did she. In a way, she was grateful that he'd given her an excuse; getting mad was better than feeling helpless and vulnerable. "Then quit," she said, "and do something else. Maybe we'll finally earn enough money to live decently."

"It's not that easy."

"If you had any balls, it would be easier than whining and screwing up until they fire you."

He stood up and started emptying his pockets, flinging down coins and keys to crack against the glass-topped coffee table. "I don't know why I tried to talk to you. It's not like

you've said a single word to show me that you missed me or
worried about me last night."

Of course not; she wouldn't give him the satisfaction.
"Frankly, I wish you'd stayed away a little longer, long
enough to get bored with self-pity. But I don't suppose a
hundred years would be long enough for that."

"Is that what you think I'm all about?" He thrust his hand
into another pocket.

"You're damn right I do. You're healthy, you have a
home—"

His eyes widened in surprise; she realized that his groping
fingers had encountered something he hadn't remembered
he had.

"What is it?" she asked.

"Nothing!" Strangely, for a moment his voice seemed rich
with over- and undertones, seemed to resonate like the
church organ. She was probably getting another headache.

"Oh, it's something," she said. "Some charming souvenir
of last night's adventures. Please, give me a treat and let me
see." If it was some woman's phone number, she'd kill him.

"I told you, it's *nothing*!" he shouted; the final word split
the air like a thunderclap.

It rocked Becky backward in her chair. She knew his
voice couldn't possibly have been as loud as it sounded, but
nonetheless her heart started pounding and she shuddered.

"All right," she stammered. "I just thought—I don't know
what I thought."

"It's not like you really believed I was carrying evidence
of some heinous crime," he said in a normal tone. "You were
just fishing for something else you could hold against me. I
love you, Beck, but it's no wonder our marriage is falling
apart when your greatest pleasure in life is putting me
down."

Suddenly she felt giddy; her anger and consternation began to swirl away like water down a drain.

She struggled to hold on to them. After all, she had a right
to take him to task when he was hurting himself. Surely their
marital problems weren't *all* her fault. And it was obvious

from his reactions that there *was* something peculiar, maybe even something damning, in his pocket.

But rationalizing her feelings didn't help. A few seconds later she couldn't even remember what she'd been thinking.

She sniffled. "I'm sorry," she said.

"Good Lord, you really are, aren't you?"

"More than you'll ever know. I just want to make you happy, and when you're not, I feel like a terrible failure. For some reason that makes me snipe at you, and then of course everything gets a thousand times worse."

Tom shook his head. "Heaven knows I'm not complaining, but how did you go from sour to sweet so fast? You sound like a different person."

"I sound like the *real* me now. Oh, Tom, I love you so much, and whatever you do I'll support you and try very hard not to hassle you about anything ever again. Can I have a hug?"

He gave her one, one-armed for the first few moments. He was slow taking his other hand out of his pocket.

4

BY THE TIME Tom finished dressing, the morning sun was flashing rainbows through the crystal suspended in the bedroom window. His hangover was little more than a memory; the aroma of fresh coffee and the sound of something sizzling were actually making him hungry.

But before he went downstairs he wanted to make certain everything was all right. He pulled down the shade, listened until he heard Becky still bustling around in the kitchen, then carefully pulled open the top drawer of the old pine dresser and looked underneath the layer of pocket handkerchiefs. Just to be sure the High Priest was still there.

It was, of course. He'd stashed it only twenty minutes ago.

Now that he was looking at it again, he wanted to pick it up. Separated from its fellows, its odor was almost imperceptible. It still felt a little squishy, but not unpleasant. The priest's face still resembled Tom's to a degree, but not nearly as much as it had seemed to last night.

Funny that the cartomancer had given it to him. If it really was part of a unique set and over three hundred years old.

Yeah, right. The little man probably had crates of them. They were probably printed in Taiwan and aged with chemicals.

He'd said that if Tom kept the pasteboard on his person, the celestial power associated with it would intervene in his life more quickly. Well, now that it was the morning after, Tom was embarrassed that he'd entertained the notion that the Tarot deck might actually be magical for even a single instant, so of course he didn't feel obliged to carry it around.

But it was interesting-looking—fascinating, really—and he'd enjoyed keeping it as a souvenir.

He regretted having to lie to Becky, but his instincts had probably been sound. She would have gone off like an H-bomb if he'd told her that he'd participated in something that many of his parishioners would consider a satanic ritual.

Or maybe not. Maybe she would suddenly have turned conciliatory anyway. He still couldn't quite believe how her attitude had flip-flopped; she'd pretty much taken all the blame for their problems on herself.

Which wasn't fair, and he'd felt a little guilty. He hadn't contradicted her, though. He'd waited too long to hear her apologize for *anything*.

And that was why he certainly wouldn't show her the card now. It would be stupid to do anything that could rock the boat now that things were finally going better.

He replaced the card and shut the drawer, wincing when it gave a tiny squeak. Then he tugged the bottom of the blind and it snapped back up.

His good mood began to curdle.

The parsonage stood behind the church parking lot and a hedge; from the upper story there was an unobstructed view of the street. Two women, one white and one black, were standing on the curb, right in front of the sign that announced the schedule of services and the topic of Sunday's sermon. The white one was a short-haired willowy redhead dressed in tight jeans and a denim jacket with a silvery fake-fur collar. The shorter, plumper, black one was wearing a platinum wig, an orange minidress, and high-heeled vinyl boots.

It would be pointless to call the police. They wouldn't do any more than they'd done yesterday. It was time he dealt with the situation himself.

He strode through the door, stopped on the landing, came back. Perhaps he would carry the High Priest, just because he felt like it. After all, a lot of people carried mementos and good-luck charms, and the card was fun to look at. He re-opened the drawer and slipped the pasteboard into his inside jacket pocket.

Becky spotted him when he stepped off the stairs. Her

wide mouth was still smiling, her green eyes bright. "It's breakfast," she said.

She looked so pretty that he wanted to forget about the hookers, forget about eating, for that matter. But he supposed he'd better take care of business. "I hope I'll be back in just a few minutes."

"Where are you going?"

"Our streetwalkers are back. This time I'm going to handle them myself."

Her smile slipped a notch. "What are you going to do?"

"Talk." What did she think he was going to do, punch them out?

"Are you sure you should?" She picked at a bit of egg yolk stuck to the front of her KISS THE COOK apron. "You haven't made those calls yet, and if people see you involved in some kind of altercation—"

"Jesus worked with the whores, the lepers, and the tax collectors, and I'm supposed to also. I promise you, nothing untoward will happen. You said you were going to be on my side from now on, and I'm about to try to do my job properly like you wanted in the first place, so don't give me a hard time, okay?"

He was sure he hadn't snarled or raised his voice, but she almost seemed to cringe. "I'm sorry. Just please, be careful."

"Sure will." He pecked her on the cheek and headed for the door.

The redhead glanced back and saw him approaching. She murmured something in her companion's ear and the black woman turned around too.

Tom said, "Good morning. I'm Tom Carpenter, the pastor of the church."

The black woman smiled, revealing a gold star inlaid on an upper front tooth. The redhead just stared.

Tom asked, "May I know your names?"

The black woman looked at her friend as though asking permission to reply. Tom didn't see even a tiny nod or the slightest change of expression, but after a moment she said, "I'm Grace and my friend is Miriam."

"I, uh, know what you do for a living. Aren't you out a little early?"

"We've been out since last night; we're supposed to keep working till Lester picks us up. We might get a little more business, you'd be surprised. One time—"

Miriam silenced her with an upraised hand. "What is it, Padre? Do you want to fuck?"

Tom felt his cheeks grow warm. "You can call me Tom, or Reverend if you want to be formal, and no, thank you, I don't."

"Then do us all a favor and go away."

"To tell you the truth, I was hoping that *you* would go away. You're not exactly helping the church's image."

Grace said, "I never thought of that. I'm sorry. But this is where Lester said he'd pick us up."

"Don't apologize!" Miriam rapped. "He doesn't own the fucking street."

"Of course I don't, and I'm not trying to *order* you away. I just hoped that if I pointed out the problem, you'd be willing to help me out."

"Maybe tomorrow—" Grace began.

"You're some piece of work, Padre," Miriam interrupted. "When you trotted out here, I thought you were going to try to change our sinful ways. But I guess you're like every other preacher; all you care about is whether your operation makes a good impression on the suckers who put money in the plate. Well, here's what I think of that." She tore open her large, glossy black handbag, rooted inside, then tossed some wrapped condoms, a few wadded-up lipstick-stained tissues, and three empty Cocktails-for-Two Tequila Sunrise bottles onto the dewy grass.

Tom took a deep breath, let it out slowly; some of his anger drained away. "It's not my job to judge people, and I don't usually confront them about the way they live unless they invite me to. Now, that sounded like an invitation.

"Do you really feel good about the way you live?" he said. "Are you proud of what you just did?"

"Hell, yes. I just fucking love myself to death."

"You don't sound like it. But God loves you. He loves you

so much, He gave you your life, an eternal life if you choose to make it one. So why do you want to defile His house?"

"I'll show you how glad I've always been that God put me in the world." She yanked back her left sleeve. The inside of her forearm was crosshatched with pink cracks and ridges. Two near the elbow were only half healed.

Tom felt the familiar helpless confusion rise again. What an agonizing life she must have had. Where did he get off, standing here prattling about a deity he wasn't even sure he believed in?

He lifted his hand, started fingering the top button of his sport coat.

"You've obviously had a rotten time," he said, "and I don't blame you for being angry. But—"

"You don't blame me? You don't *blame* me? Well, isn't that nice of you, and doesn't it just do me a ton of good!"

Grace said, "What's the point of us getting each other all upset? Lester will still find us down the street." She tried to take Miriam's arm but the redhead shook her off.

Tom let go of the button, slipped his fingers into the gap between his lapels. "What I'm trying to say—"

"That's all you chaplains and nuns and whatever ever do: *say*. Do you think it changes anything? Why don't you make God reach back in time and give baby Miriam to a mom who didn't drink. Or bring my little girl Karen back to life. Or just take away some of my memories. And if you can't, then what the hell use are you or Him either?"

Tom didn't know what to say.

He hooked his finger into his pocket and touched the High Priest.

Exhilaration flared through his flesh; he drew himself up straight.

"How did your little girl die?" he asked. "You killed her, didn't you?"

Grace gasped. Miriam said, "That's a dirty lie!"

"No. You didn't mean for it to happen, but it was your fault. If I'm wrong, then you tell me what really happened."

"I don't have to tell you shit!"

"No, he's got to be told," said Grace. "He wouldn't be

able to see as much as he has if God didn't want him to know."

Miriam's fingers curled into claws. "Don't you say another word to him or I swear I'll make you sorry."

"No, you won't." She tried to take Miriam's hand but the redhead jerked back out of her reach. "She told me about it a few months ago, when she was kind of drunk. The baby was a year old. She left her alone and she swallowed a piece of plastic and choked to death."

"Don't come home," Miriam said. She turned and began to walk away.

Tom grabbed her shoulder and spun her around.

"How dare you blame God for your misfortunes?" he demanded. "*He* gave you a child and *you* made her *die!*"

She tried to scratch his face; he caught her wrist. Tears streaked her mascara. "It was an accident! There was nobody to watch her and I couldn't feed us without money!"

"You didn't have to leave her unattended. If you'd prayed, God would have found a way to help you. Instead you chose to go and sell your body. Maybe God took your daughter because you were a dirty slut and didn't deserve to have her!"

She'd stopped thrashing. Now she was just quivering, weeping, and shaking her head.

"And you didn't learn a thing from it, did you? You're still sinning. In fact, I imagine you spit in God's eye every chance you get, just like here this morning. It's too bad, because sinners who won't repent wind up in Hell.

"And I think I know what your corner of Hell will be like. They'll chain you up in a room with your baby and a piece of plastic. You'll have to watch as she swallows it. She'll make little retching sounds. Turn blue. Convulse, get weaker, and finally stop moving.

"Then they'll stick a red-hot poker up her vagina, or do some other horrible thing to bring her back to life and make her spit out the plastic, and it'll all start over."

Miriam's makeup was an utter ruin now. Her nose was red, her upper lip glistening with snot. She was thoroughly cowed, so he rounded on Grace.

"And there's something equally painful waiting for you.

Maybe you never murdered a baby, but you're just as filthy a sinner in the eyes of God."

"I don't want to be! Dear Jesus, please forgive me!" Her dismay was almost comical.

Now that his sudden rush of energy was waning, Tom felt a little dismayed himself. Where had all this fire-and-brimstone stuff come from? He almost never talked about damnation; he'd always believed that people should embrace God out of love, not fear and guilt. In retrospect, what he'd said seemed alien. Even cruel.

Still, when the women dropped to their knees and folded their hands, he had to admit that it had got results.

5

WILLIE HARPER RAN home from school, his brown arms pumping and his rubber soles pounding the sidewalk. And it wasn't because he was afraid some other kid would want to harass him, not today; he just felt too good to go slow. Just before the start of algebra, Chuck Gutierrez, somebody *everybody* liked, had invited him to hang out with him at the football game Friday night.

When Willie razzed Reverend Carpenter, it was like he'd broken through a wall. Suddenly he wasn't the new kid anymore.

Actually, he felt a little bad about giving the minister a hard time, particularly since he'd gotten so upset. It was Reverend Carpenter who'd encouraged him to try to make friends with the other guys in the first place. But everybody else hated catechism class, or at least pretended to, and when they started goofing around, he just got swept up in it.

Maybe he could make it up to Reverend Carpenter some time when nobody else was around.

He dodged around a muttering bag lady and a man carrying cartons from a van into a storefront cigar factory. The grubby little secondhand furniture store and the pizza-and-subs shop that had closed last month flashed by, and then he was home.

The superintendent still hadn't fixed the broken lock, so he didn't have to stop and dig out his keys; he tore open the door and bounded up the stairs. By now he was gasping, and his long, skinny legs felt rubbery, but it would be pussy to stop running this close to the end. Besides, the stairwell smelled of piss.

His shoe crunched down on bits of broken glass. He grabbed the wooden knob on top of the newel post, swung himself onto the third-story landing, plunged through another door. A final exultant sprint down a dimly lit hallway and he skidded to a halt outside his own apartment.

The door was standing open several inches. The scent of marijuana hung in the air and cartoon music sounded from the television.

For a second, Willie tried to convince himself it didn't mean a thing. The building often smelled like grass, and maybe his mom had gotten off work early.

But he couldn't believe it, would have been too wary to enter even if he had. He started backing away.

The door swung open. "Hey, partner, long time no see. I got to warn you, you're going to rile the neighbors if you keep tearing around the halls like that."

Gary hadn't changed much; perhaps his short, stocky body was a little fatter, his grizzled black shoulder-length hair a little more tangled and greasy. But he was still wearing his favorite Rolling Stones tongue-logo T-shirt and tire-soled sandals; his piggish eyes still twinkled, and his grin was still wide and deceptively affable.

"So where's my welcome?" Gary asked.

Willie swallowed, croaked out, "Hi." Shoulders hunched, he sidled past the white man into the foyer.

He started toward his bedroom. But Gary said, "No, in here. We should get reacquainted." So he turned and followed him into the living room.

Gary lifted his backpack, duffel bag, and guitar case off the couch so they could both sit down. "I guess you can tell, I'm moving back in," he said.

Willie shrugged.

"This time I know it'll work," Gary continued. "The club scene is really booming along the beaches, and all those new studios in Orlando need musicians too. So now I can have a hell of a career right here.

"Your mama was mighty glad to see me, and I hope you are too. You should be; you need a man around the house."

Willie didn't want to answer, but he couldn't help himself. "I have a father."

"Well, kind of, but you hardly ever see him."

"That'll be different if he and Mom can ever work things out. He *wants* to see me."

Gary lifted the roach clip out of the ashtray, ignited his lighter, and applied the flame to the matter clasped at the end. "Let's not fight about it. I'm sure that's what he tells you, and all I know is what your mom says he tells her. Everybody knows about black dads, but maybe he's the exception.

"Anyway, it's not an either-or situation. You can love him and me both."

Willie wished he were brave enough to spit right in his face.

Gary sucked at the roach, then coughed. "Paulie says things have been tight lately. I bet you miss having all that money you used to cruise around with."

Willie shivered. "I'm all right."

"I know your mama would like to get her hands on some bucks. She can't like living in this rat-hole or seeing you walk around with six inches of leg sticking out of the bottom of last year's jeans."

"We're *okay*."

Gary shook his head. "You know you're not, and to be straight with you, I'm not in such great shape either. I had to hock my amp to get back home."

"Please, I don't want to do it anymore."

"Come on, let's look at the big picture. It's not like you ever got hurt or anything, and it's just to tide the family over until I get a gig; just one more time and then you'll never have to do it again. So what do you say we make your mother happy?"

Willie could *see* himself leaping up and dashing out the door; the image was as vivid as a movie. But he also felt faint, just like all the times before, and he knew he couldn't. "It's not right," he whimpered. "I could tell somebody."

Gary sighed. "We already talked about that, don't you remember? Sure, I guess you could turn tattletale, but who would you snitch *to*? Paulie loves me too much to believe you. Maybe there's an outside chance your dad would, but then he'd give your mama a bunch of shit, she'd hate him worse than ever, and she'd make sure you didn't see him at all anymore. And if you told somebody else, they'd take it to the cops. You'd wind up in a foster home, and then you wouldn't have either of your folks. Not only that, you'd make the papers, and all the other kids at school would find out exactly what you've been up to.

"I don't think you want that, so let's not have any more crap. If you give me a little cooperation, you know I'll make sure things don't get out of hand. But if you piss me off . . . well, I'm only human, and I can't guarantee that my hurt feelings won't get in the way of my taking really good care of you."

"Is this really the last time?" Willie asked. He despised himself for clutching at the lie.

"Cross my heart and hope my dick falls off. So you'll do it? Great!" Gary rose. "If you want, you can grab a soda from the fridge."

The room seemed to tilt. "It's—it's *now*?"

"No time like the present. You might as well get it over with, don't you think?"

Willie stood up. His eyes felt hot and wet, but he knew he wouldn't cry. After the first few times he'd stopped crying about anything, ever.

"Do you want that soda?" Gary asked. He shook his head. "Then come on."

Gary rested his hand on the boy's shoulder as they walked to his battered old MG. Willie wondered if he was afraid he'd try to run away. He shouldn't be; now that they were in motion, he felt even more helpless, like his body was a train and he was just a passenger locked inside.

They drove down Palm Street, right by his church. It looked remote and pristine, like a fairy-tale castle, all rough gray stone and gleaming white-painted wood. He could almost imagine that if a person had perfect faith and prayed really hard, an angel could swoop out of the belfry and carry him off to safety.

But it wouldn't; things like that only happened in the old days of the Bible stories. They turned a corner and the steeple disappeared behind a billboard.

Willie had avoided the intersection of Havana and Bolivar. As long as he didn't see the old factory, he could hope that it had been torn down or rented out. But it was still crouching there between two other empty buildings, looking as desolate as a crumbling tomb, its windows sealed with brick and plastered over so that they resembled the rolled-back eyes of someone having a seizure.

They picked their way through the weeds and trash to the rusty side door. Gary pushed the button twice, one short and one long; they couldn't hear the buzzer from outside.

After a minute the clown opened the door.

He hadn't changed much either. The greasepaint grin, the shaggy red wig, the shiny round nose, and the incongruous, expensive-looking blazer, dress shirt, slacks, and patent leather shoes were all the same.

Willie realized now that *nothing* had changed. He'd thought he could get over being scared and sad and ashamed all the time, but that was just some kind of stupid dream.

The clown led them inside, past the dusty, cobwebbed workbenches and piles of forgotten crates and boxes, and up the concrete stairs. The "studio" was ready, the still camera positioned on its tripod and the floodlights aimed. A little blond girl, probably a sixth- or fifth-grader, a year or two younger than him, was sitting on the edge of the bed playing with a tabby kitten, her eyes squinched up against the glare. The clown liked to tell kids that animals would have to be killed if they didn't do what he wanted.

Willie realized that he'd started undressing before they'd even told him to.

6

THE DEMON TOOK the baby's foot in its mouth and bit down. Karen writhed, blinked madly; she retched the plastic out and started screaming.

Miriam wailed and woke up. When the dream began to fade, she felt how cold she was.

A black form heaved in the darkness, Grace sitting up on her side of the waterbed. A moment later the lamp on the headboard clicked on.

"The noises you make, a person would think you were dying," Grace complained. "And I don't know why you bother to steal all the covers if you're just going to throw them on the floor."

"Sorry," Miriam muttered. She reached down to retrieve the tangled sheets and blankets.

"No, I'm sorry. I didn't mean to fuss. Was it the same dream?"

"You know it was." She tore at the covers, trying to separate them. "And I don't feel like talking about it anymore."

Grace snorted. "Now, how did I know you were going to say that?"

"Because I'm not a wimp."

"You never want to lean on anybody, but you can't live like that. Everyone needs a helping hand sometimes. Reverend Carpenter says so."

" 'Reverend Carpenter says so,' " Miriam mocked. "I hate that Bible-banging son of a bitch!"

"No you don't."

"All right, maybe I don't. But it's hard. I used to feel like dirt about half the time. Now I feel like *shit*, *all* the time, and I have the dream over and over again every night."

Grace pulled a flap of blanket over her legs. "I don't like myself much anymore, either. But I suppose that's what repentance means."

"The way Carpenter made it sound, even fucking saints sin once in a while, so nobody can ever stop repenting. So great, we get to feel this way forever."

"I don't think it'll be like that."

"I can take feeling low and guilty, but the dream is driving me crazy. I keep thinking, what if I really am seeing Hell and what if that baby really is Karen?"

"Oh, no! That couldn't possibly be!"

Miriam rolled over to face the wall. "It could. I never had her baptized."

"That doesn't mean anything. God loves innocent little children."

Miriam sank her long, lacquered nails into her palm to keep from crying. "I *want* to believe that, but how can I really *know*?"

"You just have to trust."

"Why can't you understand, that isn't an answer!"

"It's the best answer. We'll get Reverend Carpenter to explain it to you, better than I can. Right now why don't you try to fall back asleep?"

"Fat chance."

"Maybe you can if we get you warmed up." She pulled the covers up to Miriam's neck, then slipped her hands underneath to massage her shoulders and bare, goose-fleshed arms. "Hm. Let's get you loosened up, too. Your muscles feel like rocks."

"Damn it, you brainless slut, I don't want to be babied!" But she arched her spine in pleasure despite herself. She'd always loved Grace's back rubs.

"Of course you don't. Why would you want to get comfortable when you can stay frozen and tense?"

One of Miriam's vertebrae popped; she sighed. "Do you really think it's just a nightmare?"

"I think it's your conscience grumbling at you, but not a real vision of Hell."

"This does feel nice. It used to be that I was always the one who took care of you."

Grace gave a low, throaty chuckle. "That's not the way I remember it, but if you're right, then I guess it's my turn."

Miriam's flesh warmed, tingled. Her nipples came erect and her loins ached. Without letting herself think about what she was doing, she rolled over, caught Grace's wrists, and set her hands on her breasts.

Grace's full lips parted; her lustrous brown eyes glowed. Her fingers squeezing, she leaned forward for a kiss.

Then she snatched her hands away and wrenched herself back across the bed. "I'm sorry!" she stammered. "I shouldn't have touched you; it wasn't a good idea."

"Please, Grace. Just one last time, to help me get through tonight."

"You can have the bed. I'll take the couch."

"I'm hurting and I *need* you!"

"Don't you think I know that? I feel the same way. But it's part of what we're trying to put behind us. If we don't clean all the nastiness out of our lives, we never will feel better."

"It never seemed nasty till that bastard Carpenter started playing with our heads." Miriam shuddered, dug her nails into her flesh again. "Since Karen died, you're all I've ever had."

"You still do; it just can't be quite like it was. We're like sisters now."

"If that's the way you want it." She stood up.

Grace began to get up too. "Miriam—"

"Just stay in the fucking bed, *Sis*. I don't want to have to look at you till morning." She started to slam the door, forced herself to close it softly instead.

She threw herself down on the couch, grabbed the remote and turned on Letterman, switched him off and jumped back up an instant later. She stalked back and forth through the apartment, yearning to smash everything in sight.

She hated Grace for rejecting her, despised herself for craving an abomination.

But was it really? Why? Just because the Scriptures said so? The fucking Bible was written about a million years ago by a bunch of scuzzy fishermen and goat-herders so primitive they didn't even have soap or toilet paper. Why should any modern person take it seriously?

A few days ago she'd relished thoughts like that. She'd been proud that, although she might be a loser, at least she wasn't a sheep. Unlike most people, she had brains enough to see that religion was a crock and guts enough to spurn the hollow comfort it provided.

But now her guilt was crushing her. She was terrified that she was on the verge of seeing Karen's death while she was awake, that the dream was about to swallow her forever. And only fervently promising God and herself that she'd embrace salvation and be a good little Christian girl brought her any measure of relief.

Tonight even that wasn't helping much.

She strode into the kitchen and slid open a drawer. The knives gleamed.

She picked up the little paring knife she used to peel potatoes, rubbed her thumb across the edge. The metal tugged at her skin.

People who hadn't tried to kill themselves could never understand how good it felt. When the blood started flowing, it would wash away all her self-hatred and despair. She'd feel so peaceful it would be like she was already in her grave.

But she mustn't do it. Suicide was a sin, just like turning tricks or craving another woman's touch. This so-called God of love was merciless; He wouldn't permit her to do *anything* that could make her feel better.

Gritting her teeth, she put the knife back and began to close the drawer.

Then she remembered a show she'd seen one afternoon on PBS.

It was about the time of the Black Death, when people were afraid that God was totally pissed off at humanity and had decided to end the world. Back then, penitents used to starve themselves, and pray kneeling for hours on cold stone floors. Sand their skins with hair shirts and even flog them-

selves. They called it mortifying the flesh, and the Church
said it was a good way to get right with the Lord.

She took up the knife again, sat down at the kitchen table.
The molded plastic chair was cold and hard. She wished she
could do it on the sofa, but the kitchen would be a lot easier
to clean.

She poised the blade above her forearm. As always, she
felt eager but squeamish too; she had to close her eyes.

Please God, let this work, she prayed. *Let it make me feel
better, just like it always did, even though this time I'm not
trying to die.*

She incised a row of shallow notches, not the one long,
deep slice she always had before. The cutting didn't hurt; it
was just pressure. The pain started when she pulled the knife
out.

A wave of warmth swept through her. She moaned and
tossed her head from side to side.

Suddenly her misery was gone. It was better than Grace's
hands and mouth would have been, better than anything else
could be. When it became a chore to position new cuts between the ones she'd already made, she pulled up her pajama
top and started on her stomach.

It became increasingly difficult to keep the incisions superficial, even harder to remember that soon she should stop.
But she finally did manage to quit. She needed some of her
skin intact for next time.

When she opened her eyes, her pajamas were soaked red,
blood was pattering down onto the linoleum, and Grace was
standing in the doorway staring at her.

"I had to," Miriam said. "I swear I wasn't trying to kill
myself. It was a special offering to God."

"I know," Grace replied. She pulled her purple satin
nightgown off her shoulders and it dropped around her feet.
"Do me."

7

Tom NOTICED WITH amused exasperation that he had his right hand stuck in his coat again. For what seemed like the hundredth time that morning, he took it out. If he couldn't shake the habit, people were going to start suspecting that he'd cracked up and imagined he was Napoleon.

Just as he got his hand off his shirt front and down on his doodle-covered blotter where it belonged, Becky appeared in the office doorway, her curls tousled and two Styrofoam take-out in containers in her hands. "Good gosh, is it that time already?" he asked.

She grinned. "Gee, Parson, you sure do know just what to say to make a gal feel welcome."

"You know I didn't mean it that way, so just get your butt and my lunch in here." He shifted a stack of ledgers to clear a space for the food and lifted the shoe box of receipts off the chair beside his desk so she could sit down. "It's just that it's not supposed to be lunch time yet. People kept dropping by all morning; I didn't have a chance to get my act together for my meeting."

She fished plastic silverware and paper napkins out of her raincoat pocket. "It's the price you pay for jazzing up your sermons. Now that Miriam's playing receptionist, can't she keep people off your back?"

"I guess she could if I wanted her to, but I don't. They're more important than anything else. I just need a few more hours in my day."

He opened the warm container; steam wafted up. She'd brought him boliche, yellow rice, black beans with onions, and a hunk of Cuban bread. It looked and smelled wonderful.

At least it should have; it was just what he liked. But for some reason the moist-looking colors and pungent aroma were making him queasy. He hurriedly snapped the container closed again.

Becky dug some coins out of her purse. "Before I start, I'll hit the Coke machine. What do you—what's wrong?"

"Nothing. I'm just not very hungry yet. I'll eat it later."

She frowned. "The fridge is full of meals you were supposed to eat 'later.' Are you sick? I know how you feel about going to the doctor, but we can afford a measly five bucks for Cigna if you are."

"But I'm not. I guess my metabolism is readjusting itself or something."

"Right. Whatever that means."

A potbellied man with a square, ruddy face bulled into the room. "Reverend!" he boomed. "I just though I'd—oh. You're eating. Hi, Mrs. Carpenter."

"Hello, Mr. Meade."

Tom stood up. "It's all right, Bubba. What can we do you for?"

Bubba stuck his black-nailed hand into the pocket of his greasy coverall and brought out a check. "I want the church to have this. Thanks for the advice."

Tom goggled at the figure on the check. "Wow. This wasn't necessary. I hope it means that everything turned out all right."

Bubba sighed. "Well, sort of. We had it out and it got pretty hot toward the end. I talked until I was blue in the face, but he wouldn't agree to go back to school, so of course I wound up kicking him out of the house. He said we wouldn't ever see him again. I got to admit, I kind of miss him already, but until he comes to his senses and dumps his little bitch girlfriend, that's fine with me.

"My only problem now is, I got the brat's *mother* giving me shit. Excuse my mouth, Mrs. Carpenter. Do you think you could talk to her some time?"

"Any time she likes," Tom said.

"Great. I better run. I need a bite myself, and the boss isn't a big fan of long dinner breaks." He lumbered out the door.

"Look at this," Tom said. "The man just gave us five hundred dollars."

"I suppose that's good."

He was a little annoyed that she didn't seem the least bit excited. "Sure it is, and he's not the only one who's been feeling generous. Donations are pouring in.

"We're going to hire that visiting nurse and those social workers after all. I think I can sell the elders on another contribution to the Coalition. If the money keeps coming, eventually they might even vote a salary increase for that fabulous fund-raiser, Thomas Carpenter. How would you like some new clothes and a real vacation next year? How would you like to go back to that adoption agency and tell them that now we've got a healthy bank balance?"

She dropped the change back in her bag, closed the lid on her untouched meal. "That all sounds fine. But what did you tell Bubba?"

He shrugged. "I told him that he wasn't under any moral or legal obligation to provide an adult child with free room and board. I said that if he was really mad about Dean quitting college to become a writer, he should confront him."

"In other words, you encouraged him to order his son to knuckle under or get out of the house."

Somehow, without understanding it, he knew he could shut her up as easily as he could throw a switch; he'd been doing it for days. But it was wrong; a loving husband should listen patiently and respond. "I didn't say exactly that."

"Isn't that what it came down to?"

"Look, he had a right to do what he did, and he's obviously satisfied with the way things turned out. They aren't perfect, but he feels better now that the kid isn't taking advantage of him."

"But I can't believe that *you're* satisfied. A father and son are estranged. Is that the way you *wanted* to resolve it?"

Of course not, or at least he didn't think so. Suddenly perplexed, he started nervously fingering his lapel.

"And another thing," she continued. "You know he can't

afford that big donation. He's like most of your parishioners, barely keeping his head above water. It's great that he'd like to contribute, but you don't really want his grocery money, do you?

"I'm starting to worry about you, Tom. God knows you've got your faults, but a lack of genuine concern for your congregation didn't used to be one of them. Not long ago you would have thought of this stuff yourself."

His index finger slipped into his interior pocket like a snake fleeing down a hole. He felt a tingling surge of energy; his uncertainty vanished.

"As usual," he said, "you're not giving me nearly enough credit. Bubba and Dean are the kind of guys who have to assert their manhood before they can get down to cases and actually settle a dispute. Bubba needed to give the kid his ultimatum to prove that he makes the rules in his own house. The kid had to split to show that no one can push him around. Now that that's all established, Dean won't stay gone long. By the time he comes back, they'll both have calmed down, they'll have missed each other some, and they'll be ready to work something out.

"Now, if I hadn't encouraged Bubba to speak out, he might have stewed in his own resentment for months longer, and when the blowup finally came, it would have been ten times worse.

"As far as the offering goes, I have a pretty good idea of how much Bubba takes home, and I'd say he *can* afford it, barely. I'll keep an eye on him and Lucille, and if they're not making it, I'll find a way to get some money back to him.

"You have to understand, when someone who doesn't have a lot of money makes a big donation, it's because he wants to make an actual sacrifice. Either he loves God so much that he's impelled to express it with an extravagant gesture, or he feels that he *needs* to do it, to make peace with his conscience. I wouldn't interfere in that without a good reason. Heck, if I refused a contribution from a good old boy like Bubba, he'd take it as a mortal insult. In effect, I'd be driving him out of the church."

Becky pressed her fingers against her temples. Tendons

stood out on the backs of her hands; her lips worked sound-lessly. She was obviously straining to say something, but it wouldn't come out.

After another moment she gave up, or perhaps she'd lost the thought she was striving to articulate. Her facial muscles slackened. Her hands dropped into her lap and her shoulders slumped. "I'm sorry," she droned. "Of course you're right. I just couldn't see it before."

Suddenly she seemed so *dull*, as if a stroke or a psychotic breakdown had blunted her personality. For a second he was shocked. But his fingertip stroked across the High Priest again, and then he couldn't perceive it anymore.

"It's all right," he assured her. "I'm glad you care about the parishioners too." He glanced up at his mother's old pen-dulum clock where it hung beside Mrs. Ortega's hideous oil painting of the Nativity. Good Lord, only half an hour left! "Sweetheart, I really wanted to have a lunch date, but I'm swamped and you're due back at the gift shop in a few min-utes, anyway. You going to hate me if I jump back into this paperwork?"

"No. I'll get out of your way so you can concentrate. And I'll take that to the house if you're sure you don't want it." She gathered up the containers and departed.

He'd just found his place among the columns of figures when someone else rapped on the open door. It was a frown-ing black man with the rangy physique of a basketball player. He wore a conservative suit and wire-rimmed glass-es; his intelligent-looking features were marred by a pale, puckered scar at the left corner of his mouth.

For some reason, Tom disliked him on sight. Maybe it was just because he really couldn't afford another interrup-tion.

He tried his best to mask his irritation. "May I help you?"

"That depends," the tall man said. His manner seemed al-most suspicious. "Are you Carpenter?"

"Yes. You seem surprised."

He shrugged. "Sorry. I didn't mean anything by it. I just expected that Paulie would take Willie to a black church."

Tom thought he knew who he was talking to, and he decided that his first impression was right on the money. "There aren't many churches left open in Corona City, so we get some of everybody. Fortunately, most people don't seem to have a problem with it. I'm guessing you're Paulie's ex." He rose and offered his hand.

The tall man shook it. His palm was callused and he squeezed a little too hard. "Yeah, I'm Roger Harper. I want to talk to you about my son."

"It's really a bad time. Maybe we could set up an appointment."

Harper scowled. "It's not easy for me to get down here. And I think this is important."

"All right. Shut the door if you want to, and have a seat."

Harper dropped into the chair that Becky had just vacated. "Thanks," he grunted. "How much do you know about Willie's background?"

He knew that Harper had abandoned his family to shack up with some bimbo and that both his wife and son had been absolutely devastated. Fortunately, Paulie had found someone else, a white musician named Gary Saunders, who'd helped her get through the breakup. He'd accompanied her to church social events a time or two. "According to Paulie, your divorce was pretty messy and Willie took it hard."

Harper nodded. "I'm ashamed to say that Paulie and I got so bitter and vicious that that we did the worst thing that two parents in that situation can do: we each tried to use Willie as a weapon against the other. I threatened to take him away from her, and it was just bullshit; I wasn't really in any position to give him a home. She kept me away from him, then told him I didn't come around because I didn't love him anymore. As a matter of fact, she still tries to do the same damn thing today."

"The way she tells it, you don't pay your child support and you don't show up when you're supposed to."

"That lying bitch. Okay, I admit that I've been late with a few checks. Even that I've stood Willie up once or twice. But there was always a reason, and most of the time I've come through."

Tom surreptitiously checked the clock again: twenty minutes left. "I'm sure you've done your best. What is it exactly that's bothering you now?"

Harper picked at his scar. "When he was younger, Willie was an outgoing kid, but after I left, he turned shy. He stopped playing sports, stopped associating with other children his age, acted scared of his own shadow. At first I thought it was just a natural reaction to the shock and expected him to get over it pretty quickly. But for a long time it just got worse, especially after Paulie took up with this white jerk Gary Saunders. Eventually Willie became so withdrawn that, on those rare days when Paulie would actually let me take him, I could tell he was glad to see me but I could hardly draw a smile or a word out of him even so.

"Finally Gary dumped Paulie, she and Willie moved down here, and the boy started attending Roosevelt and your church. It seemed like the change helped him, because he gradually started coming out of his shell. You can't imagine how relieved I was."

Tom wondered if Harper's truculent demeanor was deceptive. Was it possible that he'd simply come to express his thanks? "Paulie probably told you that we tried to give him some extra attention in Sunday School and Youth Fellowship."

Harper snorted. "No. Paulie doesn't tell me much. And whatever you did, it didn't really take."

"What do you mean?"

"When I picked him up last Saturday I found out that Gary has moved into the apartment. And Willie was as bad as he's ever been. He looked sick, exhausted, like he isn't eating or sleeping. After I got him alone, I begged him to tell me what's wrong, but he just clammed up like always."

Tom wondered fleetingly whether Willie had ever spoken as insolently to his father as he had in catechism class; if he had, the tall man might not think it was such a terrible thing for the kid to keep his mouth shut. "Mr. Harper, you have to understand that when someone experiences a loss, the loss of his stable, loving family life or whatever, he doesn't just start recovering, come to feel better, and that's the end of it. The process is more complicated than that. His emotions run in cycles; he'll cope well for a while, then all the negative feelings that have been aroused rise up and overwhelm him. Eventually the bouts of depression become less frequent and less severe, but that can take a long time."

"So you wouldn't worry."

"Not really, not unless there's something you haven't told me."

Harper shook his head. "I just can't buy that. I left his mother three years ago; a normal kid would have adjusted by now. I think something else is wrong. I was hoping you could shed some light on it, but apparently you can't. But maybe you can still help me out."

"I'm not seeing the situation the same way you are, but I'll do anything to help Willie that I can."

"I'm remarried, and I *can* take the boy in now. I think he should come live with me and my wife and start seeing a child psychiatrist. I want you to help me convince Paulie."

The skin above Tom's heart began to itch. He stuck his hand in his coat and scratched, then absently slipped his first two fingers into his pocket and clasped the High Priest between them. "I can't," he said, "because I think it's a bad idea. Let me try to persuade *you* of *that*."

Harper stood up. "Don't bother. I don't know why I wasted my time on you. I could tell from the second you opened your mouth that the bitch had you brainwashed."

Tom squeezed the pasteboard; the sweet, familiar jolt whipped his back straight and snapped his chin up. "Sit down, Mr. Harper. I made time to counsel you, even though I'm busy and you don't belong to my congregation, and now you *will* do me the courtesy of at least listening to my advice."

The tall man sank back into his chair. "I'm sorry," he faltered. "I didn't mean to be rude."

Tom smiled; he realized he didn't dislike Harper anymore, now that he was finally in control. "That's all right. I can imagine how much it distressed you to see Willie looking so unhappy again, and I don't blame you for taking your frustration out on the first target that came along.

"Now, look. It's tough to think objectively when someone

you love is hurting, but you have to try. Willie's problems all started when his home life was disrupted, right?"

"You know they did, but—"

"Then isn't it obvious that if you disrupt it again, he really will regress?"

"But it shouldn't take three years—"

"Willie was very young three years ago. The younger a kid is when he's traumatized, the longer he needs to recover.

"Don't you think you may be going off half-cocked? So what if Willie seemed a little down the last time you saw him? Even grown-ups have bad days. I spend more time with him than you do, and I haven't noticed him climbing back into his shell. If anything, he's a little too boisterous sometimes."

Harper fidgeted. "Sure, it's *possible* . . ."

"Have you thought about how Paulie will react to this proposal? She won't go along with it, no matter what *anybody* says, and since she has custody, you can't force her. All you'll accomplish will be to make her so angry that she'll completely cut off your visitation again.

"And are you *really* in a good position to take Willie now? How does your new wife feel about it?"

"She said we could do it if we have to."

"That doesn't sound very enthusiastic."

Harper grimaced. "Okay, she's not. She's already got her own kids to take care of, and one we made together on the way. But she's willing to try."

"Don't wreck your new marriage just to deal with the emotional baggage you're still dragging around from your last one."

"What the hell does that mean? I'm trying to protect my son!"

"I know that, but your unconscious feelings are distorting your perceptions and your judgment. You *want* to think Willie is in trouble."

"That's complete garbage."

"I think you can feel it's not. If you could rescue the boy from some terrible problem, then you wouldn't have to feel guilty for abandoning him anymore. And if you managed to punish Paulie at the same time, that would be the icing on the cake."

The tall man sneered. "Oh, brilliant, Dr. Freud." There was something forced about his sarcasm, as though he were trying to convince himself. "Why do I want to take revenge on her, when *I'm* the one who walked out?"

"Because then she tried to turn your son against you. She also found another lover, and even though you no longer wanted her yourself, it made you jealous."

Harper shook his head. His face was sweaty. "I don't like her being with Gary because he's scum. I'm sure he's part of whatever's bothering Willie."

"You don't have any legitimate reason to believe that. The truth is that you took a particular dislike to him because he's white."

"Hey, I'm not prejudiced!"

"You don't like to admit it, but yes, you are. Considering the society you live in, who can blame you? You usually try to resist it, and that's all anyone could reasonably ask. But you *have* to resist it now. Don't let it influence you into a decision that could hurt people you love."

Harper sagged, pulled his glasses off, and rubbed his eyes. "Jesus. It all seemed simple when I came in here. You really think Willie will be better off if I don't try to take him?"

"Him and everybody else."

"He could still go to the psychiatrist."

"If Paulie agrees, and you and your new family can afford it. But what Willie really needs right now is to feel normal and accepted. He might not if you tell him you think he needs to see a shrink. You could give him a chance to work through whatever problems he may be having on his own. If he doesn't, you can always take some action later on."

"Okay. I don't know how you talked me into it, but okay. We'll leave the boy just like he is for now."

8

Two BIG MEN in dark suits climbed out of a black sedan. Price's heart started pounding. He spun behind the hedge, thrust his hand into his coat, and grabbed his .38. The men advanced through the rows of parked cars, their shoes crunching the gravel.

But after a few seconds he saw that they weren't wiseguys after all, just a pair of flabby, fiftyish, vacuous-looking local citizens dressed in fine K-Mart polyester. They looked about as menacing as Captain fucking Kangaroo, and of course they passed him by without a glance.

Price exhaled. He hoped no one had seen him jump for cover. At least he hadn't actually drawn his gun.

Goddamn this time of day. Twilight played tricks on you; you thought you could see at a distance, but you couldn't.

But he knew that wasn't really the problem. He ought to be thinking, goddamn his jittery nerves.

Not, he reflected as he strode up the sidewalk to join the crowd pushing through the double doors at the front of the church, that he didn't have plenty to be jittery about. He'd phoned Miami that morning and the news was all bad.

Some muscleheads had tossed and trashed his apartment. Also questioned people who knew him, leaned on some and waved a lot of cash in front of others.

Obviously, this time the proprietors of the Diamond Oasis Resort Hotel and Casino were taking the matter of his indebtedness very seriously indeed. He was lucky he hadn't told anyone where he was going; someone would have fingered him and he'd be dead.

The nave seemed drab and incomplete. The stained glass

windows were pretty, even with the last of the dusk light failing, and the vaulted ceiling was appropriately lofty, but it hardly seemed like a real church without statues, a font, or candles. Not that he was an authority; before this case he hadn't been inside a church since he'd served a subpoena on a bridesmaid back during Reagan's first term.

The pews in front were packed but he managed to squeeze into one in the back.

Too bad he wasn't religious, or he could say a prayer while he was here. Ask Jesus to fix him so he didn't need to gamble anymore.

If he'd learned anything from being a detective, it was that people shouldn't *need* anything. When you had a jones, booze, drugs, too much pride, too strong an attachment to another person, whatever, eventually it was likely to destroy you. Survivors stayed cold and hard.

Right, he'd learned it, but knowing it didn't help. Sooner or later he always picked up a deck of cards or a pair of dice, and once he had them in his hands he turned into a feeb, no better than the weak, victimized chumps he saw in his work every day.

He might as well face it, he wasn't going to change, and if he had to have a habit, it could be worse. Sometimes he went for months without betting, and he did win just about as often as he lost. If he could save his ass now, maybe he could stay out of poker games and casinos for a while, and maybe he'd be luckier next time.

Short of paying for a new face and maybe relocating to Antarctica, the only way to get the Diamond Oasis goombahs off his back was to buy back his markers. Unfortunately, even though Vasquez had given him a substantial retainer as promised, it wasn't anywhere near substantial enough. He wouldn't see the really big money until he found a way to excise Carpenter from the old man's life, and that was turning out not to be easy.

His investigation hadn't come up completely empty; he'd established that something weird was going on. When Carpenter first arrived in Corona City, he'd had a dynamite reputation as a gung-ho social activist clergyman. He'd ministered to the mentally ill, the imported stoop laborers in the south Florida cane fields, and lots of other wretched and downtrodden types. And at the start, when he was just beginning to annoy Vasquez, he'd lived up to his congregation's expectations.

But then he seemed to get tired. He still put just as much effort into his work, but because he felt obligated, not because he enjoyed it. And even though they put up a good front in public, people noticed a coldness growing between him and his wife. The parish gossips had somehow learned about the miscarriage that had left her barren, and they speculated that he'd begun to hold it against her.

To Price, it sounded like burnout. It nailed a lot of professional do-gooders after they watched enough losers go down the tubes despite everything they'd tried to do for them.

But after walking out on a classroom full of kids and getting smashed, Carpenter had abruptly turned himself around. In fact, he'd never been so eloquent and enthusiastic; he was solving everyone's problems, converting hookers in the street, and giving sermons that really rock-and-rolled. Which was too bad for Vasquez, because now that the pastor was becoming so damn influential, he could probably talk the little people into giving him his rent strike after all.

People didn't suddenly change for no reason. At first Price suspected that Carpenter was using drugs or going crazy, and when he went through his refrigerator and garbage and saw all the uneaten food, for a moment he was sure of it. But he'd searched the rest of the house and then the preacher's car and office and couldn't find a stash, drug paraphernalia, psychotropic medication, or canceled checks made out to a shrink. His background check didn't reveal any history of substance abuse or psychiatric treatment, and except for the night Carpenter had blown off his catechism class, no one could recall him doing anything flaky.

Then he'd theorized that Carpenter was cheating on his wife. If not with the choirboys, then maybe with the ex-whores who were hanging around the church looking as frumpy as Old Mother Hubbard in their long-sleeved, baggy turtlenecks and ankle-length skirts. But he'd kept the guy under surveillance for days, and if he was slipping away to get something on the side, Price sure couldn't tell when or how.

Yeah, *something* strange had happened, but he couldn't figure out what. He'd come to the evening service in the hope that watching the minister preach would trigger a hunch. If it didn't, he'd have to tell Vasquez that it was time to start the rough stuff.

The murmuring stopped; the pews creaked as the parishioners sat up straighter or leaned forward. The organ and choir rang out from the clerestory, and Carpenter came through the door behind the altar.

He was a fairly handsome guy, and there was no question that he looked impressive in the pulpit, his slim body framed by a long purple banner emblazoned with a gold cross that was hanging on the back wall. His level stare seemed to burn with conviction, and the hand-on-his-heart bit was probably supposed to convey the same thing.

Still, he was just your basic Holy Joe. Price couldn't understand why the congregation had decided he was so fascinating all of a sudden after he'd already been around for years, why the black lady on his left was staring open-mouthed like she was starving and he was a plate of barbecue and the scrawny little redneck on his right was nodding like a toy dog in a car window.

But he started to understand when the sermon began.

Later on, Price decided that neither Carpenter's ideas nor the words he'd chosen to express them were anything special. He talked about Christ's healing and "the infinite power of faith to transform our lives." Even to Price it seemed stale, and to people who listened to sermons every week it should have been worse.

But Carpenter's delivery was irresistible.

He had the most compelling voice Price had ever heard. Sometimes it thundered and sometimes it sang like an orchestra; it bypassed the intellect and stabbed straight at the heart. The parishioners swayed and shouted, blubbered and moaned; Holy Assembly wasn't supposed to be a charismatic church, but Price wouldn't have been surprised if the black woman had fallen to the floor and writhed, or the redneck had started gibbering in tongues.

He wouldn't have been surprised if he'd done it himself. His disbelief should have rendered him immune to the general hysteria, but as Carpenter spoke on, the detective found himself anguished and teary-eyed because he *didn't* believe, cringing with shame over hard-nosed attitudes and practices he'd always been proud of before. He was actually fighting an impulse to babble out some kind of lunatic confession when the old woman started pushing the wheelchair up the center aisle.

She was hobbling, and her gnarled white fingers kept opening and closing on the rubber grips; if she weren't clutching the chair, she probably would have needed a cane or walker to retain her balance. Her blue eyes were bright behind her glasses, her mouth resolute. She'd applied her rouge and lipstick carefully, and her gray suit and matching pillbox with veil were neat and clean.

The bald, liver-spotted man in the chair sprawled bonelessly, his right arm dangling so that his fingers were in constant danger of becoming entangled in the wheel. His face sagged like a hand puppet with no hand inside it. Somehow she'd managed to dress him in his navy brass-buttoned blazer, striped tie, and charcoal slacks; his crotch was stinking wet and dripping a trail of piss-drops on the carpet.

When he saw them coming, Carpenter stopped preaching; Price's crazy yearning to turn himself into some kind of Holy Roller began to fade. The minister jumped down from his dais and hustled up the aisle to meet them halfway.

"What is it, Mrs. Donovan?" he asked. "Are you all right? Does one of you need a doctor?"

She smiled. "You know as well as I do, the doctors can't help Lloyd any longer. But you can."

"I don't understand."

"Yes, you do; you were just talking about it. Please, heal him."

For a moment Carpenter seemingly couldn't do anything but stare. Then he shook his head, raised his hand in supplication. "Mrs. Donovan . . . Vina . . . I just don't . . . I *can't*."

Disgusted that he'd been manipulated, Price relished the pastor's discomfiture. *That's right*, he thought, *you hypnotic piece of dogshit. You conned all us poor suckers into believing in Christ and his healing miracles, so now let's see you make one happen.*

"Please," Vina repeated. "I know you've never done it before, but *try*."

"I could lead a prayer for him," Carpenter offered, "but faith healing isn't a part of our church's beliefs."

"You don't want to attempt it because you're afraid you'll fail," Vina said. "But that's only because you're humble. Everyone here has faith in you; we can see God's grace burning inside you."

Carpenter stuck his hand back in his coat. His fingers flexed spasmodically; it looked like there was a knot of insects squirming under the cloth. "I'm glad if you all think I'm a good man. But I'm certainly no saint, and it would be blasphemous for me to pretend that I am."

"Try!" called a man in the front row.

"Please," Carpenter said, "put your trust in the Lord, not any human be—"

"You can do it, Reverend!" howled the woman beside Price.

"Try!" yelled someone else.

An instant later, they all started chanting it. "Try, try, try, *try*, TRY!"

"No!" Carpenter shouted. The magical properties of his voice seemed to have deserted him; Price could barely hear him above the chorus. "This is wrong, and if you don't stop, we'll have to end the service! All right then, it's ended!" He turned and took a step, then doubled over and dropped to one knee.

The chanting died; for a second, everyone sat frozen. Eventually someone moved to help him, but by then he was already climbing back to his feet, right hand still inside his coat.

Trembling, smiling, he slowly turned, taking in all the anxious faces watching him. He licked away the smear of blood beneath his bitten lip. "All right," he said at last. "But if nothing happens, you mustn't let it shake your faith. God exists, and He really does work miracles, but not every time anybody asks Him to. And if something does happen, thank Him and not me."

He set his left hand on the old man's shoulder, squeezed it, and said, " 'In the name of Jesus Christ of Nazareth, rise up and walk.' "

Then he hunched over again and gasped and sobbed as his body thrashed. He reminded Price of someone fucking and trying desperately to finish. The way he was lashing himself back and forth and from side to side, the detective couldn't see how he maintained his grip on Donovan. But somehow he did, and his right hand never jerked free of his jacket.

After half a minute, Donovan started convulsing too. His limbs twitched, then spasmed so violently that he rocked the wheelchair. His head snapped up and down and saliva sprayed through his gnashing yellow teeth.

And as it heaved, his body seemed to *inflate*, as though Carpenter's bunching, straining muscles were pumping substance into it. The neck thickened, shoulders broadened, chest deepened, the calves, thighs, and forearms swelled.

They cried out in unison. The chair lurched over again and this time Vina couldn't hold it. It wrenched its occupant away from the minister's hand, overturned, and dashed him face-down on the floor. Carpenter just stared for a moment; then his quivering legs gave way and he collapsed back against a pew.

Grasping the upended wheelchair, Vina painfully lowered herself to her knees, then tugged at her husband, trying to turn him over. She couldn't quite manage it, but after a few seconds he groaned and rolled over by himself.

She started. People shifted, craned, rose, even climbed up on their seats for a better view; parents hoisted children into the air.

Donovan's skin was smoother and unspotted; the whites of his eyes were no longer yellow. He blinked, peered up uncertainly, winced when he began to sit up and something twinged.

Eventually he tried to speak; nothing came out. He swallowed, cleared his throat, tried again. "Vina?"

"Yes!" she replied. "Talk some more."

"I don't understand. You're . . . older."

Carpenter still looked dazed. Some of the parishioners set him back on his feet, straightened his clothing, and brushed him off. Their hands lingered.

"You've been sick," Vina said. "Reverend Carpenter— you don't know him, but he replaced Reverend Garcia—has made you well again. Can you get up?"

"I don't see why not," Donovan said. He stood up with far more agility than his wife did.

For some reason the organist picked that moment to strike up a hymn, and as though it were a cue, the crowd surged into the aisles. Everyone wanted to press closer to Carpenter and the Donovans.

Everyone but Price; he bolted for the door.

He ran to his Mustang, sped down the block, swung into a parking space in front of a boarded-up Spanish-language cinema and sat there nearly hyperventilating. He despised himself for getting so rattled, but Carpenter's "healing" was the spookiest thing he'd ever seen. He was lucky he'd escaped before the minister climbed back into the pulpit, or the bastard might actually have managed to brainwash him.

He hoped he could prove it had all been a trick, that the Donovans were shills. That would give Vasquez all the ammunition he needed.

But he had a horrible premonition that he wouldn't discover anything of the sort. He wondered how he could possibly convince his clients that he'd watched this freak Carpenter perform a bona fide miracle.

9

LLOYD DONOVAN LEANED to the side to double-check the angle, then lined up his shot and stroked. The cue ball clacked into the fifteen; the fifteen bounced off two rails and dropped into the corner pocket.

He grinned, delighted he hadn't lost his touch. He peered around the bar to see if anyone was watching. Some were, but not because they were admiring his skill; he could tell by the way they averted their eyes that they were gawking at the man who'd risen from the living dead.

It made him feel like his dick was hanging out. But he guessed they'd stop eventually, when they figured out that he wasn't going to breathe fire or flap his arms and fly around the room. He stuck his hand in his pocket and discovered that he didn't have another quarter.

"Got any more change?" he asked.

Vina shifted uneasily on her stool by the cue rack. "No. I thought perhaps we could go when you finished that last game."

"If you just let me teach you, you could enjoy this, too."

"I couldn't bend over like that; it would hurt my back. And I understand that ladies patronize saloons nowadays, but I can't forget the way my mother raised me."

He'd been afraid she'd be uncomfortable, but he hadn't had anyone else to go with. It was a hell of a thing to suddenly wake up one evening and discover that all your old buddies were dead. "All right." He drained his beer.

"Besides," Vina added, "the doctor told me to avoid smoke, and we really do have to watch our pennies."

"I said it's all right. We'll go." He strode past the pinball machines and dart board toward the door, stopped two-thirds of the way there and stood tapping his foot until she caught up with him. He could handle the new wrinkles in her face, but he couldn't get used to the way she crept along leaning on that steel tripodal cane.

He took her arm to make sure he wouldn't leave her behind again and they pushed through the door. The night breeze nipped pleasantly at his face. After they'd walked a block in silence, she asked, "Are you upset with me?"

He smiled and gave her a squeeze. "How could I be upset with the prettiest girl in the world? I was just thinking how strange it was to hear you say we have to be careful about money."

"You really don't remember the plant going out of business? That there was no pension fund?"

"The last I remember, I was foreman." That wasn't quite true; he dimly recalled an explosion of pain in his chest and left arm, which must have been one of his heart attacks, and a gray time when he didn't have any thoughts, just sensations—hunger, thirst, fatigue, aches, and itches. But it gave him the willies to even think about it; he sure didn't want to discuss it. "I don't see how you've made it on nothing but Social Security," he said. "After I get used to being conscious again, I'm going to find a job."

"That's a little silly. Last week you couldn't even feed yourself. You're a thousand times better now, but that doesn't mean you're well enough to go back to work. We'll get by; try to enjoy being retired."

What nonsense, he thought. But he supposed it was difficult for her to think of him as strong and capable after she'd spent years taking care of him like a mother or grandmother tending a helpless infant. They'd talk about it later, when she was more accustomed to his renewed vitality, or maybe he'd find a job on the sly and surprise her. "Well, we'll see," he said aloud. "Since you don't want to hang around a den of iniquity, what *do* you want to do?"

"There are two services this evening. We could be in time for the second."

He could hardly believe she wanted to go to church *again.*

Everybody would stare at him there, like he was Moses' burning bush or something. "Please, not tonight."

She looked up at him reproachfully. "I think we ought to show God we're grateful."

He was grateful, really he was, but he'd never been the most religious guy in town, and somehow, even being the recipient of a miracle, hadn't changed that. Maybe it would be different if he could remember the actual healing, but that really was a total blank. Anyhow, the way he saw it, a second life was too precious to waste it praying; he intended to spend his having fun. "I think so too, and I promise we'll go Sunday morning."

"All right," she said, sighing. "Then what do *you* want to do?"

Good question; he peered up and down the street. So much darkness and trash, so many empty storefronts, and hardly anyone but ragged tramps and punk kids in leather and slashed, faded denim on the street. Corona City had been decaying even before he got sick, but in the intervening years it had really turned into a hellhole. And if you'd already eaten supper and couldn't hit the bars, what *was* there to do?

"I'm not sure," he said at last. "But it's nice out. Let's do what we used to do, stroll until we find something entertaining."

"I always liked that," she said wistfully. "But this wind is cold, and I'm getting tired. There are some good programs on tonight."

Obviously she wouldn't be happy until she could sit down and vegetate. "All right, sounds like a winner. Even if they're reruns, they'll be new to me."

They set off down Martin, passed beneath a balcony where two drunks were quarreling in Spanish, went by another grubby tavern with Motown playing inside. He did his best not to hurry her, but by the time they turned down Tampa Street, she was wheezing anyway.

As always, he winced at the sight of their small two-story house. He'd always kept it up, but now most of the grass in the tiny yard was dead and there were strips of gray-white paint peeling off the walls and picket fence. Someday soon he'd have to do something about it. Or else move out of this slum to someplace decent.

He unlocked the front door, switched the interior light on and the porch light off. The living room looked too cramped, overstuffed with Vina's needlepoint, framed photographs, porcelain chickens, and corner cabinet full of pink and amber Depression glass.

His wheelchair sat in the corner where he'd stuck it after Carpenter healed him.

He realized he was staring at it, and then he began to feel faint; he was afraid he'd pass out if he didn't get off his feet. He stumbled forward past the couch, fumbled the chair away from the wall, and tried to unfold it.

Vina pursued as quickly as she could, her breath rasping and her cane thumping down on the wooden floor. When she pawed at him, his dizziness abated. "Lloyd, what is it? What's wrong?"

He didn't know. Couldn't explain why he'd felt so weak, and had even less idea why he'd been so intent on sitting in the cripple's chair that he'd staggered by other pieces of perfectly good furniture to reach it.

But he did know that he didn't want to talk about it; if they ignored it, maybe it wouldn't happen again. "I'm fine."

"You acted sick."

"No. I'm okay. Fit as a fiddle." He shook her hand off, then stepped back and swung his arms vigorously to prove it. To his surprise, the exertion was intensely pleasurable. His malaise had completely vanished, supplanted by an exhilarating glow.

He would have kept it up for a long time, but she was staring at him like he'd gone crazy. "Why were you setting up the wheelchair?"

He dropped his arms. "I don't know; I just felt like taking a good look at it. And I'm glad I did, because now I see how nasty it is." It was true; the stained, cracked seat and backrest looked so disgusting that it was like having a filthy bedpan lying around. "I'm going to put it out on the curb."

"Please don't."

"Why not? I don't need it anymore!" Seeing her flinch, he realized that he'd shouted.

"I know that! But it cost a lot of money and there are others who'd be grateful to have it."

"Okay, fine. Just as long as we get it out of here first thing tomorrow."

"Sweetheart, are you . . . are you *sure* you're all right?"

Jesus Christ, if she hadn't been the one who'd asked Carpenter to heal him, he might have thought that she *wanted* him to be sick. "Of course. How could I not be, when it was *God* that made me well? Come on, show me these programs you're so keen on."

At first it was torture to sit still. The television voices were too shrill and the laugh track brayed. Vina was spying on him out of the corner of her eye. The house smelled faintly, a foul, overripe odor that might be the signature of his own long illness. It all combined to fray his nerves to shreds.

But after a while the stink disappeared; he supposed a breath of fresh air had blown it away. Then the TV noise began to fade. When it stopped ripping at this ears, he finally started to relax.

Soon the sound track became so faint that he couldn't catch all the words, and those he did hear somehow didn't make sense. But he didn't care if he couldn't follow the plot; it was pleasant just to let the droning soothe him.

The images on the screen softened. First they blurred; then the colors bled away.

He didn't like losing the colors; they were pretty. His head lolling, he turned to ask Vina to adjust the set, but now she and the rest of the room were in black and white too. For some reason, it made him want to giggle.

His weary neck let his head droop and he noticed the hands resting in his lap. They were withering; veins and tendons stood out in stark relief and blemishes were coalescing in the skin.

He started to feel afraid, though he didn't know why. Grimacing at the discomfort, he lifted his head and looked around again. Everything was hazy but the wheelchair.

It was painfully distinct; it *loomed*, as though it were ten feet tall. The curved steel tubing gleamed like a vampire's grin.

Donovan lurched to his feet, staggered across the room, and grabbed the chair. When he tried to swing it over his head, he fell against a knickknack shelf. Wood cracked and bric-a-brac exploded on the floor.

Vina screamed something but he couldn't understand her.

He disentangled himself from the wreckage and kicked the chair. As his shoe slammed into the spokes, his strength and coordination trickled back. When he tried again to lift it, he succeeded.

He smashed it down repeatedly, then jumped up and down on it until it was so twisted and flattened that it was difficult to discern what it had been.

And every violent motion invigorated him, but even after he'd utterly destroyed it, there was still an aching weakness in his right knee, and the red roses on the sampler in the corner were still gray. He stamped the broken shelf to slivers and then he was all right again.

Vina was shaking. When he tried to touch her, she recoiled.

He sat back down beside her and put his arm around her so she couldn't get up or pull away. She was as rigid as an iron bar. "Don't be afraid," he said.

"Please," she whimpered, "we've got to call Reverend Carpenter right now."

"Don't jump to any crazy conclusions; hear me out."

"Or Dr. Eagleton. Somebody! Please, Lloyd, something's *wrong* with you!"

"Well, yes," he admitted. "This is going to sound silly, but at first I thought the chair was making me sick again, and that if I broke it, I'd be okay. But now I can tell that the problem is inside me."

"Let me call someone."

"*No!* Listen, dammit. I've got everything figured out. Your pal Carpenter helped me, but he couldn't quite fix me back like a regular person.

"Everybody knows you get weak if you don't exercise,

and now I've got the problem worse than ordinary people. My brain and body will turn back into mush if I don't keep using them. I swear to God, it was happening five minutes ago! I had to tear up the chair and your shelf to jump-start myself."

"If you understand that you're sick—"

"Then why won't I ask someone to help me? Because nobody understands this gift I've been given, and I'm scared to let anyone mess around with it. It's not like Carpenter claims to know what he's doing; he healed me halfway, but if he tried again, he might undo everything he already accomplished. And all a doctor would know to do would be to dump me flat on my back in a hospital bed and run tests, and the inactivity would ruin my mind and muscles for sure!

"Anyway, I'm not bad off. I'll stay healthy as long as I keep thinking and moving, and that's the way I want to live anyway.

"Remember how you loved dancing? New cars and pretty clothes? Riding, skiing, and parties at the beach house? Hell, screwing, for that matter!" He remembered the way she'd looked naked on their wedding night and his penis stiffened. "I want to make things the way they used to be."

"Don't be like this," she begged.

"Like what, alive? Are you saying you liked me better the way I was?"

"No!" she wailed. "Dear Lord, no! But don't you see, I can't be exactly what *I* was. I'm *old*!"

"You have to get over thinking that way," he told her. "We were born the same year; I'm not old, so you can't be." He yanked her over into his lap and bent down to kiss her.

He was sure that when he did, she'd melt, just like she always had in the old days. But she tried to avert her face, pleaded, squirmed, and finally scratched. She caught him by surprise and scored his cheek.

"Damn it!" he snarled. "I just want to love you and prove we're still breathing!" He pinned her wrists with his left hand and tore at her dress with his right.

Her flesh was sickly pale and flaccid, like something that

lived underground. But she was still his darling, and he didn't let it put him off.

When she was naked, he tumbled her onto the floor, then ripped open his pants and threw himself on top of her.

Through it all, she screamed about her back, and afterwards, when she curled up and sobbed, he was a little chagrined that he'd been so rough. But what did she expect, when she wouldn't stop struggling and stayed as dry as sandpaper?

And even though she'd tried to hide it, he was pretty sure she'd started getting excited toward the end.

Now that he'd broken the ice, perhaps it would be as wonderful as he remembered the second time. He pressed himself against her spine and nibbled her ear, reached around her side to grope her tits.

10

RAINDROPS PATTERED OVERHEAD; the wind moaned. Thunder rumbled and the windows rattled in their casements. When lightning flashed, the glass winked into life; Eve extended her apple and the serpent's tongue flickered.

Tom stood in the pulpit, feeling a little foolish. Sensible people were all in their beds. But even though he was tired, for some reason he wasn't sleepy, and he knew he'd rest better here than he would tossing and turning in bed.

It was funny. A few weeks ago, he'd been sick to death of playing minister. Now he really only felt alive when he was preaching, addressing a meeting, or counseling someone. Even when he wasn't, he felt more comfortable behind this lectern than anywhere else. He liked to picture the ranks of enraptured faces.

The door behind him squeaked open and bumped closed. As he turned, Becky said, "I hope that's you and not a burglar."

Another lightning bolt lit up the windows, changing her momentarily from a shadow into a human being. Her robe was sodden and mud and grass clung to her bare feet; water oozed out of her hair and down her face.

"It is," he said. "Don't you know better than to come out in a storm half-dressed? If you get sick, I'm never going to let you hear the end of it."

"When my husband disappears, I get scared. I'm glad you're not bar-crawling again."

"You're not still mad about that, are you?"

"No. I suppose I'm just teasing. What *are* you doing here, all alone in the dark?"

"I don't know. Thinking. Lately I think better up here than anyplace else."

She came closer. For a moment, it annoyed him. He knew it was petty and maybe even irrational, but it was hard to shake the feeling that she didn't belong in the front of his church, especially when she was dripping. "About your Co- alition powwow?" she asked.

"Yeah, partly."

She pulled her hair back from her face, wringing some of the water from the black curls. "I hope you're not worried about it. They'll throw you a rent strike this time if you still think it's a good idea. They're all convinced you piss and shit perfume."

He chuckled. "You always talk so elegantly."

"You know it. Me and the Queen."

"Actually, I'm going to propose more than a rent strike. I think the time has come to bring our greedy little slumlord to his knees."

He slipped his right hand into his coat and fingered the High Priest. "I want to bring his businesses to a standstill," he continued. "Not just the ones in Corona City; all of them. We can picket and stage sit-ins. Interfere with his employees as they try to do their jobs. Phone in bomb threats. Visit the stores in large groups and walk out with armloads of mer- chandise. Break into his unrented buildings and gut them, sell the plumbing, electrical fixtures, and everything else we can haul away for scrap.

"If he doesn't accede to our demands, he'll go broke!"

"You can't be serious."

"Sure I am. I know it sounds pretty radical, but we can do it all nonviolently."

"Oh, did God promise you that no one will lose his temper and take a swing at anyone else?"

He stroked his fingertip across the pasteboard. "God—"

She clapped her hands over her ears. "Don't talk like that!"

He gaped in astonishment. "Like what?"

"In your preacher voice! And take your hand out of your coat!"

He reached out with his left hand; she jerked away. The storm wailed. "You sound hysterical. I don't know if you're already sick or just punchy from lack of sleep, but—"

"I mean it!" she said, her ears still sealed. "Drop the . . . the *act*, the *tones* and the *mannerisms*, or I swear I'll run away!"

He supposed that if he didn't want her flying through the downpour in her nightclothes, he'd better do what she said. But it irked him to have to reposition his arm just to humor her, and afterward it ached as it dangled at his side. "I honestly don't know what you mean about my voice, but is this better?"

She lowered her hands. "Yes."

"Great, but why? It's just a stupid habit I picked up."

Becky shook her head. "I wish I could remember how you started doing it. It changes you in a way that scares me."

It just bugged her, he thought, *that he'd started winning their arguments.* "I still don't know what you mean," he said, "and I wonder if you do. But we can hash it out tomorrow. Right now let's get you dry and back into bed."

"No! Tomorrow I might not be able to put my thoughts into words and you might not be willing to talk like a regular person. And then you'll put this crazy scheme into motion."

Tom sighed. "All right, but let's at least be comfortable." They sat down in one of the front pews; the gilt cross on the banner seemed to float in the darkness. "You were saying you thought our people would go berserk."

"No, I wasn't, although I do think there's a possibility someone could get hurt. But even if no one does, they'll be arrested."

"They know that."

"Oh, well, that's okay then. They can't afford fines, legal fees, or missing work, the ones that are lucky enough to even have jobs in the first place, but if they understand the risks and they're still willing to follow their glorious leader into battle, then what do you care?"

"I do care. But a lot of these people are going to live abso-

lutely wretched lives until we turn this community around.
So it's not cruel or Machiavellian to ask them to make sacri-
fices to accomplish that.

"Besides, they won't pull big fines or stay locked up long.
The public will support us."

"No, Tom, they won't."

He realized he was reaching for his sport coat's interior
pocket, scowled, and folded his hands in his lap. "They *will*.
Corona City's part of Florida history. Not so long ago it had
the same kind of reputation as the French Quarter and
Greenwich Village. Don't you think people would like to see
it flourish again?"

"Yeah, I guess," Becky said. "The *Register* does run an
editorial every year or two about what a swell tourist at-
traction it could make. But that won't matter if you harass
and steal.

"Sure, when Gandhi's followers and Martin Luther
King's protesters went to jail for practicing civil disobedi-
ence, lots of people thought they were heroes. But the public
only condoned their tactics because they were fighting for
freedom itself and because their oppressors were so much
more powerful than they were.

"Your cause is urban renewal, Tom. It's important, but
most people wouldn't agree that it warrants a jihad. And
your enemy is just one old man managing his property as he
thinks best, not obviously denying anyone his basic human
rights and not committing any overt atrocities. If you break
the law trying to cripple his businesses, everyone's going to
regard your precious Coalition as a bullying mob. And when
the Regional Council hears about it, they'll can you so fast
it'll make your head spin."

Tom took a deep breath and let it out slowly; he didn't
want to show how angry he was. "The Council and everyone
else will understand why we did what we did once they've
heard me explain it."

"Do you think you're ready to con the whole South?
What's next, TV? Maybe you can revive the PTL Club."

"It's funny, the parishioners really like me; every day

someone tells me I'm the best minister Holy Assembly's ever had. I guess what happened with Lloyd impressed them. And yet my own wife persists in slamming me. Just what do I have to do to win *your* respect?"

Thunder boomed louder; the lighting was striking closer. "You could try acting sane," Becky said.

"There's only one crazy-acting person here, and babe, it is not the one who's dry."

"A few weeks ago you felt bad because you didn't pray anymore."

"Yeah, I remember. So what?"

"Do you pray now?"

"I . . . no," he admitted, then shivered.

"I didn't think so. It never even occurs to you, does it? Not even after you worked your miracle."

He shuddered again, his teeth chattered. At last he could see she was right, something was *wrong* with him. He was losing not his reason but his identity, turning into someone or something else. And impossible as it seemed, it must be his new good luck charm that was causing it.

The windows flamed; an earsplitting crack sounded just outside. Intending to hurl the card away, he thrust his hand into his coat—

"Don't!" Becky cried.

—but when he touched the card, a cold fire blazed up his arms, searing away all his fear and irrational notions. It was funny and unnerving at the same time, how an articulate but deluded person could nearly convince you her delusions were true. He supposed that sitting alone in a dark, spooky church with a storm raging outside had made him more suggestible.

"Take your hand out!" Becky said. She jerked at his forearm; he tensed his muscles and resisted.

"I don't think I should," he replied. "When we worked at the state hospital, I learned that if you pander to a person's phobias and false beliefs, he'll never get over them."

"You admitted you don't pray!"

"But I don't have to. People pray for divine guidance. I already feel a presence inside me, guiding me all the time. I always think I know what to say and do, and darned if I don't always turn out to be right."

"How can you know that?"

"Because everybody says so. Well, everybody but you."

She sobbed, pressed her hands back over her ears. "I told you I wouldn't listen if you used that voice!"

"I wish you could find it in your heart to believe in me," he said. "To be proud of me and show me some support. I wonder if you aren't feeling a little jealous of my accomplishments. Or maybe you're worried that if I become some kind of big shot, I won't want you anymore. Why don't you take stock for a moment and see if that isn't what's *really* bothering you. If it is, I won't think any less of you. We can talk out the problem and make everything all right."

"Don't put thoughts in my head!" She tried to stand, but it was easy for him to hold her down, even with one hand.

"I wasn't," he said. "I was just trying to help us both understand your attitude."

"I'm afraid," she whimpered. "Afraid you're going to destroy my mind."

"I know where you're coming from. When I think about how drastically I've changed, sometimes I almost scare myself. I was falling apart, and now suddenly I feel like I'm destined to do great things.

"But it doesn't really frighten me, because I know God's responsible. Most of the parishioners seem to sense it too. But I can understand why you wouldn't. The congregation never perceived me as a human being in the first place; the collar tricked them into expecting a junior angel. But you know all too well that I'm just a dumb, sinful slob like everyone else, so you can't believe Christ would choose me to receive a special gift. But you'd *like* to believe it, wouldn't you?"

"Yes," she whispered.

"Maybe you could, if you felt the power directly. If it did something for you."

"I . . . I don't see how it could."

"I do. I'm no saint, but God did send me one healing miracle, and if we ask Him, it's just possible that He'll work another. If you could conceive another baby, I'll bet you wouldn't doubt me anymore!"

She shook her head, flinging icy droplets in his face. She tried to rise on wobbly legs and he tugged her back down.

"I don't think it hurts," he said. "Lloyd didn't say it did."

Of course he really didn't understand how the healing worked, but he suspected that it might be easier if he rested his palm on her bare abdomen. She sat mute and trembling as he untied the sash of her robe.

He didn't think she really wanted to defy him, because she didn't try to run away again. But apparently she was still afraid, because she wasn't quite done resisting. She abruptly hunched over and hugged herself, pressing her thighs together with the folds of her nightgown between them.

"Come on, relax," he told her. But she wouldn't.

At first he was gentle; after half a minute he was gripping and pulling a little harder than he wanted to. He still couldn't move her with only his weaker hand.

So he reluctantly took the other one out of his pocket.

Using both hands, he managed to straighten her up. Unwrap her arms and pry her knees apart. Hitch the hem of her nightgown up around her waist.

She screamed and hit him.

The blow caught him on the ear, snapped his head to the side. He turned back, opened his mouth to ask her not to do that, and a second punch smashed into his nose.

He could understand her being timid, but this was ridiculous. He was trying to help her!

She sprang up; he did too. He pushed her and she fell.

He pounced, attempting to straddle her. If he had to slap the hysteria out of her or hold her down while he healed her, then so be it.

His vision clouded with tears and darkness; he missed seeing her roll over and draw up her legs.

The double kick slammed into his midsection, hurled him back to crack his skull against the pew.

He tried to rise and lunge again, but his head was on fire and he couldn't catch his breath. She scrambled to her feet and vanished through the door.

11

THE RAIN HAD slacked off by the time Becky reached Prudy's apartment building; the lightning was flickering westward out over the bay. Thoroughly spent but still trying to run, she stumbled through the wrought-iron gate into a courtyard full of trash cans, bicycles, and hanging plants, blundered up the stairs to the second-story walkway and pressed her boss's doorbell.

The windows were dark and only the door chime sounded inside. Prudy had a boyfriend and often slept over at his place, but please, not tonight! Becky pressed the button again and then again.

Finally a light came on behind the yellow curtains. Feet padded up to the other side of the door. A moment later it cracked open and Prudy's round, good-natured face appeared above the chain. At least the eyes, ears, and lips did; a layer of greenish mud obscured the rest.

"Holy shit!" Prudy said. She hastily released the chain and ushered her inside.

Becky stared stupidly at the bright room with its posters of unicorns and handsome rock stars adorning the walls and its hordes of dolls and teddy bears taking up most of the furniture. It was hard to believe she was finally somewhere safe.

"Are you hurt?" Prudy asked.

"I don't think so."

"I asked partly because you're limping," the plump woman said.

"Oh." Now that Prudy mentioned it, her foot did hurt. When she inspected it, she found two tiny stars stuck to her heel. "It's nothing, I just picked up a couple of sand spurs."

She plucked them off and then didn't know what to do with them. After a few moments Prudy took them.

Then she fetched a stack of towels and a spare pair of pajamas, helped Becky strip, dry off, wrap her hair in a turban, and dress again. After that she swept a Raggedy Ann and a Fozzie Bear off the couch, sat her in their place, spread a blanket over her, and gave her a brandy snifter full of something brown, warm, and subtly sweet.

Halfway through her second glass, the world slipped back into focus. "What *is* this?" she asked.

"Passion fruit liqueur."

"How come you never drink anything normal?"

"It's part of my exotic mystique. Better now?" Becky nodded. "Then tell me about it."

Suddenly Becky felt like she might start bawling. "I can't. You'd think I was crazy."

"Come on, you walked through a storm barefoot and in your nightgown at whatever ungodly hour this is to get here. I can guarantee you that I'll think you're looney tunes if you *don't* explain, so you might as well spill your guts. I assume it was husband trouble."

Becky took another sip. "Yeah."

"Men are such festering pigs. But you've been so chipper lately that I thought you and His Holiness were getting along better."

"I didn't know you knew we were having problems."

"You hid it pretty well, but the mask slipped once in a while."

"Lately it has seemed better most of the time. But occasionally I come to my senses and realize that it *shouldn't*, that Tom's turning into something creepy and I should be scared to death. Then he puts the whammy on me and makes me think he's Mister Wonderful again. If I'm lucky, he just convinces me my fears are stupid; sometimes I can't even remember that I *was* afraid. And tonight—"

"Whoa!" Prudy said. "I didn't follow any of that. Start at the beginning."

"All right," Becky said, then told her everything.

"Jeez," the plump woman said an hour later. "Do you honestly believe he has some kind of special powers?"

Becky shook her head. "I don't know. It sure looked like he healed Mr. Donovan, but maybe it was a coincidence. Maybe his doctor put him on a new medication that kicked in right at that moment, or maybe it was just his time to get better. I sure don't *want* to believe it; I'd much rather think that Tom just came out of his midlife crisis a borderline megalomaniac with serious powers of persuasion."

"But if he did work a miracle, wouldn't that mean he *is* some kind of saint?"

"No. A saint wouldn't lead all those poor people into trouble. And when he tried to 'heal' me, somehow I could just feel that if anything did happen in my body, it would be something horrible."

"Maybe he's a pod person from outer space."

Becky snorted. "Maybe. Whatever he is, I have to figure out what to do about him.

"Part of me doesn't want to do anything. I could just go home and let him convince me that everything's fine. I've been happy most of the time these last few weeks, and before then I felt lousy. And the whole world seems to think that Tom's turning into a hero; it's just my paranoid, unsupported intuition that says different.

"But I know him better and see him closer than anyone else, and damn it, I trust my feelings!

"Which is why I keep thinking I should run away. If I stay in town, he might find me, hit me with the voice, seduce me, erase more of my personality or kill more of my brain cells or whatever the hell he does. A little more of that and I might not be the same person anymore either.

"Why should I risk it? He hasn't busted his butt trying to take care of *me* these past few years, and I don't think I owe it to him."

Prudy opened the bottle, refilled their glasses. "Long-suffering wives and girlfriends in every age and nation would agree with you. So why do I get the feeling you're going to do it anyway?"

"You're right," Becky replied. "I'm afraid to stay involved, but I have to.

"Because when we were younger, we cherished each other, and that and Tom's enthusiasm for the ministry made every day exciting. Life felt romantic and adventurous and I treasured that feeling like I've never treasured anything else. But we lost it anyway.

"Things began to go wrong about the time I had a miscarriage and found out I could never have children. Tom and I both come from big families and we'd always taken it for granted that we'd have a bunch of kids. I think we needed it to feel complete, that we were living our lives the way people are supposed to.

"Losing the baby broke something inside him, or maybe he was breaking already and it just sped things up. From time to time he had failures and disappointments at work, just like the rest of us, and they started getting to him. First he doubted that he was really doing anybody any good and then he began doubting the existence of God."

"Not very comfortable thoughts for a man of the cloth," Prudy interjected.

Becky grimaced. "Tell me about it. He wouldn't quit the ministry. I guess he didn't want to let anyone down, didn't want to let God down if it turned out He was really up there in Heaven after all. But he felt like a hypocrite for staying.

"He didn't tell me he lost his faith until recently, but of course I could tell something was wrong. I tried to comfort him, but I couldn't; maybe I was still too upset about the baby myself to do a good job. Anyway, he stayed cold and morose and kept me just as miserable as he was. I finally got mad and turned cold, even bitchy, myself. I think it was a kind of self-defense.

"But it screwed up our relationship even worse, and I can't tell you how much I regret it now. I feel so bad about so many things! If Tom had married someone who could give him kids, maybe he wouldn't have changed. And if I'd been more perceptive or had more faith in God myself, maybe I could have helped him recover his. It's funny, when we first got together, I felt like I didn't deserve him. He wasn't pompous or preachy at all, but you could tell he had a calling; I believed when I bothered to think about it, but religion was something I pretty much took for granted. Even then I suspected I was going to fail him."

"Don't talk dumb," Prudy interrupted. "Your mother should have taught you that whatever goes wrong in this life is always entirely the male's fault. So if you honestly believe that Tom could permanently mess up your head or even, God help us, your uterus, don't chance it out of guilt. Guilt's usually a bad reason to do anything."

"But that won't be the reason," Becky objected. "Well, not the only reason. I still do *care* about Tom, at least a little. And many of the Coalition members belong to the church, and whether anybody recognizes it or not, they're *my* congregation too. I spend most of my time away from work visiting their shut-ins, chaperoning their teen dances, and organizing their bake sales. Some days I hate it, but I still can't stand by and watch him march them off a cliff."

"So what are you going to do, squeal to his superiors?"

Becky shook her head. "Either he'd captivate them too or they'd fire him, and then he might keep on leading the Coalition anyway. I have to find a way to put him back in his right mind.

"Level with me, Prudy. Do you believe what I've been telling you, or have you just been humoring a nut case?"

Prudy shrugged. "I've never believed in miracles. On the other hand, I know you're not a liar or any crazier than the average wacko roaming the streets. So I don't know what to think. I guess I at least believe that Tom's falling apart, that maybe he's had a nervous breakdown or something. And that he might be about to hurt a lot of people."

"Then help me stop him."

"What do you want me to do?"

"The Coalition meets in three days, so that's how long I have to bring him to his senses. Obviously I can't just argue with him; even if he didn't warp my thoughts again, I wouldn't persuade him, because he's absolutely sure he's always right.

"I think my only chance is to shake that conviction. He's

counseled or otherwise tried to help a lot of people in the past few weeks, and fortunately, I know who most of them are. If I can find someone that his efforts seriously, undeniably *harmed*, and shove the proof in his face, perhaps I can finally get through to him."

"Could be," Prudy said. "Or he might just shrug it off like he did when you pointed out that he'd stopped worrying about not praying."

"I know," Becky admitted. "But it's the best idea I've got.

"My immediate problem is that I can't go home before I'm ready to confront him, for fear that he'll hypnotize me again. So I need to stay here and I need you to buy me some clothes. To loan me some money and your car, and let me off work so I can talk to people. And you mustn't tell anyone I'm here, especially Tom. If he tries to speak to you, you'll have to end the conversation as soon as possible, before he has a chance to affect *your* mind."

"Don't want much, do you?"

"I know I'm asking for the moon. You don't make much more than I do, nobody else is supposed to take vacation until Maria comes back, and you're expected to have your car to make pickups and deliveries. If you can't help me, or have to fire me when I don't show up in the morning, I'll understand."

Prudy snorted. "Don't be so sympathetic; it makes me want to barf. Of course I'll give you everything you need, and lie us both out of trouble with dear old Mr. Hotchkiss somehow. I just wish I could shake the feeling that by helping you I'll be sinking you deeper into the worst trouble of your life."

12

Donovan hurled himself into a series of jumping jacks, his legs scissoring and his arms sweeping up and down. The breath huffed in and out of his chest and the new dumbbells clenched in his fists flashed in the afternoon sun.

He'd hoped the calisthenics would work off his frustrations, but, if anything, he felt angrier than when he'd started. He could feel the neighbors peeking through their curtains and he resented it; a man had a right to privacy in his own back yard.

A man had a right to work, too, but he'd spent the morning pounding the pavement and none of the snot-nose kids in charge of hiring would give him a chance. They all thought he belonged in a museum with the rest of the dinosaurs.

And at the very least a man had a right to expect that when the rest of the world was handing him shit, his wife would support him. He'd assured Vina that if he maintained a steady regimen of physical and mental activity, he wouldn't crumble back into the half-dead monstrosity he'd been before, and sure enough, he hadn't. You'd think she could admit she'd been wrong, rejoice that the problem was more or less behind them, and get on with leading a normal life. Instead she just kept whining and nagging; she still wanted to run to Carpenter or some quack, even though he'd explained a hundred times that it could wind up really hurting him. Dearly as he loved her, if she didn't see reason soon, he was damned if he knew what he was going to do about her.

At least he hadn't had an attack in over forty-eight hours. Maybe his condition was finally stable.

He set the dumbbells down, wiped sweat off his forehead.

He was trying to decide among the barbell, the jump rope, and the Everlast heavy bag hanging from the poinsettia tree when the preacher's pretty wife peered around the rusty fuel oil drum mounted on the side wall of the house.

He owed Carpenter his life, so he supposed he owed her a welcome. He made himself smile and say hello.

"Hi," she answered. "I rang the doorbell, but nobody came. Then I heard noise back here."

"Sorry, I didn't hear the bell. Come on in."

She unlatched the gate, walked forward past a row of rosebushes gnarled and brown from years of neglect. "I just wanted to check in with you and make sure everything's all right."

In other words, she was another damn snoop. "You people make me feel like I've gotten mighty interesting."

" 'You people'?"

"Some reporter dropped by yesterday. I didn't lie but I didn't tell him much either, because if they print a story about me in the newspaper, people won't leave me alone. I hope Reverend Carpenter wasn't counting on me to make him famous."

She grimaced. "Publicity's the last thing he needs right now. I hope you know that *I'm* here because I'm sincerely concerned about your welfare."

Maybe, but she was also morbidly curious and just doing her job as the minister's wife. "Sure. But hey, I'm fine."

"I'm glad. Still—do you suppose we could talk inside?"

"No!" he blurted. "I mean, I'm not done working out." He picked up the barbell and started doing curls.

Her eyes narrowed. "How much weight do you have on there?"

"Just a hundred pounds." He hoisted it up and down, up and down. "When I think of how much I used to lift, it makes me feel like a pantywaist. But you're supposed to work up gradually."

"Are you sure you should be doing it at all? You just got over being terribly ill."

"But thanks to your husband, I *did* get over it. And Dr. Eagleton said it'll be good for me," he lied.

"Well, obviously he'd know better than I would," Becky said dubiously. Then her bright red lipstick turned gray.

Donovan had never had an attack in the presence of anyone but Vina, and for some reason he'd assumed he wouldn't. But the shit was hitting the fan now, and he had to get rid of this prying bitch fast so he could deal with it. "Was there anything else?" he asked.

"Well, actually, I would like to chat a while longer, so I can give Tom the *details* of what you've been doing. How you spend your time and things like that." She brushed off the concrete steps that led up to the back door, then sat down.

"There's really nothing to tell; we're just taking it easy." He swung the barbell up again. He didn't know whether to keep exercising or not. Simple exertion wouldn't reverse his deterioration, but it might slow it. But his heart was already hammering, his limbs trembling; if his movements became too feeble and uncoordinated, she'd know something was wrong with him.

"Someone told me you're looking for work," she said.

Right, "someone," some miserable gossiping spy. His lower back twinged. "Yeah, but . . . I haven't found . . . any yet." As the weight grew heavier, it became more and more difficult to force his words out.

"I'm afraid it may take a while," Becky said. "There aren't that many jobs to begin with, and unfortunately, you have to expect that some of the employers are going to practice age discrimination." Her voice faded in and out like a weak radio signal.

Jesus Christ, why wouldn't she leave? She was just babbling! Grunting, teeth gritted, he wrenched the barbell up another time. Pain shot through his left hand. When he looked at it, it began to shrivel.

He bent his knees and dropped the weight; his back ached worse, and for one horrible second he thought he wouldn't be able to straighten up again. He hastily thrust his hands in his pockets.

No matter how rude or crazy he seemed, no matter how suspicious it made her, he had to dispose of her *now*, before the degeneration showed in his face. "I have to go to the bathroom," he said.

"All right."

"I'm not coming back out. I guess I wore myself out; I want to lie down."

"Oh. Could I come inside with you and talk to Vina?"

He wondered crazily if he was going to have to kill her. "No. Because she's not here right now."

"Then may I wait? I really would like to see her too. I don't mean to be pushy; it's just that I have this . . . intuition that I might be able to help the two of you in some way, and—"

"How many times do I have to tell you, we're fine! At least we would be if people would leave us in peace. I know you mean well, but you're making me feel like a freak, just like that newspaperman did. I'm grateful to your husband and I'll be glad to talk to you or to him at church, but I don't want you coming to my house anymore."

She just stared. She probably *still* wouldn't go; he wanted to break down and cry.

But then she blushed. "I understand, and I apologize. Please tell Vina I asked about her." She rose and strode to the gate.

Donovan tottered up to the steps, fumbled the screen and inner doors open, and staggered on through the kitchen into the front of the house.

The weakness was maddening, and the erosion of his senses and mental faculties was worse. But he still peeked around the edge of one of the shades he'd thumbtacked to the windowsill, to make sure she really did leave before he set about recovering. It wouldn't do to let her hear the commotion.

When she climbed into her car and drove away, he wheeled, grabbed one of the branches he'd collected, and lashed it against the wall. When it snapped, he snatched up one of the plates from the Goodwill store and hurled it to the floor.

He kept destroying until his vitality seeped back. Finally, panting, rejuvenated, he stood and ruefully surveyed the wreckage that filled the living and dining rooms, the kicked-in television, tatters of cloth, wisps of upholstery stuffing, broken-off furniture legs, and jagged shards of ceramic and glass. It was almost scary how much damage he'd done tearing and battering his way out of only—what, half a dozen?—seizures.

In one sense it had been unavoidable. He'd discovered that when he was having an attack only actual violence revitalized him; even pummeling the heavy bag didn't produce the same effect. He supposed that really hurting something started the heart pumping and the adrenaline surging in a way that nothing else could.

Still, he should have had the intelligence to lay in his supply of fragile junk *before* he ruined all this stuff that Vina treasured. But he'd hoped that each attack would be the last. He was still confident that they'd be over soon, despite the fact that this last one had come on with disconcerting swiftness. Somehow he could feel that it was just a matter of convincing his brain and other organs to shift gears.

Once the seizures did stop, when he was working again and Vina had gotten over her silly fears, they'd clear out the debris and replace it with things that were ten times nicer than her original possessions.

Speaking of Vina, she hadn't touched her breakfast, so she ought to be starving by now. He was hungry himself. Returning to the kitchen, he wolfed down a leftover slab of meat loaf, then poured a glass of lemonade, heated a bowl of tomato soup, and made a chicken salad sandwich, loaded everything on a tray and carried it upstairs.

Her blankets were on the floor; perhaps she'd struggled. If so, it hadn't done any harm. She was still bound spread-eagled to the bed.

He inspected her wrists and ankles, was glad to see that even if she had been thrashing around, the cuffs he'd fashioned out of foam rubber had prevented the ropes from galling her. He was also relieved that so far today she hadn't wet herself, although he would have changed the sheets without complaining if she had. He was sure she'd cheerfully taken perfect care of him when he was helpless, and he didn't intend to do any less for her.

He untied the gag and pulled the wadded scarf from her mouth. "I brought your lunch," he said.

She tried to answer but her mouth was too dry. He released her arms, propped her up, and tilted the lemonade to her lips. Her first gulp spewed liquid down her chin and onto her naked breasts. "Don't drink it too fast," he warned, "or you'll make yourself sick."

After two more swallows she pushed his hand and the glass away. "I've been thinking about what you said," she wheezed. "And now I see you're absolutely right. I don't have to talk to anyone, because your problems are under control. And I *shouldn't*, because they wouldn't understand."

He studied her eyes for a moment, then sighed. "You never could lie to me."

"No, really—"

"Hush." He piled the pillows up and leaned her shoulders against them, then began freeing her ankles. "You're going to upset us both if you go on, so just stop. I'll tell you about my morning."

"I know about it. I heard you breaking things."

Her gaunt white legs were crawling with varicose veins. He helped her swing her feet down onto the floor. "Thank goodness that will all be over soon. What do you say we talk about something more pleasant?"

"It'll never be over until you get some help."

For an instant he felt like slapping her; he wouldn't have wanted to listen to this again even if he'd been in a good mood. He picked up her glasses from the night stand, inspected the lenses, grimaced, and polished them with a tissue. "There," he said as he handed them to her. "Crystal clear. Do you want to use the lavatory before you eat?"

She set the trifocals on her nose, pulled a strand of her thin, snowy hair out from between the left stem and her cheek. "You can't go on like this," she said.

"I'm doing just fine, thank you. A lot better than if I let people . . . *confine* me, or *tamper* with me. You have to trust me on this; I can *feel* what's happening inside my body, so I understand better than anyone else could exactly what to do about it."

"But you don't! You don't understand at all! When you have a spell, you think you see your skin change, but it *doesn't!*"

He tried to feel amused. "I don't know how such a faithful, church-going Christian can stand to tell such terrible fibs. Especially when you already know I don't believe that particular fib anyway. Heck, even if it was true, it wouldn't make any difference. If the attacks only affected my brain and eyes and left the rest of me alone, I'd still have to fight them off, or I'd wind up back in a wheelchair just the same.

"Now then. Would you like your tray?"

Her lips drew down into her familiar stubborn frown. "No. You talked about trust. If you love me, *you* trust *me*; come with me now to Dr. Eagleton. He's a good doctor and he won't do anything that could hurt you. If you weren't sick in your mind, you'd know that."

"God, you're obstinate. I've always heard that when people get old, they get cranky and unreasonable and repeat themselves over and over, but I never dreamed it would happen to you."

"I'm sorry if I'm boring you. Let me see if I can offer something new. I can't stand to live like this, not tied up like an animal and watching the husband I've loved for over fifty years turn into a madman." She blinked furiously, sniffed twice. "So if you won't let me help you, I won't need that meal and I won't need any food ever. I'm going to fast until I die."

"That's the dumbest thing I've ever heard."

"Perhaps, but it's what I've decided."

"Things aren't that bad. I don't keep you tied when I'm home, and as soon as you realize that I'm getting well, I won't have to do it at all."

"But I never will realize it. Because it isn't so."

"Even if you're not bluffing, it won't work. I won't let you do it and neither will your stomach. I'll bring you your favorite foods. You'll see and smell them, your mouth'll water and your belly will ache, and eventually—"

He swayed and snatched the bedpost to steady himself. The lilacs on the wallpaper turned gray.

It was terrifying; he'd never had two attacks in the same day. Perhaps Vina was right, he *did* need a doctor, he *wasn't* getting better!

But there was no time to think about it now. If he didn't rage his way out of this current seizure, he'd go into a decline, turn back into the decrepit husk Carpenter had revitalized, and then no physician could help him. After all, they hadn't before.

Vina dragged herself across the bed and laboriously stood up on the other side. Her own unsteady legs trembling and her hands pressed against the wall for equilibrium, she inched toward her cane where it stood beside the closet door.

He wondered whether she meant to pause to grab her robe or run out of the house bareass. He couldn't afford to let her do either. He had to restrain her fast, then fight off the attack before it was too late.

Arms extended, he limped around the foot of the bed. She glanced to the side, was probably considering throwing herself back across the mattress to keep it between them, but he lurched forward and caught her by the shoulders before she could.

She clenched her fists, hammered; he ducked and the blows hit his bald spot instead of his face. Snarling at the stinging pain, he tried to wrestle her down onto the bed, but another wave of dizziness forced him to stop and fight for balance. She clutched his forearms and butted him.

A worse pain exploded in his mouth; she jerked backward and rammed into him again. He lost his grip, stumbled, and fell.

Black blood welling from a gash above her nose, Vina labored to step over him. By the time he caught his breath, she was extending her hand to seize the cane.

He grabbed her ankle and yanked. She wailed, scrabbled at the wall, toppled. When she slammed into the floor, a hanging photograph of her parents' wedding leaped off its nail.

He grasped her hair, wrenched her head up, and pounded it down. She yelped and ripped free, leaving him with a handful of silky hair. He snatched at her head again, held on, yanked it up and then down, pounding the floor; this time she went limp.

Donovan was nearly choking; he squandered a precious second spitting out his broken tooth and the coppery taste of the blood. Then, groaning with strain, he lifted Vina and placed her on the bed.

He struggled to retie her bonds, but his fingers were numb. The room was murky and he couldn't hear himself panting.

He'd just have to hope she wouldn't wake up; there was no more time to fool with the ropes or to stagger downstairs to his stockpile of disposable objects either. He raked his hand along a wall, hurling down more photos; stamping and kicking, he smashed the glass in their frames.

Then he threw Vina's tray across the room, ground her fallen glasses under his heel, and split open his knuckles punching the dresser mirror.

This time it wasn't helping.

She'd delayed him too long; apparently the deterioration had progressed so far that even violent exertion couldn't reverse it. All but blind now, he barely had the strength to stand. Consciousness itself was guttering out.

A part of him understood that it was futile to battle on any further, but he was too terrified to stop. Sobbing, he spun, lashed out, battered the chest of drawers, and drove his shoe through the closet door.

Soon he was only a frenzied beast oblivious to everything but agony and horror.

But after a while gray blobs floated out of the darkness, then turned into lilacs. Something produced a rhythmic, rubbery smacking. The all-encompassing pain diminished, defined itself into pulsing aches in his mouth, joints, and hands.

Thank God, thank God, it hadn't been too late after all. He was going to be all right.

As his senses sharpened and his vitality returned, he realized he was standing over the bed hammering his fists down.

Beating Vina. Her flesh, her hair, and the sheets were streaked with blood.

For an instant, certain that he'd killed her, he fully expected to drop dead himself; how could he live having done such a thing, even if Vina had brought it on herself? Then her diaphragm rose. Closer examination revealed that she had only one superficial cut on her forehead; most of the gore must have fallen from his own lacerated knuckles.

He still hated himself for hurting her. Although he supposed he was lucky he'd been delirious enough to do it. Apparently harming a living being was more energizing than breaking an inanimate object, and after she'd interfered with his recovery, he'd needed that level of stimulation.

But even that was no excuse. He stroked her hair tenderly, grimaced when he inadvertently smeared it with crimson. He promised himself that, no matter what the provocation or necessity, he'd never strike her again.

Even though, just a few short minutes ago, she had essentially asked him to kill her.

13

RAIN HAD BEGUN spitting out of the slate-gray sky half an hour ago. The traffic reporter on the radio was already tallying up the accidents, and a horde of mothers had ventured forth into the inclement weather to collect their kids. By the time Becky found a parking place, beside the towering sign that read ROOSEVELT JUNIOR HIGH SCHOOL—HOME OF THE ROUGH RIDERS, class was letting out.

Prudy hadn't bought her a raincoat to throw on over her bottle-green blouse, stone-washed jeans, and Reeboks, nor had she ever bothered to toss an umbrella into the back seat of the Taurus. And unfortunately, if Becky stayed inside the car, she wouldn't be able to watch both exits past the line of grimy yellow buses. As she picked her way through the ranks of parked cars, shoulders tightening when drops plopped down on her head, she wondered why the Nancy Drew books hadn't warned her that detectives stay wet, cold, and miserable.

Perhaps not all of them did, just the Lestrades and Clousseaus who never managed to unravel anything.

She certainly hadn't uncovered anything helpful in her first day and a half of investigating. Few of the parishioners she'd spoken with seemed happy. Many were clearly anxious or despondent, and one or two, like Lloyd Donovan, had gotten positively weird. But none reported that Tom's efforts on their behalf had backfired; even the overtly miserable ones claimed that he'd helped them to some degree. And on the basis of the information she'd managed to elicit, she couldn't prove any different.

Perhaps Willie Harper could provide the facts she needed.

Tom had affected his life; he might be living with his father instead of his mother if the pastor hadn't intervened. But Tom hadn't counseled him, which ought to mean that he hadn't been mesmerized into believing that the adult could do no wrong.

A lot of the kids obviously didn't like the rain either. Streaming out the doors, they rushed to the waiting cars and buses or set off quickly down the street; Becky had to weave and jostle through them. She was still halfway across the parking lot when Willie emerged from the north exit.

Fortunately, horrible as it was to think that way, he still looked morose as hell. His eyes were downcast and his shoulders slumped; he wasn't talking to any of the chattering kids around him. She waved and shouted his name, but he didn't look up, and the growling of the engines and the students' laughter and shouted farewells drowned her voice out.

She started to run, but two boys carrying trombone cases stepped in front of her. By the time she evaded them, a bus had pulled out, blocking her view of the exit. It paused partway out of its space to let a primer-blotched Corolla creep by. She dodged around the bus's rear bumper just as Gary Saunders intercepted Willie at the bottom of the steps.

The boy seemed to recoil; she had the feeling he would have dashed in the opposite direction if he didn't feel absolutely trapped. Gary grinned, fastened his hand on his shoulder, and ushered him to the beat-up white MG parked on the grass by the bicycle rack.

Becky shouted again; they climbed in the car. The brake lights flashed on. An instant later it bumped down off the curb, cutting off a green Pacer whose driver shot them a bird, and headed for the street.

Becky cursed. Gary was *probably* taking Willie straight home. But she was running out of time, and if she wanted to be sure she got to question the boy this afternoon, she'd have to follow them. She spun around and sprinted for the Taurus.

When she pulled out of the parking lot, the MG was turning a corner a block ahead. She pressed the accelerator and wrenched the wheel. Its tires hissing through the puddles, the Taurus swerved left of center, whipped around two cars, a bus, and a pickup to catch up.

She considered blowing her horn to signal Gary to stop, but she didn't want to startle him; he could lose control and have an accident on these wet streets. Besides, no matter where they all wound up, no doubt she and Willie could talk more comfortably there than they could standing in the rain.

Five minutes later Gary pulled up in front of a row of derelict buildings.

As she applied the brake, Becky frowned in puzzlement. She couldn't imagine why he'd want to bring Willie here. When he peered up and down the street, there was something furtive in his manner; she sensed he was making sure no one was watching him.

She reacted out of instinct, stepped on the gas, and sped on by before she realized she intended to.

By the time she turned right and parked out of sight on Bolivar, she was already feeling foolish. Running around asking nosy questions was one thing; spying on people was something else entirely. Even Nancy Drew might have scrupled to invade someone's privacy like that. If Gary caught her, it could be embarrassing at the very least; he might even have her arrested.

But she'd never really liked the stocky musician. She didn't know him all that well, but her intuition told her he was a user and a parasite. It wasn't difficult to imagine him involving Willie is something illicit, perhaps selling crack or running numbers.

If she could prove he had, it would certainly be evidence that Tom had made a bad call, and she doubted she could if she didn't follow them. Gary wouldn't be obliging enough to admit doing anything wrong if she simply questioned him, and Willie probably wouldn't either. She'd been eager to speak with the boy only because she lacked any better ideas; he'd always been reticent and she didn't expect him to change now.

So she guessed she would spy, even if it did make her feel ridiculous. She couldn't pass up what might be her only chance to bring Tom to his senses.

She jumped out of the car, scurried to the corner, peeked around. Willie and Gary disappeared between two buildings.

Running on tiptoe, praying they wouldn't hear her rubber soles squeaking on the concrete, she hastened up the sidewalk to the gap and warily peeked again. They were standing in a narrow, littered, weed-infested space. A metal door swung open; they stepped through and it clicked shut.

She waited a few seconds, then crept down to the door. Someone had mounted a bell button on the frame. She pressed her ear to the cold, rusty iron and couldn't hear anything. Then she tried to crack it open, but as she'd expected, it was locked.

Seeking another way in, she began a circuit of the walls.

As she groped through the premature twilight, her head bowed against the drizzle and her feet crunching and rustling trash, she soon realized that the structure was giving her the creeps. It was the bricked-up windows. She couldn't help imagining that people had been sealed up inside, plague-carriers or convicts, condemned to die alone in the dark.

She dismissed her morbid fancies with an effort. She had to concentrate on getting inside the building, analyze the problem in the same way a burglar would.

She'd found two other doors, one facing the street and one on a loading dock in the rear, but they were locked and tight in their frames, too. The ground floor seemed impregnable.

But above the side door a fire escape zigzagged down from the top story to the second. The building adjacent was only a few feet away and it still had glass windows the way the good Lord intended.

She returned to the Taurus and removed Prudy's tire iron from the trunk. Trotting back down the sidewalk, she wished she had a coat to hide it in. If a cop happened by, it would probably make him suspicious.

None did. No one did.

The building beside the one Willie and Gary had entered presented a row of wooden doors and painted-over windows to the street; it had probably housed stores and offices. Becky tested the first door, expecting she'd have to force it. It was already broken.

The doorway admitted just enough watery gray light to reveal that the space within had been a hat shop; a fedora and a panama still sat on the highest of the otherwise empty shelves. A nest of newspapers, a sardine can with a peeled-back top, a Hostess Twinkies wrapper, and an empty Colt .45 Malt Liquor bottle lay in the center of the floor.

Hoping there were no squatters in residence at the moment, at least no vicious or territorial ones, she stepped inside and shut the door behind her.

She had to feel her way through the darkness; Nancy Drew probably never left home without a flashlight. Dust drifted up to tickle her nose, cobwebs fell into gummy tatters around her outstretched hand, and occasionally something skittered.

After what seemed like hours she found a stairway leading up. Fortunately, no one had painted the windows on the upper floors.

Many of the rooms contained abandoned pieces of furniture, but she had to explore all the way up to the third story to find something suitable to her needs. Leaning against the wall in what might have been the conference room of a suite of offices was a long, narrow, Formica-topped table with folding legs.

She dragged it into a room that looked out on the fire escape. The window refused to open at first, but relented when she pried it with her tire iron.

The table would have to slant upward, but if she unfolded the rear pair of legs and braced them with the desk that someone had conveniently left in the corner, it shouldn't slide back. She shoved her makeshift bridge out over the windowsill, then, grunting with strain, hoisted it up. It reached the black grillwork walkway with just a couple of inches to spare.

When she saw that she really could attempt to cross, she suddenly felt a chill. What the hell was she doing? She didn't *know* Willie was in trouble, and even if he was, it didn't mean she had to risk her neck playing acrobat. If she had any brains, she'd call the police.

Except that she had nothing to tell them. She was sure

Gary had Paulie's permission to pick up Willie, and he probably had the owner or tenant's permission to visit the building next door as well. The only crime she could report was her own illegal entry.

Come on, she thought, *Tom and all the parishioners are depending on you, even if they don't know it. And it's only a few feet. Don't think, just do it.*

She stuck the tire iron in her belt and crawled out into the rain. The tabletop quivered and she clutched it.

But of course it was going to vibrate. That didn't mean anything was wrong. If she just kept moving, she'd be fine.

She let go, inched forward. The tabletop cracked and buckled.

She squawked, scrambled up, lunged. The upper half of the table dropped away and she started falling. Then her fingers locked around the guardrail; her right foot landed on the grille beneath. Shaking, eyes squinched shut, she pressed her body forward as the table section crashed to the ground below.

After a minute her pulse began to slow and she managed to climb on over.

She couldn't understand what hidden flaw had split her ramp; the damn thing had looked and felt solid enough. Perhaps she should consider a diet.

One thing was certain: after she saved Tom's sanity, she was going to make him suffer for putting her through this.

Of course, it would all have been for nothing anyway if the doors opening on the fire escape were as secure as the ones at ground level.

But they weren't. All three were locked, but they were only made of weathered wood, and the one on the third floor was particularly loose in its frame. She inserted the tire iron into the crack between the door and the jamb and pulled. The handle cut into her palms for a moment; then the door splintered and snapped open.

Beyond was a large room full of high worktables with vises mounted on them. A cockroach scuttled away from the sudden light. Twin stacks of crates framed an opening in the far wall.

She listened; except for the raindrops pattering on the fire escape, everything was silent. She slipped inside.

She left the door ajar, but after she crossed the first room, she ran out of light. Her shoes crushed roach turds and squashed rodent droppings as she fumbled on.

Murmuring ahead. She strained to make out words but couldn't.

She felt her way through another doorway. The space ahead might have been slightly less black than the one behind, but she felt more than saw the stairs falling away to the floor below.

Groping, shuffling, she found the first step and the handrail running down the wall; if there'd ever been a railing across the top of the landing or along the outside of the steps, it was gone now. It made her shiver to think how easily she could have plunged over the edge. She was probably going to emerge from this delightful adventure with a severe case of acrophobia.

Assuming, of course, that she emerged from it at all.

But that was a wimpy way to think. It shouldn't be all that hard to sneak close enough to find out what was going on and then steal away again. Treading softly, she descended.

At the bottom of the stairs the light was brighter; it was coming through an opening to her left. She still couldn't quite discern what the speakers were saying, but with any luck the heaps of crates and cartons stacked on the floor would permit her to approach unseen. Bending low, she crept forward.

The floodlights dazzled her. Until her eyes adjusted, she wasn't quite sure she was really seeing what she thought she was.

After all, why would Willie be naked? And why would the man fussing with the camera on the tripod be made up like a clown?

"There we go," the clown said at last. "But my stuff's never as good when I use the timer. Are you sure you won't pose?"

"Forget it," Gary replied. He opened a gold-toned cigarette case, removed a joint and a book of matches.

"No one will recognize you if you wear a mask."

The musician lit up, sucked in the first hit, blew it out a few seconds later. "No way. At least, not unless you're willing to pay a lot more."

"You've got to be kidding. I was trying to keep you from being bored. But if you're too chicken to join in, you can just sit and watch while Willie and I have all the fun ourselves. Okay, big guy, assume the position."

Willie stood up and bent over in front of the camera, his hands clenched on one of the bedposts and his skinny buttocks more or less pointed at the lens.

"Good," the clown said. He jammed a black leather hood like an executioner's mask on over his bushy scarlet wig, then exchanged his expensive-looking double-breasted suit coat for a motorcycle jacket jingling with chains and zippers. "But look back over your shoulder. Now wet your lips. And when the camera starts shooting, try to look scared but turned on at the same time."

He flipped a switch on the camera, then lifted a cat-o'-nine-tails off a stool. Hastily positioning himself beside the boy, he started lashing his bottom. The shutter clicked and the film advance whirred.

Kneeling behind a cardboard box, sickened yet fascinated, Becky looked on. She knew she should flee and call the police that instant, but she couldn't, partly because she was almost positive that she'd seen the lanky, slouching clown somewhere before. When he took off the hood again, she might recognize him even through his greasepaint, wig, and round rubber nose disguise.

The whip slapped down, raising welts. Willie jerked with every blow, but he struggled to keep his face contorted in a sickly smile.

"I hope that didn't sting *too* much," the hooded man said at last. Willie didn't reply. "It has to look authentic. Don't worry, I'll make it feel better." He crossed to a table just outside the circle of illumination, rummaged in a box on top of it, and produced a jar of petroleum jelly.

The black boy shot Gary a look of forlorn appeal. The musician smiled and shrugged.

Becky abruptly felt that if she witnessed any more, she'd gag. She began to rise and something touched her leg.

An instant later, as it raced away into the shadows, she saw it was only a tiny, harmless mouse. But by then she was already flailing. Her forearm thumped the carton in front of her and knocked it skidding forward across the floor.

Gary's head snapped around; he almost tumbled off his stool. "Jesus Christ," he hissed, "somebody's in here!"

The clown simply dropped the jar. By the time it shattered, he'd already spun back to the table and snatched up something else.

Becky sprang up and ran; feet pounded behind. After gazing into the light, the darkness was nearly impenetrable. Obstacles popped into existence as if they were shooting up out of the floor. She dodged around a worktable and leaped over a dolly; another stack of crates reared up right in front of her. She crashed into it face first, rebounded; as she stumbled back, someone took her arm and turned her as neatly as a partner in a dance.

It was the clown. Gleaming even in the blackness, his snub-nosed revolver stared into her face.

14

GNAWING HIS LIP, Willie braced for the slimy hands kneading and cupping, the finger probing like a worm boring into an apple. He wished his flesh could suddenly glow red-hot.

Then something bumped. The two adults scrambled into the darkness. He stared after them but couldn't make out what was going on.

Running feet thudding, more bumps, then a crash. Half a minute later Gary dragged Mrs. Carpenter into the light. She swayed like a drunk and her nose was bleeding.

The boy's face burned with shame. But even so, he knew he shouldn't worry about the minister's wife seeing him naked, not now. What mattered was the gun the clown held leveled at her back.

"This is real trouble," Gary quavered. "She knows me. She knows the kid."

"Get a grip on yourself," the clown replied. "And bring me the handcuffs."

"Do you hear what I'm telling you? She—"

"If we don't panic, everything will work out. Now move." Gary drew a deep breath, then wheeled and moved to the box that had held the vaseline.

Mrs. Carpenter blinked, shook her head like she was trying to start it working again. "You better not hurt me," she said. "People know where I am."

"You can tell us all about it," said the clown. "Just as soon as we get you situated. Willie, could you please move out of the way? Go sit where Uncle Gary was sitting. Becky, you bend over like he was, only hold onto that piece that runs between the bedposts."

Willie scurried to the stool. Mrs. Carpenter said, "I don't have to—"

"You *do*," said the clown. "Or I'll shoot you this instant. Really."

She stared into his hooded face for a moment, then turned, bent, and gripped. Gary looped the manacles around the rail, then snapped them on.

"Do you think someone really knows she's here?" he asked.

"Oh, sure," said the clown. "The police or her husband or somebody. They sent her off to investigate the big, bad child pornographers all by herself, and if she's not home by next week at the latest, they'll send out a search party. Give me a break."

"It's true," Mrs. Carpenter said. "They didn't expect me to get into this kind of trouble, but they knew I was going to try to find out what was wrong with Willie, and—"

"I don't think so," the clown interrupted. "So let's cut the crap and discuss how we can get ourselves out of this sticky situation you've created without anybody getting hurt."

He set the revolver on the bed. "Because, believe it or not, I wouldn't want to have to hurt anybody. I know you think I hurt kids, but I don't. I give them what they want. Teenagers go horny-crazy wishing some kind grown-up would teach them about sex, don't they, Willie?"

Willie's face grew hot again; he couldn't speak. Fortunately the clown, as usual, didn't actually seem to expect an answer.

"Maybe so," Mrs. Carpenter said. "I don't care anymore either way. Just let me go and I'll never mention this to anyone."

"That sounds great," said the clown. "Except that I'd be afraid to trust you without a little insurance. Now the way I figure it, a preacher's wife wouldn't turn in a pornographer if it meant everybody would see nasty pictures he'd taken of her. So here's the deal: we'll have a little party in front of Mister Camera and *afterwards* you can go."

"I don't think—" Gary began; the clown glared and Gary's eyes narrowed in sudden comprehension.

"All right," Mrs. Carpenter said, "if that's what it takes. I'll do anything you want. Just don't hurt me."

"This is going to be *great!*" crowed the clown. He pulled off his hood.

When he did, Willie realized he was lying about letting Mrs. Carpenter go. He wouldn't have unmasked unless he meant to shoot her no matter what she did.

He reached around from behind and unbuckled her belt. She stiffened, then made herself relax.

"Now that we have an understanding, you can take the cuffs off," she said. "They're just going to cramp my style."

The clown pulled her jeans and panties down around her ankles. "I like B and D shots. But maybe later."

The boy could tell she knew her captors were going to kill her; she was only pretending she didn't so they'd free her hands. Unfortunately, he was sure the clown could tell it too.

But maybe *he* could grab the gun.

It was only a few feet away, and Gary and the clown were so focused on Mrs. Carpenter, it was like they'd forgotten he was even there. It made him mad that they considered him such a tame, helpless slave that they wouldn't even think twice about raping and murdering another adult right in front of his eyes.

But he was sweating and felt like he needed to pee, not nearly as angry as he was afraid. Because his tormentors were right. He never *had* been able to resist them.

He was just a kid, sick, scared, and weak from years of abuse. He wanted to help Mrs. Carpenter more than he'd ever wanted anything, but he simply couldn't.

The clown started ripping her shirt off. She sobbed once, then brought herself back under control.

Willie remembered the day that Gary had returned.

He'd imagined an angel flying out of the church steeple to rescue him. It had been a sort of prayer.

And now, when he'd abandoned hope, here was Mrs. Carpenter miraculously come from the church to save him, if not an angel then the next best thing. God *answered* the prayer; He'd decided to set Willie free. Surely He'd send him the strength he needed to liberate His messenger, if only he had faith enough to try.

Slowly, silently, Willie stood up. His pulse beat in his neck. His legs felt rubbery.

The clown unhooked Mrs. Carpenter's bra, left it draped around her manacled wrists. Gary chuckled. The boy edged past him.

"Almost show time," said the clown. "Remember, the hotter you get us, the sooner we'll finish." He straightened up and turned back toward the camera. "Willie! What are you doing?"

Willie sprang forward. Gary wheeled, gaped, lunged. The boy ducked under his hand and dove. Belly-flopping on the mattress, he snatched the gun, rolled, bounced to his feet, and swept it frantically back and forth. "Stay back!" he shrilled. "Staybackstaybackstayback!"

The two men froze.

"Why don't you put that down before you hurt yourself," Gary quavered after a moment.

"Let her go," Willie said.

"Listen to Uncle Gary," purred the clown. "Nobody has a problem here. The lady and I have already worked out a deal—"

"He's *not* my uncle! Unlock the handcuffs or I'll kill you!"

"Could we talk about this?" Gary asked. His voice was still shaking but he was trying hard to sound calm. "It's cruel to threaten people who love you. How would your mom feel—"

Willie pointed the revolver at his chest and jerked the trigger.

The gun roared, bucked; he flinched.

His eyes popped back open. Gary wasn't hurt, but his face

was as white as a sheet of paper and he had a wet spot on the front of his pants.

"If I were you, I'd do what he told me," Mrs. Carpenter said.

Hands trembling, Gary fumbled the key out of his pocket and sidled forward to release her. Willie stepped back so he couldn't snatch the gun.

When her hands were free, she hastily pulled up her pants and refastened her bra. "Pass me the gun and get your clothes," she said to Willie. He handed the gun to her, and the clown backed up a step. "Stop!" she ordered.

"Sorry," said the clown. "I didn't mean to, it's just that I never had to face a gun before. What happens now?"

Willie stepped into his jockstrap. Mrs. Carpenter sidestepped to the table, scooped up a handful of photos, folded them, and stuck them through her belt. "We're leaving," she said.

"What about after that?" the clown asked, easing back another pace.

"I told you to stand still!"

"Sorry. What are you going to do after you leave?"

Willie pulled his T-shirt over his head. Mrs. Carpenter knuckled the blood on her upper lip. "That's kind of a stupid question."

"Is it? You have alternatives. You have to admit, we didn't actually hurt you, and that kind of trial would be awfully rough on the boy." He stepped back again.

"Stop!"

"Sorry. What do you say we do it this way? Gary will disappear. I'll shut down my operation and pay each of you a hundred thousand tax-free dollars. Wouldn't you agree that that—"

"If you don't walk back toward me, I'm going to kill you."

"Sorry," said the clown, and spun behind a pile of boxes. The revolver cracked an instant too late.

Gary darted for cover. Mrs. Carpenter pivoted and fired, missed him too.

And then Willie and Mrs. Carpenter stood seemingly alone. Gun and marijuana smoke hung in the air. The vast, dark space beyond the circle of light still seemed to echo faintly with the sound of the shots.

"Okay, okay, we're still okay," Mrs. Carpenter chattered. "They can't hurt us, because we've got the gun."

"Yeah," Willie said. He wondered how may bullets were left, two or three.

"But let's get out of here as quick as we can. Don't bother with your shoes, just move."

The lights went out.

He clutched at her forearm. She jumped, squealed; for a second he was afraid she was going to shoot him. Then she fumbled her arm around his shoulders and hugged him tight. "Oh, God," she moaned.

She sounded even more frightened than he was; if he didn't calm her down, she might freak out. "Don't worry," he said, trying to make his voice confident and brave. "I can find the way out. I've been here a lot."

She took a couple of deep, slow breaths; when she spoke again, it wasn't quite as shaky. "All right. Lead on. Hell, they can't see us either."

His hand clutching hers, the floor cold and gritty under his bare feet, he set off groping through the dark. Ghostly whispering and shuffling seemed to come from all around. Mrs. Carpenter kept stopping abruptly, jerking his arm as she froze to stand and listen.

How long ago had they started away from the bed? A minute? Two? Five? Should it take that long to reach the staircase? What if he was leading her in a circle?

Then the blackness ahead grayed, so imperceptibly that he had to approach a little closer before he was sure he was actually seeing it. Apparently Gary and the clown hadn't extinguished the little yellow bulb at the top of the steps; he'd been proceeding in the right direction after all.

A creak. A sense that something was rushing at him, but he couldn't tell from where. Mrs. Carpenter yanked him aside and a stack of crates crashed down where they'd just been standing. A small box hit his head, knocked him down on one knee.

She pulled him back up. His vision swirling with globs and streamers of light, he couldn't tell where the stairs were anymore; he hoped she could. They ran.

More crates fell; they barely dodged them. Mrs. Carpenter fired at the shadow that had pushed the crates over. The muzzle flash was as bright as the sun.

They wheeled and fled again. Ducked around another corner and saw the yellow bulb itself. A moment later they were stumbling down the steps.

Boxes flew. One smashed down right behind Mrs. Carpenter, rolled and bumped her thighs. She lurched forward, arms windmilling, recovered her balance just before she tumbled off the edge of the staircase.

Screaming, she fired at the landing. The revolver barked once, then clicked.

Gary and the clown started down. The clown had a tire iron in his fist.

Willie and Mrs. Carpenter dashed to the bottom of the steps and across the room to the iron door, tore at the stiff, unfamiliar bolts and latches. Their pursuers bounded onto the floor.

The door jerked inward. The clown's arm whipped up, then down; the tire iron clanged beside Mrs. Carpenter's head. She screamed again; Willie dragged her out into the rain.

They sprinted for the sidewalk. Pain flashed through his foot when he stepped on something sharp. By the time they reached the pavement, the clown had burst through the door, the tire tool in his hand again. Willie wished he'd had the sense to snatch it up.

Nobody else was on the street. They wheeled right, raced on around the corner. He would have run right by the Taurus if she hadn't grabbed him. They scrambled inside and locked their doors.

Her hand shaking, she tried to fit the key in the ignition. Dropped it. Gary and the clown dashed around the corner.

She managed to pick up the key, insert and twist it. The

starter whined. Gasping, the clown stumbled up beside her, swung back his club to smash her window.

The engine roared; the car surged forward. The tire iron shattered the window behind her, spraying bits of glass into the back seat. Then they were speeding away.

15

WHEN TOM STEPPED into his office, the doughnut and coffee Miriam had pressed on him in his hands, Becky was sitting in her accustomed spot beside his desk. She had dark smudges under her eyes and a bruise on her nose, but she was smiling. "Surprise," she said.

He hastily deposited the pastry and cup on his blotter; the coffee slopped over and seared his fingers. Oblivious to the pain, he pulled her up out of her chair and hugged her. "Thank God! I was so worried, so afraid you'd stay gone for good."

She squeezed him back. "I knew—or at least hoped—you would be. I should have come back last night. But the police kept me past eleven, and I was just too frazzled to face another confrontation."

He pulled back to look her in the face. "What were you doing with the police?"

"Frustrating them, mostly. It's amazing how a simple layer of paint can mask somebody's features. I'll tell you all about it in a minute. But first I want you to look in that envelope on your desk."

"Well, okay." Puzzled, he tore it open. A piece of cardboard and some creased color photos in plastic bags slid out.

"Be careful with them, they're evidence. I practically had to swear a blood oath to convince the cops to let me borrow them, even though I'm the one who turned them in in the first place."

They were all pictures of naked children. In the first a little boy was masturbating. In the second a pretty blond girl was fingering her nipples. In the next she was kneeling in front of a man in a leather hood and motorcycle jacket with his penis in her mouth, and in the one after that she was fellating Willie Harper.

For a moment Tom thought he was going to throw up. He squinched his eyes shut, threw the photos down.

"Willie acted depressed because Gary was renting him out to a kiddie-porn maker," Becky explained. "When you persuaded his father not to try to help him, you ensured that he'd have to experience more of the same."

Tom shook his head. "I couldn't know." His hand crept toward the High Priest.

"Don't strike your pose!" Becky rapped. "Or I'll leave again and this time I won't come back."

He let his hand drop onto the blotter. But even in the midst of his anguish and confusion, he resented her ordering him around. "All right, fine. If you're still worried about *that*. My Lord, this is terrible. But I really *couldn't know*."

"Right," she said, "you couldn't. That's the point. You're not infallible, so why do you think you are?"

His stomach squirmed again. A headache started pounding in his temples. "I don't know."

"Something terrible is happening to you, and part of you *does* know what it is. Tell me so we can fix it."

"I have to know about Willie. Is he all right?"

"Yes. Don't change the subject. Tell me what's wrong."

She was right, it was time to admit the ridiculous, hideous truth. He opened his mouth and pain exploded in his skull and gut. He gasped and doubled over; his hand shot into his coat. He tried to stop it and couldn't.

"Are you all right?" Her hand fell on his shoulder.

"I guess," he replied. "Just a little shaken up. Those poor kids!" He straightened.

"You said you wouldn't do that!"

"In a moment of weakness. As I already explained, it would be wrong for me to reinforce your delusions."

She grabbed Willie's picture and thrust it in his face. "You did this!"

"I made a mistake. Who doesn't? It doesn't mean there's anything wrong with me. It doesn't even mean that the Lord hasn't chosen me to fulfill a special purpose. Perhaps I gave *one* person poor advice because I didn't have enough information, but that doesn't change the fact that I worked a miracle."

Becky shook her head; a tear ran down her cheek. "I tried. I don't know what else to do, except get away before you mess *me* up again. I guess you'll hear from a lawyer."

It should have been a terrible moment, but all he could feel was a guilty sense of relief. "If that's what you really want. But maybe after you've had a chance to think—"

"Let me see that."

Startled, he turned. Miriam stood in the doorway, blue eyes blazing and fists clenched.

"I know, I shouldn't eavesdrop," she continued. "But there's a part of me that still doesn't like you. I knew Becky split on you, and when I caught her voice, I hoped I'd get to hear her make you crawl. Now give me the picture." Becky handed it to her. "You bastard."

Tom said, "Be fair. It's terrible, but ultimately, it's the pornographer's fault, not mine."

Miriam giggled crazily. "No. It's yours too. Want to see something else that is?" She peeled off her orange turtleneck. Tape and bloodstained gauze covered virtually all the skin beneath.

He winced. "I don't understand."

"Guilt was eating me alive. I thought that if I made a blood sacrifice, God would send me peace."

"I never told you that!"

"No, but somehow you made me need to do it anyway. The wife's right, Padre. Whether you mean to or not, you're wrecking lives."

Tom shook his head. "I'm sorry you—"

"Don't be sorry *I* bled." She tore bandages off her breasts, raked her long, pointed nails through her scabs. "I don't care about it, see? Be sorry Grace won't kiss me anymore. Be sorry I took a knife to the only person I love because I thought you were the next best thing to Jesus and all the time you were some toxic motherfucker who *hurts kids*!"

She sobbed and slapped him, then fled.

He rubbed his smarting cheek. It was wet with her blood.

The fingertips of his other hand were trembling. The Tarot card had already begun to soothe him. If he simply stroked it, it would wash his fear and guilt away.

Instead he bit down hard on his lower lip. The pain cleared his head; he managed to jerk his hand out and started pulling his jacket off.

Agony ripped through his body, worse than before. Whimpering and retching, he dropped to his knees. His heart fibrillated, a stutter of spasm in his chest. The High Priest was a part of him now; if he severed the link, he surely wouldn't survive.

All right, he thought, *if that's how it has to be*. Convulsing, bile burning in his mouth and nostrils, he dragged his right hand clear of his sleeve.

Becky was babbling questions, pawing him frantically. He wished she'd either help him remove his coat or stand back out of the way.

He felt like someone was chopping him with an axe; how could he hurt so much and not pass out? After an eternity of anguished struggle, he wrenched his left hand free of twisted, clinging cloth and feebly lobbed the jacket into the hall . . .

And immediately scrambled after it.

He savaged his lip again, sank his fingers into the ratty green carpet to anchor himself. Finally the pain and compulsion faded together. Sane, aching, and utterly spent, he collapsed on his stomach.

Becky tried to roll him over. After a while, he forced himself to help her. "Are you all right?" she asked.

"Yeah, unlikely as it seems." He raised a trembling hand, wiped at the accumulation of blood, sweat, tears, mucus, and saliva on his face. "Together you and Miriam got through to me. Not only am I all right, I think I'm even still alive."

"Thank God. So what's with your coat? Lately my whole life is this series of striptease acts."

"The thing that was corrupting me's inside it. I had to get rid of the whole jacket because I didn't dare touch it."

She stared; her mouth fell open. "Of course. That first morning. You had something in your pocket."

"Yeah. It's a Tarot card—"

For a moment she thought she'd misheard him. "A what?"

"A fortune-telling card," he said. "I got it in a *botanica*. I started carrying it as a good luck charm, and it turned out to really be magic. Somehow it was able to twist my thoughts."

She shook her head, trying to come to terms with an idea that contravened her understanding of the world. "I guess I have to believe you," she said at last. "There are magic cards, okay. But what makes me crazy is that all this time, the problem was a *physical object*. If only I could have remembered, or if only I'd had brains enough to figure out that you kept your hand in your pocket because you were fondling something, I could have swiped it while you slept. I wouldn't have had to follow Willie. I nearly got raped and murdered and it was completely unnecessary."

"Oh, Becky, no! Oh, I'm so sorry!"

"Don't be. I'm not, not really. I *didn't* get hurt, and if I hadn't done it, the kid would still be in trouble. It's just that . . . life is really perverse sometimes, you know?"

"Yeah. I've begun to notice." He took her hand, pulled it to his lips, kissed it. "Thank you. I owe you my . . . soul, I suppose."

She grinned. "So you repay me by snotting on me. Oh well, you're welcome anyway."

"You can't imagine what it was like. A part of me *did* understand what was happening, but the card wouldn't let me acknowledge it even to myself. If you and Miriam . . . Miriam. I should go after her."

"At the moment you couldn't help her. Maybe later. At least she's better off now than she was before she broke your spell."

"You're right. All those people I worked with. I'll have to check on every one, and I'd better start with Lloyd."

"I saw him yesterday. He acted odd, but he still looked healthy and he said he was okay."

Tom grimaced. "I wish I could believe it. Something foul took control of me. Usually it made me influence people in ways that hurt them, but I did worse than that to him. I put a piece of the foulness itself inside him. I don't know what it did to him, but I mean to find out *immediately*." He started to sit up; his back spasmed and he flopped back down.

"Obviously you'll have to rest a little first," Becky told him. "Then clean up so people won't think you're sick or crazy. And we can't leave your magic—Tarot card, was it?—lying around where someone could pick it up. Don't worry, we'll catch up with Lloyd in just a little while."

"All right. If you checked him recently and it didn't seem like anything terrible was about to happen, I guess a few more minutes won't make a difference."

16

DR. WARNER'S STUBBY fingers probed Vasquez's abdomen. The old man braced but couldn't control himself; he gasped and twisted away.

Warner nodded as though in satisfaction; light danced on his scalp, and his wattles jiggled. "*That's* why I want you back in the hospital."

"You son of a bitch, you hurt me on purpose."

The pudgy physician sighed. "I barely touched you. From now on the pain will be excruciating unless you allow me to take the measures necessary to manage it."

"If I ever suspect you aren't doing everything you can to help me *already*, I'll sue you for everything you've got and see you expelled from your pathetic excuse for a profession to boot."

"I can't perform surgery in your bedroom. As I explained, if we sever certain nerves—"

"I'll probably wind up a paraplegic and incontinent and may hurt just as much as before. No, thank you. Content yourself with the money I pay you for nothing. Don't try to steal what's left of my dignity too." A burly, gray-haired figure appeared in the doorway. "Come in, Mr. Price," Vasquez said, then turned back to Warner.

"We need to talk more—"

"*Go!*"

Warner scowled. "Fine. I'll see you the day after tomorrow." He snapped his bag shut and stalked out.

"Good morning," said Price. Another spasm ripped through Vasquez's middle; he stiffened and gritted his teeth to hold in a whimper. "I take it it's bad today."

"You don't care how I feel!"

Price shrugged. "Actually, no. Do you want me to?"

Vasquez chuckled; it hurt his belly. "Certainly not. I hired you because you're supposed to be tough. Sorry I snapped at you. When you find out you're dying, you promise yourself you won't let it turn you weak, but of course it does. What have you learned?"

The detective pulled up the chair beside the bed. "I showed Donovan's records to three different doctors. They all agreed that he was too far gone to feed himself or speak a coherent sentence and would stay that way till he croaked."

"For some reason I don't have as much confidence in modern medicine as I used to," Vasquez said.

Price grinned. "Guess I wouldn't either. But the neighbors confirm he'd been stuck in a wheelchair for years. Besides which, he's always been an upright citizen; I don't think he'd start shilling for a con artist at this late date. And when I told him I was a reporter and tried to interview him, he clammed up. If it was a scam, what was the point if they don't publicize it?

"This is the weirdest thing I've ever had to report to a client, but Donovan really was sick as hell, and when Carpenter touched him he got well for no reason anybody can explain.

"But the way I see it, just because we can't prove Carpenter's a charlatan doesn't mean we can't use this to get rid of him. His church doesn't believe in faith healing or inciting people to break the law either. If we tell his bosses everything we know, I bet they'll suspend him pending an investigation. I doubt that he'll defy them and keep leading the Coalition; they'd kick him out of the ministry for sure. Even if he did, the Coalition probably wouldn't *want* his leadership if they felt he'd been discredited."

The old man smiled. "It always amazes me how often people miss the obvious. Hasn't it occurred to you that my objective may have changed?"

Price blinked. "Damn. No. I feel stupid. Do you really think he can do it whenever he wants?"

"I'm still not entirely convinced that he did it at all. But I can't afford to ignore the possibility."

"Assuming he can, the question becomes, will he do it for *you*?"

"Bring him here today. I've never crawled to an enemy before, but I'll do it. Beg. Apologize. Convert to his idiot religion. Give his beggars everything they want. Make him rich. Whatever it takes."

Agony sliced up from his groin to his sternum; he sucked in a hissing breath and writhed. "If for some reason he refuses," he whispered when the pain had run its course, "then we'll coerce him however we must. And if he fails me, I'll exact revenge."

17

VINA PULLED DOWN with her arms and up with her legs. Her entire body throbbed and the raw spots on her bony wrists and ankles burned. After a few seconds it became intolerable; she moaned and went limp.

As she waited for the pain to subside, mustered the will to pull again, she wondered why she didn't just give up. Lloyd had beaten her twice during the night. With any luck, he'd put her out of her misery soon.

And after all, what did she have to live for? Only her love for her husband and her faith in the Lord had sustained her through all the heartache and tribulations of the past few years. Now, in a horrible mockery of all her cherished memories, hopes, and beliefs, Lloyd had become her deranged tormentor and it certainly seemed like it was Christ Who had made him that way.

But she'd lived such a long, rich, difficult life. After all she'd experienced and endured, she couldn't see turning fraidy cat, wouldn't lie down and die without a fight for *anyone*. As Lloyd had suspected, when she'd threatened to starve, it had only been a bluff.

Perhaps she was just too ornery to know when to quit. But her restraints were looser than they'd been an hour ago. The foam-rubber cuffs that Lloyd had fashioned to keep the ropes from chafing were gradually breaking apart. Eventually she'd be able to slip her hands and feet out.

Glass shattered. Something pounded.

Please, not again, not so soon! In just a few minutes he'd decide breaking things wasn't helping him, and shamble upstairs. Sobbing, her livid flesh twinging, she wrenched convulsively at her bonds.

They didn't release her. Any second now the crashing would stop and the risers would begin to creak.

Silence. Then something squealed. A chorus of snarling, hissing, and yipping sounds rang out.

He'd decided to try hurting animals. Somehow she knew it wouldn't satisfy him, but it would delay him a little longer. She started dragging at the ropes again.

The squealing grew louder and shriller, then suddenly stopped. A few seconds later another animal began making the same sound.

She felt the pad encircling her right wrist split. Chortling breathlessly, madly, almost choking, she pulled and twisted.

Her hand still wouldn't slide free. Another animal died.

The next one screamed. She jerked at the noose, gasping out a chant in time to her tugs. "Let—go—let—go— let—*go!*"

Her hand lurched an inch out of the loop, then caught again.

A final animal perished. Then the bottom step groaned.

Each riser sounded in turn as he slowly ascended. Twice he stumbled and thumped against the wall. Slick with blood, at last her hand tore free. Needles pricked her numbed and clumsy fingers.

She rolled onto her shoulder, fumbled with the noose securing her left hand. The knot finally came apart, but at the same moment he stepped onto the landing. Without her glasses she was so nearsighted that he was just a shadow, but she could make out the splashes of red on his hands, forearms, and chest.

It was the cruelest mockery of all to have struggled so hard and come so close for nothing. Even during one of his spells, he was stronger and at least as nimble as she was. With her legs still bound, she didn't have a chance.

Or did she?

He claimed that when he had a seizure, *his* vision deteriorated. What if he didn't see her hands were free? What if she could take him by surprise?

She hastily stretched her arms over her head, set her hands down on the ends of the ropes.

As he shuffled forward, his blurry features sharpened into focus. The animals had scratched and bitten. He had a bloody Boy Scout pocketknife in his right hand.

"I tried," he said dully, "but kittens and puppies don't work."

He looked and sounded so forlorn that for a moment her heart went out to him in spite of everything. Perhaps she could still reach him after all. "Please don't hurt me," she said, "I love you."

"I love you too," he responded. "But the attacks have been coming faster and hitting harder ever since you interfered with that one recovery. My only chance is a huge dose of therapy. Oh God, I hate this so much! Why did you have to make me do it?"

"You can still see Reverend Carpenter and Dr. Eagleton."

"No. Even if they could help, I'm out of time. And when they found out I hurt you, they'd have me locked up."

"I swear I wouldn't tell!"

He smiled, then started crying. "You never could lie to me. Look, this is all for the best. You're old and sick and miserable; you told me you *want* to die." He swayed and recovered his balance. "I should have begun already, but I wanted to say goodbye." He raised the knife.

"Wait! Just one more second!"

"What?"

"I truly do adore you, my darling. I *will* die, if that's what it takes to make you well. But won't you *kiss* me goodbye?"

"Sure." He bent down. She held her breath, praying he still wouldn't notice the ropes.

His lips fastened on hers. He kissed her gently, just as he always had. His breath was foul and his stubble scraped her.

She nibbled and tongued, prolonging it. She slid her hand slowly down the sheet. The linen rustled; she cringed, but he didn't seem to notice.

He ended the kiss, began to straighten. She grabbed him between the legs, wrenched and squeezed.

He gasped, staggered, turned pale, then stabbed at her forearm.

The blade plunged in, then out the other side. It caused a pulsing, sickening pain, but she kept crushing and yanking anyway, sat up and clawed with her other hand like the poor little baby cats must have done.

He twisted his head and her nails slashed open his cheek instead of his eye. Then he fell; she lost her grip. The pocket-knife tore free in a shower of gore.

She scrabbled at the cords around her ankles. The left noose came loose instantly but the right seemed to take an eternity. Just as the knot finally yielded, Lloyd grabbed the edge of the mattress and hauled himself up onto his knees.

The knife sprang at her throat; she blocked and it gashed her wrist instead. She jerked her right foot free, rolled and tumbled onto the floor.

The impact jarred the wind out of her. The tiniest movement hurt and her meager strength was dwindling. She snarled and crawled toward her cane.

It was three feet away. Two. One. Her tremulant fingers fumbled their way up the tripod and onto the shaft.

Wheezing and bowlegged, his left hand cupping his groin, Lloyd lurched around the foot of the bed.

Somehow, for one final instant, Vina transcended pain, age, and illness. She swung herself to her feet in one fluid motion.

But then her head spun; she had to lean back against the wall to keep from falling. Her heart was pounding as though it was about to burst, and when she raised the cane, it shook like a twig in a hurricane.

Lloyd let go of his crotch. Still crouching, he minced closer, waving the knife back and forth. Vina's blood pattered onto the floor.

He lunged, blade driving in low. She yelped, swung, batted him across the face. Grunting, he stumbled back.

He leaped again; she struck. He caught her cane and ripped it out of her grasp, tossed it into the corner behind him.

Vina realized she wasn't afraid; it was a relief to have it nearly over. She hoped he'd know she forgave him.

He grabbed her arm and swung the knife back. Someone stepped through the door. "No!" shouted Reverend Carpenter.

Lloyd shoved her away. When she hit the floor, her hip snapped, the worst pain yet. Her husband pivoted.

"Please, let's talk—" the Reverend began; Lloyd thrust at his chest.

He goggled and twisted aside. The blade snagged the loose folds of jacket at his waist.

Lloyd ripped it free. The minister punched him twice, once in the mouth and once in the stomach.

Lloyd darted in again. The pocketknife seemed to flash at the pastor's belly, but when his hands dropped, it suddenly arced at his head. He recoiled at the last instant, escaped with only a long red scratch on his cheek.

Lloyd jerked his weapon back. Reverend Carpenter feinted a grab at it, then kicked him in the knee.

Lloyd hobbled back two steps. Lightheaded with agony, Vina stuck her good leg between his ankles.

He tripped and fell sideways, cracked his skull against the closet doorknob. Slumping down onto the floor, he lay inert.

Becky Carpenter burst through the bedroom doorway. The Reverend eyed Lloyd warily for a second, then knelt beside Vina.

"I could almost *always* fool him," she whispered, then started sobbing.

18

TOM PEEKED THROUGH the door behind the altar. The church was packed; the Coalition members who couldn't jam into the pews crowded the back of the chamber and the aisles along the wall. Murmured conversations droned.

"You sure you want to do this?" Becky asked.

He picked at the bandage on his cheek. "I'm sure I don't. But I have to."

She caught his hand, pulled it away from his face, squeezed it. "Maybe so. But don't be too hard on yourself, okay?"

"I'll try," he said. "I guess it's show time." He picked up the cardboard box.

As he strode to the pulpit, he felt naked and ordinary. He fancied they were already scowling and muttering in puzzled disappointment.

He raised his hand and they gradually quieted down.

"Hi," he began. "I know you came here tonight to decide how we can best exert more pressure on Howard Vasquez. And if you still want to, you can discuss that later. But it's vitally important that I make a confession first.

"A while ago I started doubting the existence of God." Someone in one of the front pews gasped. "It made my entire life seem like a worthless lie."

A skinhead rose and raised his hand. His silver earring and the safety pins decorating his black Iron Maiden T-shirt glittered.

Tom reflected wryly that if he still had the High Priest in his pocket, no one would interrupt him. "Yes, Alan?"

"Uh, do you feel all right?"

"I know what I'm saying, if that's what you mean."

"Huh," said Alan. "Well, it's your funeral." He sank back down.

"Eventually," Tom continued, "I felt so miserable that I walked out on a catechism class and got drunk. A lot of you know about that already. What you don't know is that after I got loaded, I inadvertently wandered into a *botanica*."

Their eyes bored into him. "Maybe if I'd been sober, I would have walked right out again, but I wasn't and I didn't. I wound up chatting with the proprietor.

"Even when I believed in God, I never believed in black magic or demonic possession. I always preached that they were silly superstitions.

"I'm sorry to say that I taught my parishioners wrong. Such things exist. I know, because I fell victim to them in that shop."

He wiped his forehead. "The shopkeeper sensed how unhappy I was. He invited me to draw a card from what he claimed was a special Tarot deck. If I kept it, supposedly the spirit associated with it would exercise his unique powers on my behalf.

"To make a long story short, I gave it a try." He bent and reached into the box, slipped his fingers through the loops at the ends of the tongs and lifted them out. "This is the card I picked. The shopkeeper called it the High Priest."

His audience whispered and growled; people leaned and stretched for a better look.

"After he gave it to me, I stumbled home. The next morning I started carrying it like a good luck piece.

"If you think about it, you'll realize that I became more . . . *charismatic* about that time. People who hadn't been attending church regularly, started. Others with personal problems begged my advice. Coalition members who opposed my ideas suddenly decided I was right after all. It wasn't because I'd gotten smarter or more eloquent; the card just made you think I was.

"It affected my mind too. It replaced my doubts with vanity, persuaded me I *deserved* your adulation. After it enabled

me to heal Lloyd Donovan, I was absolutely convinced I was
a modern saint."

A tiny Hispanic woman in the third pew back sighed and
shook her head. A couple dragging a baby carriage started
shoving their way down the right-hand aisle toward the exit.

"If the card had only compelled you to love me," Tom
continued, "that would have been bad enough. But—"

Bubba Meade stood up. "Reverend, please. It seems to me
like you must have been working too hard. You don't—"

"It seems to you like I've gone crazy, and most of the
other people in the room agree. The rest are appalled that
their minister would traffic with the powers of darkness, and
they don't see why they should listen anymore either. But I
promise, there's a reason. In fact, I was just getting to it."

Bubba grimaced, shrugged, and sat back down.

"You see, the *most* evil thing about this card, the true
curse of it, is that apparently every time I tried to help somebody, it turned out horribly wrong. Two sweethearts wound
up abandoning loving sexual practices for a vicious sado-
masochistic ritual. A little boy had a chance to escape abuse,
but thanks to me, he didn't. Even my glorious *miracle* fell
apart. Lloyd ran amok and tried to murder his wife. She's in
Mount Carmel in serious condition. He's there too, his body
still youthful but his mind senile again. I imagine the story
will be in tomorrow's *Register*."

"You bastard!" cried a man in the back of the room. "You
screwed people up for fun!"

"No! The *card* did. It made me say and do the wrong
things, but I honestly thought I was taking care of you." He
wiped his brow again. "I know it's hard to believe a scrap of
grubby pasteboard took control of me. So don't worry about
that part of it. The important thing is that everyone who
asked my advice in the last few weeks understands that the
advice was almost certainly bad. Following it might not in-
jure you as spectacularly as I hurt Vina Donovan, but it's
sure to undermine your happiness somehow.

"This organization can't afford to take my advice either.
Many of you already know I proposed an extremely militant
strategy; you expected to ratify it tonight. Well, we mustn't.

Now that I've severed my link with the card, now that I'm not hypnotizing you, if you reconsider, you'll realize it would be a disaster."

He scanned the staring faces. Some reflected horror, some pity, some anger, some derision, and some incomprehension; none looked adoring. He took a deep breath. "For what little it's worth, I'm sorry. And that's pretty much all I had to tell you. I'll tell the same stuff to my bosses at the Regional Council in the morning.

"I'm going to get out of here in a minute. I imagine you'd like to talk without me present, and I'd like some time alone anyway.

"But first I'm going to destroy this miserable piece of Hell. It hurt a lot of you, and you have a right to see it die." Stooping, he lifted a can of lighter fluid out of the box.

At the rear of the chamber a massive, gray-haired man bellowed, "Don't!"

"Got to." He squeezed the can and doused the pasteboard. Acrid fumes stung his nose.

The gray-haired man started shoving and elbowing people aside, frantically fighting his way through the press toward the unobstructed center aisle.

Perhaps the High Priest had somehow reached out and affected his mind. If so, it didn't matter; he was out of time. Tom switched on the long-handled electric lighter.

The High Priest didn't ignite; it exploded. Orange, green, and blue flames blazed up to the vaulted ceiling. Waves of heat and stench beat like hammers. People screamed; several in the first few rows threw up.

The fire blew out as abruptly as it began. Something screeched by Tom's averted face, perhaps only a final blast of searing, reeking air. Black curls of ash crumbled out of the tongs.

Snarling, fists clenched, the gray-haired man wheeled and bulled his way to the door.

People started babbling, rising. Dropping the tongs and lighter, Tom loped to the rear exit, Becky at his side.

"They have questions," Becky said.

"They'll keep. I can't handle any more right now." He

opened the outer door; they stepped onto the sidewalk. The cool night breeze soothed his blistered skin, carried some of the lingering stink away. "What do you think they're thinking?"

"Damned if I know." She grinned. "I'll tell you one thing, though. If you just destroyed your career, at least you did it with flair."

19

"WHY DIDN'T YOU see him earlier?" Vasquez demanded.

"I tried," said Price, "but he was off dealing with the Donovans."

Vasquez wiped at the yellowish spit on his chin. Scuttling forward, Steven ripped a tissue out of the dispenser on the night stand; the old man shoved him away. "You should have pulled your gun!"

"I was working alone in the midst of hundreds of people. I said I'd take risks for you. I didn't say I'd commit suicide."

Vasquez arched his back and clutched at his blankets. "All right," he wheezed when the spasm passed. "I suppose there was no way you could have predicted or prevented it. Go see him tonight."

"Okay. Why?"

"Perhaps the man lied; maybe the card wasn't the source of his abilities. But if it was, you'll just have to persuade him to go back to his *botanica* and get another."

"Fine by me. But do you understand he claims the magic doesn't work right?"

Vasquez's face contorted. "By God, he'll make it work for me. Stop arguing and do as I say."

Price stood up. "All right. I'll report as soon as I have something to tell you."

"I'll walk you down," Steven said.

They traversed the long hall and descended the stairs in silence; whatever the kid had on his mind, he didn't want his father overhearing. "I'd like to speak with you before you go," he said at last.

"Okay," said Price.

Steven smiled and ushered him into the study. Maps of Corona City, the county, Florida, the southeastern United States, and the Caribbean adorned the walls, and a three-foot globe sat in the middle of the floor. Tiffany lamps glowed like jewels, their soft light glinting on the leather armchairs, the oak paneling, the bindings of the ledgers and law books on the shelves, and the crystal tumblers and decanters on the bar.

The door clicked shut behind him. The lock snicked. "Four Presidents have sat in this room," Steven said.

Price let him blather until he was ensconced in one of the easy chairs with a glass of Wild Turkey in his hand. Then he said, "Why don't we get down to business?"

"You aren't much for small talk, are you?"

"I don't know if your father really expects me to deliver Carpenter tonight, but I'd like to at least be able to say I set the wheels in motion."

"Okay." Steven took a sip of his cognac. "If I tell you something, will you keep it confidential?"

"If it won't hurt your dad. *He's* my client."

"This could only hurt him if it *did* come out. Unfortunately, there's a chance it could." He took some photos out of his breast pocket. "Take a look at these."

The detective riffled through them. Two little girls sixty-nining. A towheaded kid pissing on a black one. Another girl in a split-beaver shot. "Did you take them?"

"Yes." He drank again. "I want you to understand, I don't do it for the money. I don't need it. This is an act of love. The kids understand, and they enjoy it just as much as I do.

"They have sexual feelings just like you and me. That's why so many adults respond to them sexually. If we didn't live in such a repressive society—"

"Hold it," said Price. "I don't care why you do it, or if anybody gets hurt. Stick to the facts."

"But I don't want you to think—"

"It doesn't matter. Just tell me the problem. Is somebody blackmailing you?"

"Worse than that. I set up my studio in an abandoned factory on the other side of the district. Yesterday my friend

Gary Saunders brought me a kid. Becky Carpenter sneaked in and spied."

Price raised his eyebrows. "These church people lead interesting lives."

"Gary and I caught her and—well, we were going to dispose of her. It didn't seem like there was anything else we could do. But the damn kid grabbed a gun that was lying around. He and the bitch got away and talked to the cops."

Price didn't bother remarking on the fact that evidently at least one child hadn't relished Steven's attentions. "Why aren't you in jail?"

"Gary's hiding. I haven't had to, because I was wearing clown makeup. I always figured it was only prudent to use a disguise, and that particular get-up helped set the kids at ease."

"The police may still be able to trace you."

Steven grimaced. "I hope not. The Vasquez family has never owned that particular building; a dummy corporation in Grand Cayman does. They may find fingerprints, but they don't have mine on file. And I set a fire before I took off. With luck, it destroyed at least some of whatever evidence was there.

"What worries me more is that Becky knows me. I've bought cards and flowers where she works. Obviously she didn't recognize me past the greasepaint and rubber-ball nose at the time, but as she mulls over what happened, she still might."

The older man took a swig of bourbon, savored the sweet burn as it went down. "Do you want to scare her or kill her?"

"I wouldn't trust her to stay intimidated. If I'm going to be really safe, I need her dead." He tried unsuccessfully to suppress a smirk. His pale eyes shone and his sallow cheeks flushed. "And of course, I want you to help me. After all, you're the professional.

"I've got it mostly figured out already." He tossed off the rest of his brandy, rose, and returned to the bar. "You're going to have to force Carpenter to do what Papa wants."

"Don't know. We haven't tried buying him yet."

"Do you really think that could work?"

"Probably not. Carpenter's smart enough to understand that he could have sold healing for big bucks. If that's what he wanted, he wouldn't have told an audience that his first miracle didn't work out right or torched the thing that was supposed to be his magic healing doodad in front of them."

"Then you might as well lean on him right away. Papa won't care, as long as you get results. He hates the man; that's why he hired you in the first place, remember?

"Here's my idea." Snifter replenished, Steven dropped back into his chair. "We collect Carpenter tonight. Gary can come too if you want another gun; I know I can persuade him if I wave a little money under his nose. We collect Becky at the same time, before she has a chance to realize who she met yesterday. The preacher does whatever he can for my father, and then we kill him and the wife. You'd have to kill him anyway, wouldn't you, so he couldn't tell anybody you forced him to do what Papa wanted."

Frowning, Price considered.

He didn't like it. The job would become too complicated if he tried to look out for the separate interests of two clients. And it was always dangerous to work with amateurs, especially sadists, frightened people, or guys who were out for revenge.

But the longer he thought about it, the more certain he became that Carpenter wouldn't help the old man voluntarily. It really was time to get rough, and when he threatened, abducted, and otherwise abused people, he liked backup. He'd particularly appreciate it this time out, when he'd be confronting something uncanny. Whenever he remembered the healing, the way the sermon had twisted his thoughts, or the unnaturally violent and malodorous conflagration of the Tarot card, he broke out in a sweat.

And unfortunately, he couldn't call any of the goons he usually hired. They all would have heard that the boys from Vegas were willing to pay for news of his whereabouts, and there wasn't a damn one of them he could trust not to sell him out.

Maybe on this occasion amateur help would be better than none. Anyway, one thing was sure: if he only took his original client's money, he could buy back his markers and that was all. It would be a lot nicer to finish the case with a fat bank account.

"All right," he said at last, "but there are two conditions. The first is that I'm in charge. We're going to do it as fast and clean as possible; it's the only way to keep this kind of job from going sour. You can't torture anybody except on my say-so, and after it makes them do what we want, you'll have to stop."

Steven nodded. "What's the second?"

"It'll cost you a hundred thousand, fifty a hit."

20

BECKY PULLED THE headphones off, tousling her curls. "Think it's safe to put the phone back on the hook?"

"Let's leave it off till tomorrow," Tom replied. He tossed his beat-up Robert Ludlum paperback on the coffee table. "Play that through the speakers if you want to. I've read the same page twenty times."

She scooted closer on the couch. "You did what you could to set things right. So stop kicking yourself."

"I would if I could. I wonder if there's any chance at all that the congregation and the Council will both want me to stay on. I guess I'm dumb to worry about it, when I don't even know if I belong in the ministry anyway."

"Whatever happens, you'll land on your feet."

He smiled; it hurt his blistered, bandaged face. "The card's gone. How come you're still acting like you like me?"

"Life's been so eventful lately that I haven't had to bitch to keep myself entertained. I can always start again when things get slow."

"That's something to look forward to."

"Seriously, Tom, don't you know I've always loved you? But after you turned all cold and bitter, I had to harden up or it would have killed me."

He stared at her. "Are you kidding? *You* turned mean first."

"Bullshit. You blamed me for losing the baby."

"Tell me you didn't really think that. I hated that it happened, but I swear I never, *ever* thought it was your fault."

"Well, it sure seemed like it. I figured you *still* did. It made me hate us both, but especially myself." She started sobbing and he folded her in his arms.

"Now we're even," he said when she finally stopped. "You snotted on me."

She snorted, sniffled, and wiped at her reddened face. "Serves you right. Because I still think you got nasty first."

"Could be. Or maybe after the miscarriage we each felt so rotten we took it out on the other without even realizing what we were doing. And maybe it doesn't matter how we started hurting each other. The important thing is to stop."

"I'd like to," she said. A car motor rumbled into the parking lot. "Come on, people, not at this hour."

"Let's turn out the lights and head upstairs," he suggested. "Hopefully they'll go away."

21

"You owe me," Gary said. His shaggy head and round, fleshy shoulders made a black hump in the rearview mirror, the tip of his marijuana cigarette a flaring orange star.

"No," Steven answered. "You understood the risks when you got involved. Twenty thousand's all I can afford, and it's plenty to get you established in a new identity."

"You've got to be kidding. I don't dare contact anyone who knows me. I can't work in music anymore!"

Price parked at the rear of the lot, switched off the lights and the ignition. "Here's the bottom line. You agreed to a price, the same money I'm making. The deal's about to go down. If you want out, you have to walk away *now*. If you don't, stop whining so we can get this over with."

"All right," said Gary, "I'm in. But I want you to know I know I'm getting fucked."

They climbed out of the van Price had boosted, a mud-splattered brown Chevy with tinted windows. A warm, dank breeze was blowing. A dog down the street began yapping, and the shadow of an owl glided across the grass.

When they peered around the hedge, the lights in the parsonage went out. "Shit!" Gary exclaimed.

"Relax," said Price. "It doesn't mean anything; they're just going to bed." A window on the second story flared. "See?" He pulled three crumpled rubber apeman masks out of his raincoat pocket. "Put these on. And don't let them hear your voices."

"Why?" Gary asked.

"Because I said so."

"If they think we're worried about being identified, and if

they don't know we're people with a score to settle, they're more likely to believe we'll let them live if they cooperate," Steven explained. "Don't worry, we'll show them who we are before the end."

The musician shrugged. "Sounds pointless, but you're paying." He dragged the stretchy, comical simian features down over his own and threaded the dwindling stub of the joint through the mouth-hole.

Price adjusted his own mask. The latex had a sharp, unpleasant smell. "Gary, you watch the back. Steven, you're coming in the front with me. Let's go."

His heart was pounding as they dashed across the yard. When he tried to slip the skeleton key into the keyhole, his hand shook.

Settle down, he told himself. *Carpenter may be a freak, but you're a professional. If he starts turning your brain to mush, you won't have any trouble making him stop.*

The lock clicked open. He pocketed his ring of keys and drew his .38, then turned the knob.

Amorphous masses of furniture squatted in the darkened living room. Pale light spilled down the stairs.

Price crept forward. Steven followed, making too much noise. At least he had the brains to close the door.

As they slowly ascended the stairs, the sounds above grew clearer. Water hissed out of a faucet. A drawer squeaked open, then thumped shut.

Halfway up, Steven planted his foot carelessly. The riser squealed.

Price ran. As he bounded onto the landing, Carpenter lurched out of the bathroom. He was barefoot and his hair was disheveled; with his eyes goggling and his mouth hanging open, he looked reassuringly like any other alarmed, helpless citizen.

"What—" he began.

Price extended the gun to make sure he saw it. "Get in your bedroom."

"What do you—"

"Now!"

Someone gasped. Price glanced to the side. The preacher's wife cowered in the master bedroom doorway, a tortoise-shell hairbrush in her hand. Crouching a few feet away, Steven had his Beretta aimed at her chest.

The detective felt himself relax. They had them.

"Both of you in there," he said. As they backed up, he stayed close so they wouldn't try to slam the door in his face. "Rev, you can park it in the chair. Lady, stand in that corner." He flicked his head toward Steven. "You get our buddy." Steven wheeled and took off.

"What do you want?" Becky wailed.

"Shut up," said Price. No point getting into it until the rest of his team arrived. Besides, it might soften them up to sit and stew.

"Please," she said. "Don't hurt us. We'll—"

"If either of you speaks again when I don't want you to, I'll shoot him in the knee."

She shivered, swallowed, and shut up.

After a minute Steven and Gary clumped up the steps. The rich kid still had his pistol out; his friend was carrying a big blue- and brown-striped carpetbag of a purse. Spying the wallet and jewelry box on the chest of drawers, he grabbed them and dropped them inside.

Price could cheerfully have shot *him*. He was supposed to be concentrating on the job, not pilfering. But it didn't seem worth hassling over, even to reestablish who was boss. If he jumped on the idiot's meat, he'd answer back.

Apparently Gary didn't see anything else he thought worth stealing, because he finally started following instructions. Sidling behind the pastor's wife, he pulled the hairbrush out of her hand and tossed it on the bedspread, then gripped her forearms. Steven positioned himself in front of her and Price edged closer to Carpenter.

"Now we'll talk," the detective said. "Here's the situation. Our employer is sick. If you make him well, you and your wife can live. If you don't, we'll kill you."

"But I can't!" Carpenter said. "Don't you know what I did in the church tonight?"

Price said, "Hurt her." Steven lashed the barrel of his Beretta against Becky's cheek.

The big man winced. It was no way to treat a gun, particularly a loaded one.

"The magic burned up!" Carpenter shouted. "There's nothing I can do!"

"Hurt her some more," Price ordered. "*Not* with your weapon."

Steven stuck the Beretta in his belt holster. Picking up the brush, he turned it over in his hands, then suddenly swiveled and rammed it into her stomach like a prod. After the first few blows, her legs went rubbery. Gary grunted when he had to catch her weight.

Carpenter lost his shit and tried to jump up. Price rapped him on the head to keep him in his chair.

Becky retched down the front of her turquoise T-shirt. Steven hopped back so he wouldn't get splashed.

Price said, "Stop. So far this is nothing. But we're going to start breaking fingers and then we're going to start cutting. Will you cure my employer?"

Carpenter's face was ashen beneath its pink burn, his cheeks streaked with tears. "I swear I can't."

"Okay, I believe you. So you take us back to your *botanica*. We'll buy you a replacement card."

The minister rubbed the darkening bruise on his temple. "You can't. It was one of a kind."

"Then you'd better hope they sell something else that does the same stuff. Put your shoes on. You're driving."

Becky whimpered and clutched her middle as she stumbled across the yard; she probably would have fallen if they hadn't let Carpenter support her. Price peeked around the end of the hedge. The coast was clear.

"My gun and I will ride up front with you," Price told the pastor. "My partners will be in the back with your old lady. If you pull any shit, she'll pay for it." When they were all seated, he handed him the key.

They turned out onto Palm, drove half a block. "It can't work," Carpenter said.

"Just get us where we're going."

They passed two crumbling houses with CONDEMNED notices tacked to their front doors, another shrouded in an exterminator's tent. "But it *can't*," the pastor blurted. "Anything we bring out of that shop will be evil. No matter how sick your employer is, he's better off now than he would be if you exposed him to a demonic influence."

"I don't know from demonic influences," Price replied. "I just want my fee."

Carpenter stopped for a red light. An orange and white EMS truck rolled across the intersection. "There's something else you have to understand. I don't exactly know where the *botanica* is."

"What kind of bullshit is this?"

"I was drunk. I don't remember precisely where I found it. Look, don't worry. I know the general area and I'm sure I can find it again. I just don't want you to think I'm stalling if I seem to be driving in circles."

"Find it fast."

For the next half-hour they crept up and down the western half of Martin Avenue and the narrow, shabby streets surrounding it, constantly turning and doubling back. Gary and Steven shifted restlessly, their cheap, ridiculous masks somehow lifelike in the gloom. The stink of Becky's vomit gave Price a headache.

Someone lacking any artistic ability had painted a bikini-clad female matador on the side of the Aragon Street Package Store and Lounge. The fourth time they passed her, Price said, "Get out a knife."

Becky thrashed; Steven drove his elbow into her solar plexus. She made a choking sound and slumped.

"Don't," Carpenter begged, his face haggard. "I'm trying. I can't understand—I was lost, but it has to be right around here."

Gary gripped Becky's wrists. Steven opened a clasp knife. The blade shone. "Show him we're not kidding," the detective said.

"No!" Carpenter cried. *"Look!"*

When the big man glanced out the windshield, he felt a chill.

A particularly dark brick street lined with extremely dilapidated storefronts ran off at an angle to the southeast. A green light burned partway down the block.

"Son of a bitch," Gary breathed, "this stuff is for real."

"Quiet," Price said mechanically. His voice broke.

It was unsettling enough that they hadn't been able to see the intersection until that moment. Spookier still was the fact that the street couldn't exist in that exact spot. Price had a good head for spatial relationships, and he was sure there were other, brighter streets filling the same area, streets they'd driven down only minutes ago. The world had to stretch in some unimaginable way to make room for this one.

He didn't blame Carpenter for failing to comprehend that the street itself was unnatural. If he'd wandered through here drunk, he wouldn't have understood, or at least believed, the evidence of his senses either.

"Are you beginning to realize what you're getting into?" the minister asked.

This time Price made sure his tone was deep and steady. "If you can go down a street, you can come back up it. You did it already. Turn the car."

Carpenter squinched his eyes shut as if he were going to start crying again, then tore at the wheel. A few seconds later he parked in front of the door with the green light.

Price reclaimed the ignition key, Steven and Gary readied their guns, and they ushered their captives out. Becky and Carpenter quickly huddled together.

Price had a vague impression that farther ahead the street became . . . stranger. Lighter patches mottled a wall; they might have been faintly phosphorescent. A figure seemed to jump at the edge of his vision, a black silhouette of a mannequin in a window. When he turned, it wasn't moving, but it still looked oddly asymmetrical. Rats, or something that sounded like them, skittered along the roof line.

"I beg you," Becky said. "Don't make him touch magic again. We'll give you everything we own."

Price said, "I take it this is the place."

"Yes," Carpenter answered.

"Then lead the way."

The door opened on a tiny, lightless excuse for a vestibule. Pushing through the musty curtain on the other side, they found themselves in a grubby room crammed with precariously leaning bookshelves and display cases full of occult paraphernalia. A dozen guttering white candles furnished the only illumination.

"Where's your shopkeeper?" Price asked.

"Right here," said a baritone voice at his elbow.

Becky squealed, and Price was so startled it was a miracle he didn't shoot. The tubby little guy in the disheveled three-piece suit must have been kneeling behind the nearest bookcase, straightening the titles or something. He seemed to burst out of nowhere like a jack-in-the-box.

He smiled as genially as Santa Claus; if he even noticed the ape masks and the guns, Price couldn't tell it. "Hello, Mr. Carpenter, what a pleasure to see you again. How can I help you and your friends?"

"He needs another High Priest, or something else that does the same thing," said Price.

"Please," Carpenter said. "Make them understand there was only the one."

"Follow me," the little man said. "I'll show you something interesting." He turned, still seemingly oblivious to the pistol now leveled at his back, and ambled toward the counter at the back of the room.

Baffled by this nonchalance, Price gestured with the .38 and the rest of them scurried in pursuit. Gary paused briefly in transit to examine a case of silver rings, bracelets, and pendants. Apparently even the more bizarre aspects of their situation couldn't stifle his acquisitive impulses; perhaps the shopkeeper's innocuous demeanor had put him at ease.

The little man started to hook his arm behind the huge metal cash register. "Freeze!" roared Price.

The shopkeeper peered at him blankly for a moment, then grinned. "*Oh*. You thought I might be reaching for a firearm or an alarm button, didn't you? I assure you I've never seen the need for either. But if it would make you more comfortable to fetch out the deck yourself, please feel free. It's the wooden box on the first shelf down."

Price edged behind the register, squatted, and found it immediately. Setting it on the counter, he lifted the lid to reveal a stack of stained, oversize pasteboards. A faint, rotten odor wafted up.

The shopkeeper dumped them out, then spread them facedown on the counter top as deftly as any dealer or gambler Price had ever seen. Beaming, he plucked one out and turned it over.

It was the High Priest.

Carpenter recoiled. Steven planted his hand between his shoulder blades and thrust him forward again.

"Sometimes an object *can* be in two places at the same time," the little man explained. "When a card leaves the shop, it also remains, a safeguard against misadventure and improvidence."

Price didn't want to touch the thing. "You're back in business, Reverend. Pick it up."

Carpenter looked like he was about to be sick. Steven jabbed him with the Beretta and then he finally stretched out his hand.

"I'm afraid that won't work," the shopkeeper said apologetically. Carpenter froze.

"When the good pastor threw off the influence of the High Priest," the little man continued, "he spurned the gift of a haughty and unforgiving power. It won't offer it again. And to forestall your next question, no one is ever permitted a second draw. The other cards confer different boons which probably wouldn't serve your purpose anyway."

"Can somebody else take it up?"

"Regrettably, no, not intentionally. The supplicant doesn't choose which spirit will ally with him; fate does. In other words, it takes a blind selection."

Price wondered if the shopkeeper had any inkling that he'd just condemned the Carpenters to die in the next few minutes. If neither of them could cure Vasquez, there was no reason to drag them around any longer; they might as well leave the bodies here in the Magic Kingdom. "Friend, I want you to understand something. I've killed people before and I wouldn't mind killing you now. If you don't want me to, give me something that'll heal a guy dying of cancer."

"Here's what I suggest," the little man said, still entirely composed. "No two cards work exactly alike, but each labors after its own fashion to make its possessor content, and the mortally ill are rarely that. Why don't you carry the deck to your ailing friend and let him draw. The spirit that answers his call is quite likely to cure him in addition to whatever other benefits it bestows."

"Okay," said Price, "if that's the best you can do." He considered blowing him away and quickly decided against it. After all, they were disguised, and for all the shopkeeper's apparent harmlessness, there was something subtly unnerving about him which made the detective leery of fucking with him any more than necessary. Besides, it was hard to imagine him phoning the police to report the robbery of a store on a street that didn't exist. "Put them back in their box."

Gary shoved forward, leaving Steven to cover both the Carpenters. "It's nice you could help the sick guy," he said to the shopkeeper. "What are you going to do for me?"

"Shut up!" Price barked. "We're getting out of here."

"Go to hell!" the musician snarled. "This guy makes miracles and I need some. Make me rich. Make the cops forget about me. Make me live forever. Make me play like Clapton."

"Ask your sick friend if you can draw a card too," the shopkeeper said. "Since he can only take one himself, I doubt he'll begrudge one of his benefactors another."

"That's not good enough. The Reverend says they don't work right."

"I think that's, at the very least, debatable. Mr. Carpenter was delighted with his until—please forgive my candor, Mrs. Carpenter—a certain someone started henpecking."

"I have to control what happens," Gary insisted.

The shopkeeper shrugged. "The Tarot really is the best I can offer."

Price's nerves jangled with the certainty that things were

spinning out of control. "Knock it off, or—" Behind him, something bumped.

He whirled. Obviously Gary's exchange with the shop-keeper had riveted Steven's attention as thoroughly as it had his own. Taking advantage of their distraction, the captives had crept toward the entrance, making it better than halfway there before one of them jostled a bookcase.

"Hold it!" Price shouted at the fleeing couple. "You watch them," he ordered Steven.

"I don't believe you," Gary told the shopkeeper. He shot the little man in the hand.

Blood spurted. "Ouch!" the shopkeeper said.

"You want another?"

"Oh, good grief." Gray eyes glittering, he swept the cards to the side.

An instant later, the candle flames elongated, released blobs of golden light. These drifted upward like bubbles in a water cooler, then leaped. Flaring, they danced on Gary's head and back.

The musician shrieked, slapped at them with one hand, and jerked off shot after shot with the other. The bullets slammed into the little man's torso. Making no effort to de-flect the pistol, he grappled with Gary. Vapor rose from his mouth and nostrils, then his skin. His hands glowed red and Gary blackened and sizzled under their touch.

The Carpenters bolted. Price fired; a jar full of brown powder exploded; they scrambled through the curtain. "Come on!" Price shouted at Steven. Steven came, but back-ing slowly, seemingly unable to tear his gaze away from the counter.

As he took his first stride, Price dimly sensed his mind ea-gerly locking into a kind of tunnel vision, dismissing the im-possibilities behind him to focus on the straightforward business of the chase.

He plunged through the hanging. Carpenter was waiting on the other side.

The minister drove a hard, straight right into his jaw, then spun and threw open the door. Jolted off balance, Price clutched at the drapery. It tore off its rings and tumbled down in dusty, entangling folds.

If he'd burst out onto the sidewalk a second later, he would have lost them. Instead of fleeing back toward Aragon, which would have given him a clear shot, they'd dashed a few feet farther down the street to a gap between two buildings.

Wondering why Steven hadn't followed him, Price fired and missed again, then sprinted. The gap opened on a narrow, crooked alley. The Carpenters were racing toward a branching passage.

Something chittered, and then a shiny black squirming mass the size of a boxing glove dropped on Becky's shoulder; she screamed and fell to one knee. When Carpenter whirled, two more leaped on him. Staggering, the humans clawed and pummeled, desperately fighting to rip the creatures off.

They couldn't do that and dodge bullets too. Smiling, Price sighted in on the Reverend's chest.

More chittering sounded directly overhead. He felt the shriek building inside him before he even looked up.

A filthy brown tide surged down the wall. Jointed legs pumped, antennae quivered, and double sets of mandibles gnashed open and closed.

Two of them pounced. Hurling himself backward, swinging his Colt wildly, he bashed one out of the air. The other landed on his forearm. Its claws hooking through his coat and shirt into the flesh beneath, it began biting.

He clubbed it off; it hit the ground and darted at his ankle. As he stamped it into slime and bits of chitin, more of them jumped. He reeled under the impact.

He threw himself down and rolled. Bug-things crunched under his weight.

At last the biting stopped. Leaping to his feet, he ran from the alley, a rustling carpet seething along behind. When he reached the middle of the street, he turned and started shooting.

It scared them, or perhaps they disliked venturing far from the deeper darknesses and cramped, twisting recesses of the alleyways. At any rate, they abruptly scuttled back the way they came.

Price fumbled in his pocket for a fresh clip, made himself take slow, deep breaths. He was okay; they'd barely scratched him. He'd make it through like he always did, if he just kept functioning like a pro.

Once his heart stopped hammering, he peered down the gap. The Carpenters were nowhere to be seen.

Fuck it. It would take a miracle to catch them now. He trotted back to the *botanica*. Mask gone, Steven sat on the curb by the Chevy's front bumper, hyperventilating.

"I could have used some help with those bugs," the detective growled.

Steven gave him a dopey, quizzical smile. "Help?"

Price realized he hadn't even seen the creatures. "Skip it. Is your pal dead?"

The younger man tittered. "Oh, hell, yes, *really* dead. I never dreamed that . . . well, I just never did."

Price wondered if a slap or a shaking would snap him out of his daze. "Is the shopkeeper dead?"

"Get real."

"Can't get a break tonight," Price muttered. He moved to the door.

Steven blinked the glaze out of his eyes. "Are you going back in there?"

"Unless you have the cards."

Rising, Steven pulled his mask out of his jacket. "I'm right behind you."

Price was surprised. The little pervert was either tougher or even crazier than he'd suspected. "Good, but don't do anything unless I tell you to." He waited for Steven to adjust his false face and draw his Beretta, then gripped the brass handle and pulled.

The room reeked of burnt meat. A charred husk lay in front of the counter; behind it sat the shopkeeper, fanning himself with his tie. His clothes were singed, riddled with holes and bloody, but he didn't seem to be wounded anymore.

"That was altogether too strenuous," he said. "I'm glad I usually lead a peaceful life."

"We came back for the cards," said Price.

"And I suppose that if I decline to hand them over, you'll fill me full of lead."

"We'll try. Can you take one in the eye?"

"Probably. But I'm only teasing. Don't you understand, I *want* you to take them." Smiling, he proffered the inlaid box.

22

STEVEN TURNED IN without letting up on the gas. Price braced for a collision, but the radio-controlled wrought-iron gate rolled out of their way just in time. The Porsche, to which they'd returned after ditching the van, hurtled up the palm-lined semicircular drive.

"It really upsets me that the Carpenters got away," Steven said.

"Maybe they didn't. Something could have eaten them before they made it out. Even if they are okay, you didn't talk or show your face, so with luck they still didn't recognize you and you aren't any worse off than you were before."

Brakes squealing, the car jerked to a stop before the front door. "If you were as tough as you're supposed to be," Steven said sullenly, "you would have gone in after them."

"Fuck you. If you don't like my work, then if they do turn back up, you can hire somebody else."

The younger man smirked. "Hey, I'm sorry, I was just mouthing off. I'm still wired from what we went through."

Price nodded. "It was a bitch."

"Yeah, but it was also the most exciting thing that ever happened to me. I wouldn't have missed it for anything."

"I wish you could have had my share," Price said. He un-buckled his seat belt. "Let's deliver the goods."

Vasquez lived in a huge, gabled, three-story brownstone. In the darkness, with no lights visible anywhere, it looked like an ancient crumbling fortress.

As Price started toward the door, Steven said, "Wait."

The detective turned. "What is it?"

"Let's think about this for a second. I imagine I'd enjoy being the *senior* Vasquez, and if I was, I could pay you a lot more than my father intends to. Are we absolutely certain we want to follow through?"

"I am. Sometimes I do things my clients wouldn't like if they found out about them, but I always give them what they hired me to get if I possibly can. Besides, I thought you weren't sure about the will."

Steven snorted. "I could probably make sure before the end, and if there were any nasty surprises, a good lawyer could almost certainly convince a judge that Papa was incompetent when he wrote it. But if you want to hand over the deck, then of course that's what we'll do. I do more or less love the old buzzard, and I'm really curious to see what'll happen when he draws a card."

Perhaps it was just an illusion, but Vasquez looked even sicker than he had only a few hours before, even more shriveled inside his baggy envelope of jaundiced skin. He smelled worse, too, as though he'd begun to decay. He tried to sit upright but only managed to flop. "Medicine," he croaked.

Scurrying to the night stand, Steven popped the cap off an orange plastic bottle, dumped two pills out, and placed them on his father's grayish tongue. Then he picked up a pitcher.

"No, idiot!" the old man snarled.

Hastily setting it down again, Steven brought a liter of Bacardi Black out of the cabinet in the bottom of the stand. Vasquez guzzled for a while, golden rum dribbling down his stubbly chin, then pushed the bottle away. Liquor splashed on his pillows.

"You should have called the nurse," Steven said.

"I couldn't get my finger on the button."

"You should have had her stay in the room."

Vasquez sneered. "Shut up and let someone with something to say talk. What's the story with Carpenter?"

"I interrogated him and the guy who gave him the card," said Price. "It really was the source of his abilities. There's a . . . call it a duplicate, but because of the way the damn things work, neither the Reverend nor anybody else can simply pick it up and use it."

"No!" The old man grunted and arched his back; tears squeezed out off his bloodshot eyes. "They must have been lying," he groaned when his body unclenched.

"It's all right," Steven said. "We found a different way to cure you."

" 'We'?"

"I was there too. With your welfare at stake, I had to be."

"Of course you did," Vasquez said sardonically. He shifted his gaze back to Price. "What's he talking about?"

"I have the whole magic Tarot pack right here in my pocket," the detective replied. "If you draw a card the way Carpenter did, there's a good chance it'll take away your cancer."

"Then get it out!"

"Hold on one more minute."

Vasquez smiled crookedly. "Oh. You want to renegotiate."

Price shook his head. "We have a deal. I just don't want you saying afterwards that I didn't warn you. Carpenter said the deck's cursed, and we saw plenty of shit tonight that makes me think he might be right. There's no *guarantee* your card's going to heal you, and whether it does or not, apparently it'll change you in some other, unpredictable way. I'd think twice about drawing even if I was as sick as you."

"What could it do to me that's worse than this? Get them out."

Price handed him the box. "There's no ritual. Just shuffle and cut."

Vasquez's palsied fingers fumbled with the catch. As it finally released, the box slipped out of his grasp. It tumbled down the blanket, spilling cards.

"I don't think I can shuffle," the old man said. "You'll have to do it for me."

Suppressing a grimace, Price leaned under the canopy and gathered the deck. The cards felt moist and soft. When he had them all, he spread them in a fan. "You should probably touch them all anyway."

Vasquez stroked them back and forth, closed his eyes and sighed.

Price swept medication bottles to the back of the night stand, clearing a space to shuffle. Despite their mushy feel, the cards riffled together as easily as a fresh deck. Their stench of putrefaction nearly choked him.

Nasty as they were to handle, he kept shuffling till they felt right, just as he would at a poker table, then turned back to the bed and fanned them again. Vasquez regarded them with narrowed eyes, then finally reached for one in the middle. His thumb and forefinger missed their hold the first time, pinched again, dragged the card out, and rolled it over.

Price cocked his head for a better look. Steven shoved up close behind him to goggle over his shoulder.

A monstrously obese man in an embroidered crimson robe and a plumed yellow hat sat on an ornately sculpted throne. He actually looked a little like Vasquez, or like Vasquez had probably looked before his cancer. He was gnawing on a huge drumstick, massive rings glittering on his fist. Arrayed at his feet were nine golden goblets crammed full of other food, bottles of wine, coins, gems, and rolls of parchment bound with ribbon. The chair and cups rested on a gray mound with an intricate line running through it.

When Price studied the line, the mound broke into separate shapes. It was made of crushed, naked human bodies, all as emaciated as concentration camp victims. Some eyes stared and some mouths gaped, but he couldn't tell if they were supposed to be alive or dead.

"I don't feel—" the old man began. "No, wait. Maybe I do." He gasped and shuddered; then, the pasteboard clutched in his hand, he threw back his covers, swung his feet to the floor, and snatched the Bacardi.

"What's happening?" Steven cried.

Vasquez upended the bottle and chugged it dry, swatted his son aside and broke into a lurching run. Trotting, Price pursued him down the hall.

The old man kept weaving and stumbling, almost tripped at the top of the stairs. Price tried to take his arm, but he struck his hand away. Blundering down to the ground floor somehow, he scrambled on toward the rear of the house.

Price realized they were heading for the kitchen. He

stopped in the doorway and Steven caught up with him there a moment later.

"What is it?" the younger man asked, his eyes shining and his voice shrill. "Is he crazy?"

"I don't know," Price answered, "but he's hungry."

Vasquez yanked open the refrigerator door. A huge, pineapple-glazed ham sat on the top shelf. Plunging his fingers into the glistening pink meat, he ripped out handful after handful. Flecks of it sprayed from his furiously gnashing jaws.

Two minutes later he jerked the platter and bone out of his way and tossed them clanging to the linoleum floor, swilled a gallon jug of milk, and chomped down a head of lettuce. When he gobbled the eggs, he ate them shells and all.

As he stuffed himself, his body swelled, tightening his sagging skin. By the time the bottom of the refrigerator was empty, he was fat again.

Price wouldn't have been surprised if he'd attacked the frozen food next, but, his movements now lithe and his equilibrium restored, he turned to the cabinets instead. Seizing a can of fruit cocktail, he punched his greasy fingers through the top and tore it off like Popeye opening his spinach. The sharp edge gashed him, but either he didn't notice or he didn't care.

Adam's apple bobbing up and down, flesh rippling as it reconfigured itself, he wolfed down peaches, plums, corn, asparagus, and ravioli, then wheeled and strode toward the door. This time neither Price nor Steven tried to question or detain him. They just pressed against the wall to clear his path, then followed.

Once again the detective surmised where he was headed and once again he turned out to be right. Marching into the study, the old man crossed to the bar, knocked back the Scotch, the brandy, and finally the sherry.

He sighed, belched, and set the last decanter down. Panting a little, blood dripping from his right hand and his pajama shirt so food-stained it resembled a painter's palette, he smiled at the watchers in the hall. "Come in and have a drink."

"Are you all right?" Price asked.

"Indeed I am, thanks to you. Free of pain, full of strength, and eager to reassert my prerogatives. And I believe I know exactly how to start."

Lifting the framed map of Corona City off the wall, he pulled the cardboard backing loose and drew the chart out, then laid it on the desk and picked up a pen.

Price and Steven moved closer. "What are you doing?" the younger man asked.

Vasquez smiled. "You'll find out soon enough. Everyone will."

Staring intently at the paper, pressing hard enough to carve a groove, he traced the generally accepted boundaries of Corona City, Iroquois Avenue to the north, Thirtieth Street to the east, Columbus Drive to the south, and the Little Seminole River to the west. He only deviated at the northeast corner, cutting diagonally across from Iroquois to Thirtieth to leave the red square representing a police station outside the line.

"There," he said as he finished. "I'll clean up and dress, and then we're going out."

23

Tom stuck his head around the corner. Surely *this* time he'd see the street where the *botanica* stood, or at least some street.

He grimaced and closed his eyes, wanted to shout and hammer his fist against the sooty brick wall. Ahead lay only another junction in the shadowy, claustrophobic maze of alleys.

He twisted his face into a smile before he looked back. "Everything's still okay. No more insects and none of those lizard-looking things, either."

"And no way out," Becky gritted. She sat down with her knees drawn up and her back against the wall. In the darkness her tanned face seemed ghostly pale, the welt under her eye a jet-black stripe. "I need to rest for a minute."

Tom looked around, making sure nothing was creeping up or down on them, then squatted down beside her and squeezed her shoulder. "We will get out."

"Oh, really? What makes you think so?"

"I don't know," he sighed. "It seemed like the thing to say. I guess 'I'm sorry' would have been a better choice."

"Don't say that either. I'm not blaming you, I'm just in a really bad mood. We already risked our lives, and you made your big confession, and that should have been enough. We paid our dues and the shit is supposed to be over."

He chuckled and the loose end of his bandage flapped against his cheek. When he peeled it off, it stuck to his fingers, and it took a few seconds to flick it away. "Sounds fair to me. You should have explained the system to Gary and Vasquez Junior."

"Damn, I'm glad I finally recognized that little shit! We *do* have to make it out of here, if only for the satisfaction of slamming his ass in jail."

"And his father has terminal cancer. Lucky for us; I have a feeling he and Gary would have turned up at the house anyway, but just killed us immediately. Funny how things come together sometimes."

Back down the alley, around the last dogleg, something rattled. Tom stifled a gasp, Becky clutched his hand, and they held their breaths till the noise receded and stopped.

"I'll laugh when we step onto Aragon Street," she said at last. "What *is* this place? We ran blindly to get away from the bugs, but even so, how can we be *this* lost?"

"I have an idea, but it's only that, and it's kind of demoralizing."

"Tell me."

"I think we're in Hell."

"That would be weird. I'm a relatively good girl and I also don't remember dying."

The insect bite on the back of his left hand itched. When he scratched, the bruised knuckles on his right hand twinged. Neither he nor Becky were seriously injured, but their ordeals were nickel-and-diming them into hamburger. "You're a very good girl and you didn't. The way I figure it, the cartomancer is a native of Hell, and when he wants to contact the living, he doesn't leave home. What happens instead is that his section of Hell reaches out and attaches itself to a particular spot in our world. Like a leech."

She smiled wanly. "Too bad he didn't just buy an RV like the other snowbirds."

"He probably saves a bundle on gas. Anyway, how could a piece of another place intrude itself into the middle of Corona City without subtracting something that's already there? Something, not precisely the geography but the medium that supports the geography—space itself, I guess you'd call it—would have to bend for it to jam itself in.

"Which could explain why we're having so much trouble reaching an exit. Maybe right isn't exactly or always right, and left isn't exactly or always left. It could be that some of these twists and branching alleys really turn in cockeyed directions we aren't equipped to perceive."

She brushed a tumble of raven hair out of her eyes, then scowled and tugged at the snarls. "You're right, that is discouraging. Although things could be worse; at least we aren't having difficulty with up and down. I have to tell you, I will *never* understand how you stumbled into this place without noticing how odd it is."

He shrugged. "I was stinking drunk, remember? Besides, you have to admit, until you scan a little way past the *botanica*, the street itself doesn't even begin to look peculiar, and even then it's subtle. And it could be that the strangeness masked itself."

"Do you think it would bother?"

"It might if all this is here because *I* summoned it. Perhaps guys—or things, whatever—in the cartomancer's line of work take a special interest in playing dirty tricks on guys in mine."

"Christ," she muttered, "if I believed that, I think I'd have to—No. I said I don't blame you and I still wouldn't. Even if you placed the call, you didn't know who'd pick up the phone. So you can't blame yourself, either. Like you said, that is all just bullshit theorizing anyway."

"I'm trying to see it that way, but it's hard."

"Don't even think about it. Concentrate on finding the way out."

"I've been doing that, too." He picked up a white pebble, then straightened his legs. "Two intelligent people using their heads and working systematically ought to be able to work their way out of a labyrinth, even one in bent space." He scratched an arrow on the wall. "These'll tell us if we're retracing our steps."

She extended her hand and he helped her to her feet. "I read in some mystery novel that when in doubt, you should always turn the same direction," she said. "I think it specified right, though I don't remember why."

"Then we'll do that too." The rattling sounded again. He stiffened and Becky shuddered. "We'd better get moving."

24

VASQUEZ DROVE ONE-HANDED, leaving the other free to cram food into his round, ruddy face. A steadily dwindling supply of steak sandwiches sat on the seat between him and Price, the frozen beef hastily microwaved into oozing, pink, half-raw edibility before they left the house. Crumbs and juice flew constantly, staining the windshield, the bronze leather upholstery, and the old man's creamy sharkskin suit. Occasionally, when he'd emptied his fingers of meat and soggy bread, he stroked the card pocketed behind his black silk handkerchief.

He'd cranked the Seville's AC up as high as it would go, but Price was sweating anyway. Every time the car slowed down, he felt an urge to leap out.

He resisted. This had turned out to be a scary job, scary in a way no case had been before, and he didn't like working for a guy who'd taken some of the scariness inside himself. But he'd never walked out on clients who hadn't fucked him, and despite everything, he didn't intend to start now, especially since he still needed their money to save his neck. The hitters from Vegas could kill him just as dead as spooks and voodoo.

"I really can drive if you don't feel up to it," said Steven from the back seat.

"Stop saying that," Vasquez replied through another mouthful. Turning off Martin onto River Street, he pulled up to the curb beside a row of newspaper dispensers. The stores on the block were dark and the sidewalks empty.

"Why did you bring us here?" asked Steven after a moment.

"Look out over the water."

In the darkness the superstructure of the Martin Avenue Bridge resembled a spider web, and a gelid-looking mist roiled above the black ripples, but it wasn't until Price peered at the downtown area on the other side that he actually sensed that anything had changed.

The towers loomed crooked, forked, and jagged, too few rectilinear and too many constructed in other shapes. Some appeared broken, as though by shelling or an earthquake. Late as it was, there should have been more lights burning, neon signs and white incandescent lamps, not wavering glows like green and violet bonfires.

A flicker of motion jerked Price's eyes back to the river. Just south of the bridge a mass of colossal tendrils that could have been either tentacles or intertwined serpentine necks squirmed above the surface for a few seconds, then slipped back below.

Vasquez chortled and put the Cadillac in gear.

"I don't understand," Steven said.

The old man grinned around his new bite of sandwich, obviously enjoying his son's bewilderment. "I'll explain once I'm absolutely sure it worked."

The car sped north, then a couple of blocks east to Twelfth Street, then north again across Iroquois. Here the buildings seemed a little grimier and more decayed, but certainly not as altered as the skyscrapers downtown. For an instant Price allowed himself to hope that Vasquez's magic *hadn't* worked, not completely, and then they rounded a sharp bend in the road.

In the middle of the pavement stood a kind of totem pole carved with leering inhuman faces, and lashed to the bottom, supported only by the blood-soaked strands of coarse hemp, slumped the naked wreckage of a man. Someone had sliced his eyes, ears, nose, lips, nipples, and genitals away.

Steven wriggled and made a funny little chirping sound, half shocked and half excited. His father swerved and stamped on the brake. Just as the Seville lurched to a stop, a creature sprang out of the shadows onto the hood.

It was the size and approximate shape of a tiger, but with

five legs, iridescent ophidian scales, and a malformed cyclopean head. Crouching, keening, its talons scoring metal and its slit-pupiled eye blazing, it glared at the men inside the car.

Steven squawked. Grabbing for his Colt, Price bellowed, "Put it in reverse!"

"No need," Vasquez said. Stroking his card, he leaned forward, bringing his face as close to the windshield as he could.

The beast cocked its head. A nictitating membrane flicked across its eye. Then it leaped off the hood and loped away.

"They won't hurt us as long as we don't interfere with them or penetrate too deep into their territory," the old man explained. "Later, when they're used to us, they might even help us."

"That was fantastic," Steven said, his voice only a little shaky. "*Now* will you tell us what's going on?"

"It's simple enough," said Vasquez, backing the Seville around. "I moved the neighborhood out of Florida and made it a kind of island in the middle of someplace else."

Price had figured it out the instant he saw the towers. When he thought of all the times he'd nearly run, after Carpenter healed Donovan, after the visit to the *botanica*, and again after Vasquez's transformation, it made him want to scream or shoot somebody. But at least he was on the old man's good side, and if he wanted to see Miami again, he'd better keep it that way. "Can you get us back to earth when you want to?" he asked.

The Cadillac rolled back across Iroquois. "This is Corona City," Vasquez said. "I can do anything I want."

"Are we going to check the south and east boundaries too?"

"No, I think we can assume those shifted as well. Let's begin showing the Corona Coalition and their sympathizers who runs this community." He pulled up in front of an apartment building constructed around a courtyard. "Let's evict somebody."

"But we don't own this complex," Steven said.

"Try not to be so stupid," the old man replied.

As he strode through the gate, the box containing the rest of the Tarot deck a bulge in his hip pocket, he gobbled his last sandwich. His belly heaved and buttons clinked on the pavement.

By the time they reached the first door, Steven was nearly prancing with excitement. "Shall I knock?"

"Can you open these?" Vasquez asked Price. The detective showed him his ring of tools and master keys. "Then why stand on ceremony?"

The detective's nerves buzzed; for a second, his hand shook, jingling the items on the ring. Housebreaking was dangerous even if your accomplices were sane.

The two locks clicked open easily enough, but someone had engaged the chain. Planting his fleshy palms against the door, Vasquez pushed. His coat split down the center of his back, then the door burst free and banged against the wall.

Art prints, concert and theatrical posters, and photos of actors and dancers performing on stage adorned the dingy white living-room walls, and a grease-blotched Domino's box with two slices of cold pepperoni-and-mushroom pizza sat in the middle of the ratty green carpet. Scooping up the leftover pie, the old man shouted, "I'm evicting you! Everybody out!"

Down the hall, springs squeaked, then something crashed to the floor. "Wake up! Wake up!" a woman cried.

Snapping down the pizza, his great mass wobbling, Vasquez marched to the bedroom door, threw it open, and flipped on the light. "Come on, get up, get out!"

A brown-haired, twentyish woman in a pink pullover nightshirt and a blond, bare-chested guy of about the same age blinked from the tangled covers. She was livid, obviously frightened, but his face was slack and befuddled, still half asleep. "Who *are* you?" she demanded.

"The new landlord," Vasquez said, "among other things. Perhaps you can arrange a lease later, but for now you'll have to go."

"That's ridiculous. We paid the rent."

Stepping out from behind Vasquez, Price leveled his .38. "If you don't go, we'll hurt you."

She stared for a moment, then shivered and mumbled, "All right."

But now her boyfriend roused into blustering life. "It's not all right with me," he growled, cheeks flushed and fists clenching. "This is our home—"

Tittering, Steven fired. The bullets punched into the wall just over the tenants' heads. They screamed and huddled flat against the mattress.

"You don't listen very well," he said when he stopped shooting. "Move your asses *right now*, and don't come back unless we say you can."

The couple scurried out of bed. The boyfriend turned out to be naked. He tried to snatch his jeans off a chair, but Steven fired again. The chair splintered, jumped, and the blond guy bolted.

"You know," said Vasquez, "some of them probably would try to sneak back, no matter what we said. But if we burn down one of the buildings an hour or so after we empty it, that just might give them second thoughts." Lumbering into the kitchen, he pulled a gallon of chocolate-swirl ice cream out of the freezer, tossed the lid to the floor, and dredged out a handful. "Let's keep moving. I'd prefer that no one warn anybody else."

The second apartment housed a Cuban divorcee and her two tiny daughters; Steven watched wistfully as she led the weeping, bewildered children into the night. In the third lived an elderly black couple who assumed the intruders belonged to the Klan, and in the next drowsed an incoherent drunk. Too sloshed to notice or be cowed by the guns, he threw a poorly aimed haymaker that knocked a dent in the plasterboard wall. Price cold-cocked him and dumped him outside, then Steven kicked him around a little.

Vasquez stole some food at every stop. Already so bloated that he almost had to wriggle through the doorways, he was still swelling, his filthy garments as tight as a sausage casing and the tortured seams gradually ripping apart. Beneath its thickening coating of flesh his skull was changing too. His chin jutted and his yellow teeth looked like the heads of shovels.

Price was still edgy. He kept reminding himself that nobody could call the cops. Nevertheless, after a while he realized that a part of him was enjoying the job. Not as much as his maniac companions, but a little.

It was always satisfying to put the heat on somebody. It proved you were smart and tough, a winner, and that was the only worthwhile thing to be, even if the game was a nightmare and the other victors were freaks.

The first apartment on the second floor was plusher than the ones below, with brighter, cleaner paint and a fancy cut-glass light fixture mounted on the living room ceiling; the tenant had probably fixed it up herself. A plump, pleasant-looking woman in a blue terry-cloth robe, she'd sprawled on the sofa to watch TV, a legion of dolls and stuffed animals watching beside her. Her head jerked around when the door swung open.

Vasquez swallowed the last of his banana. "I'm evicting you," he said.

Rising, she clutched the front of her robe together. "Mr. Vasquez, is that you? You can't . . . this has to be some kind of weird mistake."

"No. I want you off the premises immediately."

"But this is crazy. I guess you bought the building, but nobody notified me, and I'm sure there have to be some sort of proceedings—"

Price positioned himself with his back to a framed photo of Axel Rose, then aimed his Colt at her face. "Don't argue. Walk away fast or we'll shoot."

"Wait," said Steven, slipping through the door. "I know her."

"Yes!" the woman chattered. "Of course you do, you've been in the store a million times, tell them—"

"Do you want me to let her stay?" Vasquez asked.

Steven smirked. "Not hardly. I want to kill her."

"I think you're all drunk," the woman quavered. "Otherwise you wouldn't think you could scare anybody with such a stupid joke."

"I have my own grudge against Carpenter's *wife*," Steven said to his father. "I'll explain if you want; for the first time,

I feel like you'd understand. Anyway, this is Prudy somebody, her friend. Becky may be dead. If she is, the only way I can get back at her is to hurt people she cared about."

Trembling, her forehead and rosy, dimpled cheeks gleaming with perspiration, Prudy stared into Price's eyes. "For God's sake, please, don't let him do it. You have to know they're crazy."

"Quiet," the detective replied.

"If you're willing to do it quickly, go ahead," Vasquez said to his son. "If you want to fool around, you'll have to leave her for later."

Steven smiled and stroked his chin, considering or pretending to. "I'll probably regret it," he said at last, "but I can't wait."

Prudy whirled and scrambled for the hallway. Steven let her bound three steps before he opened up.

His first shot beheaded the fairyland princess on the poster to the right of the doorway, but the next three slammed into Prudy's lower back. She grunted, staggered, and sank to the floor, revealing the starbursts of blood on the wall behind her. As she took a final, rattling breath, her bladder and bowels released.

Nose wrinkled, Vasquez gingerly sidestepped the mess as he made his way to the kitchen.

After that Steven wasn't satisfied to simply drive the tenants out. He kissed and fondled the children, slapped, kicked, and spat on the adults. Occasionally his father struck somebody too.

Every citizen on the first two floors turned out to be such a helpless schlemiel that by the time they reached the third floor, the pair had lost what little caution they'd initially possessed. Price kept trying to scope out the interiors before they made their presence known, but when the locks to Apartment 304 snicked open, Vasquez shouldered him aside and hurled back the door.

"I'm evict—" he began, then it caught in his throat.

The room was blue with cigarette smoke. Half a dozen grubby teenagers in boots, jeans, and denim vests with silver cobra patches on the backs lounged on the battered furniture.

Each had a pistol or an AK-47 cradled in his lap or resting at his side. Heaped on the coffee table among the beer bottles, Chinese take-out cartons, and overflowing ashtrays were Ziploc bags stuffed with white powder.

The kids didn't say a word, just grabbed their guns. Price snatched at Vasquez's collar, hoping to yank him out of the doorway, but apparently the old man's brain hadn't gotten around to warning his feet that they were carrying him into danger. He took another step, the detective missed his hold, and then the shooting started.

Vasquez thrashed. Momentarily off balance, now unable to throw himself back out of the doorway, in his imagination Price could already see his living shield dropping, leaving him naked before the next barrage.

But Vasquez didn't fall. He stumbled backward, bright arterial blood spurting from his neck and left forearm, then roared and lunged.

Bullets smashing into his flesh at point-blank range, he grabbed a chunky kid with a crescent-moon earring, tangled his fingers in his reddish shoulder-length hair, and ripped his scalp off. As the boy started shrieking, Vasquez whirled and bashed his elbow into another kid's chest. Ribs crunched inward, shearing into his lung.

Shaking off his astonishment—what was one more miracle at this point?—Price ducked back out onto the walkway, then leaned in the door and began firing. Steven tried to do the same, but he'd forgotten to reload.

The old man tore a thin, freckle-faced kid's throat out. Blood jetted, painting even more of his enormous body red. Spinning again, he swatted a boy with pimples, snapping his neck. One of the two gang members with an assault rifle— the one who kept yelling "Ah! Ah! Ah!"—tried to press the muzzle against the back of Vasquez's skull, but Price blew him away before he had it fully lifted into position.

Babbling some incoherent plea, the last teenager threw down his pistol and ran at the door. Price was sure his client wouldn't like it if he allowed a guy who'd hurt him to get away, so he shot him through the heart.

Steven finally fumbled a fresh magazine into his Beretta, then jerked himself into position to fire. "Oh," he said sheepishly. "Gosh, Papa, that was something! I guess all that fat is like armor."

Blood still gushing from at least twenty wounds, Vasquez gurgled and collapsed.

Scurrying to his side, Steven knelt on the gory carpet. Price followed more warily, making sure that all the gang members were either dead or incapacitated.

Steven tried to press a folded handkerchief against the pumping hole at the base of his father's neck, but Vasquez feebly batted his hands away. "Food," he whispered.

Leaping up, Steven dashed into the kitchen. Price rummaged through the debris on the coffee table. The longnecks and food containers were virtually empty, but he raked them onto the floor anyway. Clutching his Tarot card with one hand, Vasquez frantically snatched them with the other, sucking the last few drops out of each bottle, gulping sauce, a water chestnut, a bamboo shoot, and a lo mein noodle. "More," he gasped.

"There's nothing here," Steven called, "just some catsup."

"Bring it," Price told him. "Do you think you could eat cocaine?" he asked Vasquez.

"I don't know," the old man said, then suddenly smiled. "But I have a better idea anyway." Rolling over, he picked up the piece of meat he'd wrenched from the skinny kid's throat and stuffed it in his newly protrusive jaws.

"Not bad," he commented as he chewed. "But let me have the catsup."

Actually looking more unnerved than excited, Steven handed him the red plastic squeeze bottle.

Vasquez chose the scalped boy, probably because he was the fleshiest one. Curled in the fetal position, whimpering, the teenager seemed to be in shock; Price couldn't tell if he understood what was about to happen or not. He squirmed, but not vigorously, and the old man didn't have any trouble pounding his lights out.

When the kid stopped moving, Vasquez started on his face, stripping it off his skull as easily as he'd torn the ham off its bone. He squirted the condiment on his first few handfuls, then tossed it aside. Price, looking on in queasy fascination, noticed that he gobbled the cartilaginous ears and nose as greedily as the softer tissues, his jaw muscles bunching as he strained to grind them up.

By the time he tore the kid's colors and shirt off, he'd stopped bleeding. His body pulsed; pulverized scraps, then bullets, oozed from his wounds. When he bit the penis's head off, the holes in his left arm closed.

In three more minutes he'd completely healed. The boy was just a crimson skeleton above the knees.

Smiling, Vasquez climbed to his feet, sauntered into the kitchen, and started washing his hands. "That was too close. I need more firepower. You should be magic too."

"Me?" Steven squeaked, eyes widening.

"Both of you." He dried off on a paper towel, then tried to take out the Tarot box. His pants had stretched so tight that he had to rip his pocket off to do it. "Here. You know the drill."

Hands trembling, Steven extracted the pasteboards and began to shuffle. Their rotten stench suffused the air, masking the smells of smoke and blood.

"Come on, please, please, make it a good one," he chanted, then abruptly flipped the uppermost card.

A gaunt man, nude except for his jester's cap and broken-chained shackles, capered on the edge of a cliff. Welts crisscrossed his shoulders, and his long, thin penis stabbed erect. Grinning, his narrow, weak-chinned countenance rather like Steven's own, the jester dangled a marionette resembling himself over the abyss; meanwhile, rock crumbled under his feet.

Steven just had time to set the rest of the pack on the coffee table before he fell to his knees. The jester card pressed to his breast, he giggled uncontrollably, moaned, then burst out giggling again.

"Your turn," Vasquez said to Price.

Price was so scared, it was a wonder he wasn't shitting in

his pants. But he knew he couldn't refuse without forfeiting the old man's trust.

Maybe he wouldn't turn into anything gross; after all, Carpenter didn't. And if he didn't like his pasteboard's influence, surely he could shake it off the way the Reverend had.

"Sure," he said. "Why not? I *like* to play cards."

25

HALFWAY TO THE next dogleg, the tiny hairs on Becky's nape stood on end. She jerked Tom to a halt.

They had yet to glimpse the thing they'd named the Rattlesnake, but they'd heard it frequently enough to be convinced that it had begun stalking them. Now, without understanding how, she sensed it lying in wait around the corner.

"What is it?" Tom whispered.

"Our friend's up there." She tugged on his hand to start him moving back the other way.

But peering ahead, he balked. "I don't see or hear anything, and I doubt it could have gotten ahead of us. What makes you think so?"

"I just know. Come on!"

He frowned. "If we double back and you're wrong, we're liable to walk right into it. Every time we come up on one of these blind turns, I get antsy too, but—"

She realized she was smelling a faint, musky odor. "Shut up and use your nose," she told him.

He sniffed. "Why didn't you say that in the first place?" Wheeling, they trotted down the alley. An angry clattering rang out.

Five dark, narrow passages twisted away from the last junction. Weary, burning eyes straining to penetrate the murk ahead, they scurried into the only other branch they hadn't ventured down before.

Rusty, stinking trash barrels choked the way, many vomiting masses of blue-green mold. When her arm brushed against some, it stung. More rustling sounded overhead; at any moment another wave of insect-creatures could pour down the endless brick canyon walls.

Then the furious clacking echoed behind them, over and over again. Before, the Rattlesnake had rattled once every ten or fifteen minutes, as though yielding to an inconvenient impulse it could no longer resist. Now, apparently, it had grown impatient with attempting to creep up on them; perhaps it had abandoned the hunt, but more likely it meant to take a shot at running them down.

"Good grief," Tom muttered. They sprinted.

After two minutes and several turns, the rattling grew faint and finally ceased. Panting, they lurched to a stop to take their bearings. On the other side of a puddle with an oily sheen, the alley divided. Several doors, their peeling paint leprous in the gloom, lined the far wall of the left-hand fork.

Tom scratched another arrow at the corner. Then they set off down that branch, examining hinges and testing handles and knobs.

Becky cocked her head to listen, heard only the sighing of the dank, malodorous breeze. "I still don't want to meet whoever lives in these buildings," she said.

"I'm not crazy about the prospect myself," Tom replied, "but in case you haven't noticed, the beasties that live *outside* them are no treat either. We're going to need to sleep eventually, and if we could find a vacant building to hole up in, that would be a safer place to do it. Plus, the Rattlesnake might go away. I don't guess we're going to find one, though. Every place is locked up tight. Without tools—"

More clattering. Aching legs and backs protesting, they ran on again.

Rounding a hairpin turn, they encountered another intersection. The left branch extended at least one hundred feet before squirming out of sight, a hundred feet visibly clear of predators, so that was the one they chose.

A pace in the lead as they rounded the bend, Becky nearly slammed into a wall; the passage dead-ended. Behind three more garbage barrels, two of them encrusted with fungus, stood another door. Tom tried the knob, but of course it wouldn't turn.

Dashing back the way they'd come, she spotted one of the rare spaces between buildings wide enough for them to sidle through. Tangled coils of thorny vines clogged the passage, rustling even though the wind had died.

She wondered if their pursuer had intended to herd them into a cul-de-sac.

If they reached the junction ahead of it, they could chose another path, but the maraca-like noise was chattering louder and louder and she knew they weren't going to make it. Sure enough, when they were only halfway up the alley, the creature finally bounded into view.

With its hooves and curling horns, the Rattlesnake looked something like the skeleton of a satyr stretched eight feet tall and narrow. Its skull-sockets gaped, and a greasy-gray integument resembling wax paper bound its bones together. Its four arms ended in sawtoothed pincers clattering rapidly open and closed like castanets.

No longer in a hurry, it minced forward, freezing every few steps like a runway model.

Tom and Becky fell back. "I'll keep it occupied," he panted. "You slip past it and run."

"No way," she replied. "*I'll* hold it off, for what I hope will be the very few seconds it'll take you to break open that door back there."

The Rattlesnake danced a yard backward, then forward again.

"I don't know if I can," he said. "It felt solid, just like all the rest. Maybe if we both fight—"

They backed around the dogleg. "Unless you're packing some heavy-duty weapon you forgot to mention," Becky argued, "I like my plan better. And since you're the big, strong man, you draw the brute-strength job."

He grimaced. "I love you."

"Likewise. Get busy."

As he started kicking, she scuttled to the trash barrels. The one on the right held shafts of broken wood. Snatching out a long, sturdy-looking one, splinters pricking her palm, she hastily rubbed one jagged end in the blue-green mold. Dark as it was, she would have missed the bent, rusty lid lodged between the barrel and the wall if the receptacle hadn't shifted and clanked against it. Grabbing it by its handle, she smeared more fungus on the opposite side.

Another furious burst of clattering made a counterpoint to the banging at the door. Makeshift sword and shield clenched in her fists, she whirled to meet the Rattlesnake's first attack.

A chela scissored at her face. She swept the lid up. Metal rang, buckled; the impact jolted her arm.

She jabbed her stick at the creature but it hopped out of reach.

The next instant, it darted in again. All four pincers suddenly extended, snapping high, low, left, right, all at once. Gasping, retreating, she lashed her shield and cudgel back and forth. Behind her, the monotonous bashing pounded on.

Claws clashed shut inches from her left biceps, then in her hair. Ripping free, she stumbled, and a third pair thrust down to snip her knee. She swung, only scored a glancing blow.

But it was good enough. Madly shaking its arm to dislodge the mold that adhered to its wrist, the Rattlesnake sprang back again.

She lunged, clubbing and stabbing wildly. If she pressed the attack while it seemed off balance, hit it hard and stuck fungus all over it, perhaps it might actually run away!

But the Rattlesnake evidently wasn't in as much distress as she'd believed. Abandoning its efforts to shake off the mold, it lashed out as aggressively as before. Becky tried to wrench herself back into a defensive posture, but she was a split second too slow. Gnashing pincers sheared her sword in two.

She threw the stub at it, missed, and the creature drove her staggering back again, pincer-strike after pincer-strike barely deflected by the punctured, crumpling lid. Sweat burning her eyes, blurring her vision, she groped behind her back for another stick.

Before she found one, claws whipped past her guard. She ducked before they could slash shut on her temples, but she couldn't stop them from beating down on her head. The lid slipped from her nerveless fingers, and she slumped to the pavement in a heap.

Clacking, chelae poised to clip her into pieces, the Rattlesnake crouched above her. Numbed and dizzy, she struggled to raise her arms.

Tom leaped into her field of vision, swung one of the moldy barrels, smashed the creature back. Two more blows hammered it against the wall. Bone grated.

Tom abruptly hurled the barrel at its hooves, then spun, yanked Becky up, and dragged her toward the now half-open door.

Kicking the trash can aside to roll clanging down the alleyway, its agility unimpaired, the Rattlesnake charged.

They reached their goal a stride ahead of it, plunged inside, and slammed the door. The tips of one set of its claws caught in the crack. Tom tried to crush them, but it jerked them free before he could.

A moment later, it started battering; they shoved back to hold the barrier closed. The panels cracked. Soon pincers might crash through the wood and stab into their flesh.

Her dizziness abating, Becky searched for a bolt, found only the lock Tom had ruined breaking in. So she looked over her shoulder.

The room was as high and occupied as much ground as the entire parsonage. Sheets of gossamer fell from the dark recesses overhead, the dimly glowing red orbs suspended in them providing the only illumination. There were no windows and only one other door, directly across from them on the far wall. A senseless miscellany of objects littered the floor, among them a tricycle, an uprooted tree stump, a wooden Indian, an astronaut's helmet, a piece of sandpaper, a kitchen chair, and a set of Tupperware bowls.

The chair was only a couple of yards away. "Can you hold the door by yourself for a second?" she asked Tom.

"If I have to," he gritted.

"Okay." She wheeled, grabbed the seat, and wedged it under the doorknob. "Now, run!"

Dashing across the crimson vault, shredding the cobweb

veils in her path, she exulted. What fool would have believed they might actually escape?

Her right foot plunged into ooze. Thrown forward, she fell face-down into a cold, clinging muck that had looked exactly like the solid wooden flooring behind her. As she struggled to raise her head, to spit out the slime in her mouth, it started to suck her down.

Above her, a deep voice laughed. The shrouds of webbing shivered as something began its descent.

Tom, still on solid wood, whirled at the sound of the splash. Dropping onto his belly, he crawled forward.

"Don't flail around!" he said. "Tread water!"

She dog-paddled. It did seem to keep her from sinking quite so fast, but the quicksand was already lapping at her chin.

Something resembling a viscous maroon jelly inched downward along the webs. The pounding and clacking grew even more frenzied, as though the Rattlesnake sensed that another demon was about to claim its prey.

Tom found the edge of the wood flooring. "I can't come any closer. Stretch out your arms."

She struggled to lift them out of the glue. When they tore free, the motion submerged the rest of her still further, brought gelid slime surging up to her lips.

She couldn't reach him.

As she opened her mouth to tell him to leave her, he crept forward. His upper chest now hanging over the quicksand, he grasped her wrist.

Hand over hand, she pulled herself up his arm. Teeth gritted, every muscle straining, somehow he kept her from dragging him into the pit.

Something soft caressed her hair.

But by that time only her legs were still mired; a final desperate effort ripped them out. Hurling themselves backward, she and Tom scrambled to their feet.

Rippling and pulsing on the webbing, looking rather like a huge, bloody booger, the jelly-thing started to extrude a pseudopod. She whirled to flee, and Tom grabbed her.

"Put your feet where the junk is sitting," he gasped. "The floor has to be solid there."

The door at their backs crashed open. Leaping from one occupied area to the next, they zigzagged toward the other exit, both the jelly and the Rattlesnake now at their heels. Maddeningly, the clawed beast could evidently distinguish the solid surface from the muck.

The castanet sound crescendoed. Certain they weren't going to make it, Becky tore a drawer out of a roll-top desk, pivoted, and threw.

The missile smashed the Rattlesnake squarely in the teeth. Stumbling, the creature blundered into the ooze. As it thrashed, the jelly centered itself above it, then sagged down to envelop it.

Tom and Becky passed through the door at last. Discovering where it led, she goggled in astonishment.

They stood on the cartomancer's street, almost directly across from the *botanica*. Nothing stirred. The Chevy van was gone.

Tom closed the door, sealing in the splashing and slurping, the rattling and gales of raucous mirth. "Why so surprised?" he asked mischievously. "It figures that if a building has two doors and one opens on an alley, the other's going to open on a street."

She shivered, brushed icy brown slime off her arms and chest. He swept some more off her back. "It figures, my ass. We can't be here. We never crossed the street."

"Bent space, remember?"

"Right, like that's really an explanation." She smiled. "Not that I'm complaining. I hate to break it to you, Dan'l, but all that nifty trailblazing was getting us nowhere. Come on, let's move out before the snot monster decides it wants dessert."

As they advanced up the sidewalk, her teeth began to chatter. Every few seconds, she glanced over her shoulder; she might have broken into a run if she hadn't been afraid it could spur some unseen shadow to attack. After all the perils of the last few hours, a part of her simply couldn't believe that the gods of this ghastly place would permit them to walk away.

But nothing happened. When at last they stepped onto Aragon Street, Tom whooped, hugged her, swung her around, and kissed her. "You're my life," he said.

She kissed him. "I'm glad, because you're mine too."

When they finally let go of each other, they walked to the pay phone outside the bar. Tom lifted the receiver and punched in 911. "I know it's vindictive," he said, "but I wish I could be there when the police arrest them."

Becky shivered again, peered back at the intersection. It was empty. Drawing a deep breath, she silently commanded her jitters to begone, then noticed the clock in a grilled pawnshop window, and the sky.

Two gray-white columns of smoke rose into blackness. A reddish moon hung frozen overhead.

She and Tom hadn't walked away from anything.

"The phone's dead," he said. "Let's find another."

"It wouldn't work either. Look up. It's almost seven-thirty in the morning. Where's the sun?"

26

GOLDEN TONES RANG out of the church speakers. Across the river, atop a squat truncated pyramid, flickering purple flames leaped higher. Perhaps the flare had nothing to do with the bell, but for a moment Tom almost expected some dissonant carillon to clang back in response.

He wished Holy Assembly had real bells. He knew the notion was irrational, but he couldn't help feeling that cast bronze might possess a power that electric bells didn't.

But why shouldn't the church have fake bells? It had a fake preacher.

As they'd limped home, he and Becky had encountered dazed and hysterical people wandering the streets. The coherent ones told of arson, molestation, and murder, of being driven from their homes by three assailants who were human in some accounts, grotesquely inhuman in others. Some of the refugees had discovered hideous creatures and altered terrain on the outskirts of the area, and nearly all were obsessed with the moon that wouldn't set and the sun that wouldn't rise.

It was like something out of Revelations, and they owed it all to him. If only he hadn't lost his faith. If only he hadn't drawn from the Tarot pack. If only this, if only that, and of course, if only the other.

He sighed, turned from the steeple window, and descended the narrow spiral stairs.

He found Becky still hard at work in the church kitchen. After they'd showered and donned fresh clothes, she'd begun preparing food. Stacks of sandwiches filled two platters, Oreos, saltines, and sliced cheddar another, and bowls of popcorn, apples, and raisins a fourth. Pots of tomato and chicken noodle soup simmered on the stove, while beside them a portable radio blathered on about President Bush.

She smiled at him. "Coffee's ready. How's it look from up there?"

He picked up a Styrofoam cup, stuck it under the urn's black plastic spigot. "Dark. Anything on the news?"

"Zip, and I wish I understood how that can be. But don't mention bent space, or I'll bust you one."

He sipped; the hot liquid seared his mouth. "That explains why we seem to have moved, but it can't account for why the rest of the city hasn't noticed we're gone. Maybe when they look at the hole where we used to be, they can't see it. Or Thirty-first Street runs along the river now, and no one remembers it didn't always. Or there's another Corona City in our place, populated by our doppelgangers. Heck, I don't know! What's the difference? All that matters is that nobody's even trying to reach us!"

"Somebody doesn't sound like a happy camper. If you take that tone with the parishioners, you'll scare them even worse than they're scared already."

"Gee, I don't know why I'm having trouble putting on a happy face."

She slapped another turkey sandwich down on the counter. "This is no day at the beach for me either."

Suddenly he saw past the cosmetics, brushed, lustrous hair, and cherry-red blouse and barrettes to the bruises, scrapes, and cuts, the gray skin, the aches and exhaustion dragging at her flesh. "I'm sorry."

She took his hand, gave it a squeeze. "No problem." One of the front doors squeaked open. "Hey, a customer."

They hurried down the hall. It was the skinhead Alan and a short, spiky-haired blonde in a suede jacket, a turquoise and silver nose clip, and enormous earrings like copper mobiles. They huddled by a rack of church newsletters and inspirational pamphlets. The skinhead had a lopsided mustache of dried blood, and the girl's face was flushed and swollen. When Tom rounded the corner, they recoiled; the earrings jangled. Alan jerked her toward the door.

"Don't go!" Tom cried. "It's only us."

"I followed the bells," Alan stammered. "They burned down our place, I didn't know where else . . . but I guess I thought somebody else . . . I mean, we don't belong to *your* church, so maybe—"

Becky stepped forward, took each of them by the arm. "Forget it. Nobody's going anywhere till your friend tells me where she bought that great coat. Besides, we've got a ton of food to get rid of."

"Please stay," Tom said. "After more people turn up, we'll figure out a way to fix this mess."

"All right," Alan said.

People trickled in for the next two hours, many members of the congregation or the Coalition, others not. Even the calmest seemed strangely reticent. Some muttered among themselves, but when Tom tried to talk to them, they ducked their heads and mumbled.

Those in tatters or pajamas received garments from the supply donated for the needy, the lost-and-found, and Tom and Becky's closets. Tom administered first aid until a thin, frowning nurse in a white short-sleeved shirt and matching overalls showed up to take over the job.

When the pews were two-thirds full, he climbed into the pulpit. Gradually a hush fell over the chamber. Familiar faces, Alan's, Bubba's, Grace's, Miriam's, Paulie's, Willie's, all haggard and lost, stared up at him.

"Last night," he began—Lord, had it really only been last night?—"I stood up here and talked about a unique Tarot deck, a genuine instrument of black magic. Those of you who heard me will remember that I unwittingly came into possession of a card from the deck, then discovered that its influence was blighting my life and the lives of the people around me. I concluded by burning the foul thing, and assumed that the problem would be over."

Someone in the back snorted.

"Right. Obviously, it isn't. Shortly after I destroyed my card, Howard Vasquez acquired one of his own. Evidently he's decided to use it to torture us, and imprisoned us under a dome of endless night so no one can come to our aid.

"To save ourselves, we'll have to capture or kill him. He has some terrifying, miraculous abilities, but take it from someone else who's owned a card, he's not omnipotent. If we band together, plan a strategy, we can beat him."

A needle-nosed guy in rimless glasses stood up. "How do you know?"

"For one thing, there are only three of them. Vasquez, his slimy little child-pornographer son, and some thug."

"You talk like they're human beings," shouted a square-faced black woman with a frosted streak in her hair. "Maybe they started out that way, but they're not anymore!"

A teenager in a denim vest with a cobra patch jumped up. "She's right! Vincenzo told me just before he died! They shot them over and over again, and it didn't do shit!"

Frightened murmuring rippled across the room.

"Even if all that's true," Tom said, raising his voice to be heard above the babble, "they must have weaknesses."

Bubba slowly rose, wrung the grimy Cincinnati Reds cap clutched in his hands, shuffled his feet. "Here's the problem, Reverend," he said at last. "You told us not to follow your advice."

"The advice I gave before, not what I'm saying now."

"But how do we know we can trust you this time?" Bubba persisted. "How did Vasquez get his hands on the cards, if not with your help?"

"I had to do it. His son and the thug had Becky and me at gunpoint."

Louder murmuring.

"If that's true, no one could blame you," Bubba said. "But maybe you're still a hoodoo. You could be in cahoots with Vasquez, and want to lead us into a trap."

"Look, it doesn't matter what anybody thinks of me," Tom said desperately. "And it sure doesn't matter if I'm the leader; one of you combat vets should take the job. But it's vitally important that we stand up and fight. Everyone who has the courage, join me at the altar."

People shifted, whispered, looked around. The double doors at the rear of the nave crashed open.

Everyone jumped, twisted in his seat. After an instant of silence, the screaming started.

Steven remained at the rear of the hall, presumably guarding that exit. His father and the thug advanced down the center aisle. The moaning, whimpering people sitting closest to the aisle cringed at their passage.

Steven was by far the least changed. Grinning, eyes dancing, he looked demented but still quite human despite the thick, six-inch string-wart that dangled from each fingertip. The excrescences protruded at odd angles from the fist grasping the pistol.

Vasquez had become so obese that he repeatedly bumped his hips against the pews. He was nude except for the gym bag strapped around his neck, a condition rendered more rather than less obscene by the way his jiggling belly hung low enough to conceal his genitals. Pink horizontal ridges crossed his cascading mounds of flesh; the one above his right knee squirmed for a moment.

His jaws, jutting like the muzzle of a carnivorous dinosaur, gaped impossibly wide as he snapped at the fleshy, purple organ clutched in his hands.

The thug's flesh had segmented and turned to silvery metal, parts fusing in the process; he probably couldn't brush his hair out of place or change his flat expression, perhaps couldn't even open his mouth. Condensation beaded on his skin. When he stepped, wet clothes slapping, or swiveled to scan the crowd, he whirred. His right hand, the gun hand, was considerably larger than his left.

Tom struggled to cast off his shock. He'd understood that the three men had undergone some kind of transformation, but the garbled, inconsistent stories told by the refugees hadn't prepared him for anything as bizarre as this.

His legs quivered; he wanted to bolt. Becky stared from the first pew, willing him to do precisely that. But if he did, none of the people he'd gathered would ever help him fight.

Vasquez gobbled the last of his meat, licked and sucked his fingers. When they were relatively clean, he raised his hands, revealing another pink ridge on each palm. The terrified crowd fell silent.

"Congratulations, Reverend," the old man said, his voice unaltered despite the malformation of his mouth. "This is quite a turnout for a weekday."

"I'm glad you looked in," Tom replied, relieved to find his voice was steady; his knees were still knocking, but fortunately no one could see it through the pulpit. "We were just talking about you."

Vasquez chuckled. "Now, why am I not surprised?"

"We've decided to offer you a deal," Tom continued. "Send us back to earth immediately and we'll let you live."

"*We*, who?" He turned like a great, wobbling globe, surveying the pews. Everyone flinched from his gaze. "I don't believe you have a *we*."

"Naturally they won't identify themselves while you've got them under your guns. But there are plenty here, and elsewhere too. More than you can possibly handle when they finish arming and come after you en masse."

"Bullshit!" Steven shouted.

Vasquez nodded. "I agree. But just on the off chance it isn't, I hope this hypothetical mob understands it won't be attacking a paltry three opponents; the beasts from beyond the borders will rush in to defend me. And I hope they're aware that only I can send us home; kill me, and you'll stay in this place forever."

"I don't believe you," Tom gritted.

Vasquez turned again to face the crowd. "It's time I explained myself, and clarified your options. Not long ago, when I was dying of cancer and thus unable to look after my interests, this so-called clergyman and a collection of shiftless malcontents formed a conspiracy to destroy my family businesses, eventually plotting a campaign of violence, theft, vandalism, and other criminal acts to accomplish that end.

"How would you feel if someone did that to you? Wouldn't you want to get even? And wouldn't you want to show the community that seemed eager to throw in with your enemies, the community where you, unlike Carpenter, had lived all your life, the community your family had nur-

tured and supported for generations, that you were a dangerous person to betray?"

He pried a scrap from between his chisel-like teeth,
wiped at the bloody filth caked around his mouth. The
ruddy stripe above his right nipple thickened, then wriggled. "Well, I do, but I don't want to hurt you unnecessar-
ily, not if you were only Carpenter's dupe or never
belonged to the Corona Coalition at all. I simply feel I
have to instill a little respect.

"So here's *my* offer. *Show* me respect, do what I tell you,
stand aside while I punish my special enemies, and I'll take
you back to earth within the week. But if you fuck with me,
I'll cut off the power and water like I did the phones, invite
the creatures in to roam the streets, and keep you here a long,
long time."

"He's lying!" Tom shouted. "He'll never take you home
of his own free will! Just look at him—he's a creature himself now, there's no place for him there anymore!"

"You're mistaken," Vasquez purred. "We can revert to our
original forms whenever we like. Enough debate. Let's find
out who was most persuasive. Fetch him, Mr. Price."

Gun leveled, his unblinking eyes riveted on the pulpit, the
metal man strode forward, each pace the mirror image of the
one before. None of the audience moved until Becky leaped
up and threw a hymnal.

The heavy book missed the back of Price's head by
inches. If he still had a human's sense of touch, he must have
felt the breeze, but even when the volume thumped down on
the floor, he didn't pause or react in any way.

Vasquez smiled. "Hello, my dear. I hope you didn't think
we'd forgotten *you*."

"Dibs!" Steven yelled. He trotted down the aisle.

Price reached up, a chill radiating from his wet, glistening
skin.

Shots rang out on the right-hand side of the room.

For a second Tom was afraid Price *still* wouldn't glance
aside. But then his head jerked, the soft, animal eyes in the
expressionless silver mask flicked, and at that instant the

minister kicked the lectern. The heavy podium crashed down on his would-be captor, dashing him to the floor.

The nave exploded into chaos. Jolted from paralysis to panic by the final, utterly unanticipated threat of the gunshots erupting in their midst, the crowd stampeded in all directions. A shrieking, shoving press jammed every exit.

Becky ran to Tom; they started fighting their way toward the door behind them.

Price threw the lectern off his body. He and Vasquez waded forward, yanking and clubbing people aside.

Tom punched, stamped, elbowed, clawed. He didn't enjoy it, but he and Becky needed to escape more desperately than any of the gibbering, thrashing obstacles blocking their path.

A man with a cheap toupee slipping off his head suddenly twisted his shoulders, shoving Becky back six precious inches. Vasquez snatched a woman close, bit her arm off, then tossed her out of the way.

Half suffocated, Tom thrust forward again, then the back of his neck turned cold. He ducked, something blasted beside his ear, and the skull of the Hispanic-looking man in front of him cracked open. Blood and flecks of tissue spattered his face.

He looked back, Price aimed again, then the throng surged, interposing another layer of bodies between them. A second later, the corpse slumped, revealing that he'd nearly reached the inner door.

Tom gripped the dead man's shoulders and rammed him to the floor, then scrambled over him into the hall. The crush suddenly abated as people spilled away in three directions, through the outer door or down either arm of the corridor. Blinking, wiping gore out of his eyes, he pivoted.

Becky pushed forward; she and three others were jammed in the doorway. Vasquez shoved closer behind her, pink spit drooling from his chomping jaws, one huge hand stretched out to grab her hair and the other throttling the skinny Oriental man squashed against his belly. Price's implacable mask gleamed over his shoulder.

Tom gripped her arms and pulled; nothing happened. The

old man shoved even nearer. His clutching fingers sprinkled red droplets in her ebony curls.

Tom heaved again. She burst free like a cork wrenched from a champagne bottle.

The three who'd been stuck beside her fell. Equally off balance, she and Tom reeled backward, but somehow he managed to keep them on their feet. They plunged through the door and he darted left, leading her toward the parsonage's carport.

Before they'd covered half the distance, Price and Vasquez lunged out onto the sidewalk. Sighting his prey at once, the metal man raised his pistol.

Tom grabbed Becky's arm, dodged left. Price's gun barked once, again, then they dove around the end of the hedge. Tom landed hard; gravel jabbed his palms and knees. As he began to scramble up, he lifted his eyes . . . and froze. Beside him, Becky did the same.

Steven stood about six feet away, his weapon trained on Becky's face. "I've got them, Papa!"

"Good," the old man called back. "We'll be there in a second."

Tom tried to surreptitiously close his hand on a mass of pebbles and grit. "Don't even think about it," Steven said.

"Please," Tom said. "You aren't as far gone as they are. You can still choose to be human."

Steven tittered. "I'm farther gone than I look. Check this out." He raised his empty hand. The flopping string-warts suddenly writhed like tentacles, lengthened.

Behind him, an engine roared. Headlights flaring into dazzling life, a car hurtled forward.

Steven leaped left, Tom and Becky right. Brakes squealing at the last instant, the car, a rust-dappled station wagon, crunched into the hedge. Grace, riding shotgun, beckoned frantically. "Get in!" Miriam snarled from behind the wheel.

Tom and Becky scrambled for the rear door. By the time he tore it open and half stuffed her inside, Miriam was already backing the vehicle around. As Tom started to swing himself in, Willie Harper charged out of the darkness.

Eyes blazing, brandishing a fallen tree limb, he meant to brain Steven from behind. But his old tormentor wheeled, lashed his pistol across his face, raised his empty hand when the boy dropped to one knee. Rippling, stretching string-warts fell like streamers.

Tom hopped back out of the door, almost tripping in the process, dashed around the station wagon's front end. As Steven pivoted back toward him, he pounced.

The gun flashed; the bullet whined past his ear. He crashed into Steven a split second later, slamming him back against the hedge.

The younger Vasquez flailed, struggled to point his pistol at Tom's midsection, slithered his impossibly long warts over his body. Tom gripped his shooting arm with his left hand and punched him repeatedly with his right.

Coiling tendrils crept around Tom's head. Suddenly he felt weak, addled, but landed a final blow to the younger man's jaw. Steven went limp.

Panting, Tom stooped to retrieve the weapon that had fallen from his adversary's hand. It was time to find out if this creep was as bulletproof as everyone thought he was; considering that he'd kayoed him, it didn't seem likely. But then Price and Vasquez rounded the hedge.

The metal man fired. Tom shot back, yanked Willie to his feet, dragged him toward the car.

On its opposite side, Vasquez lumbered toward it too. Grace emptied the revolver grasped in her hands. Holes erupted in his cicatrized, mountainous chest, but the wounds didn't even slow him down.

He grabbed for her. Miriam sent the station wagon skidding ten feet backward, out of his reach but farther from Tom and Willie as well.

Tom and the boy put on a final burst of speed, made it to their goal an instant before the hulking ogre across from them. As they scrambled inside, Vazquez lunged, snatched; the station wagon lurched back again, metal screeched, and Grace's door ripped away in his hands.

Miriam jerked the stick shift; gears grated. The car careened across the parking lot, sideswiping a VW and tumbling Tom and Willie into Becky. One of Price's bullets glanced off the hood, showering sparks, a second smashed in the rear window and out through the windshield, then the car swerved onto Palm Street and sped away.

27

TOM INSERTED THE tire iron in the crack and pried. The door snapped open.

"See?" Becky said. "Works like a charm. If I survive this nonsense, I'm taking up burglary."

The five of them stepped from the alley into a dingy hall lit by a single buzzing fluorescent fixture. Tom counted down the row of doors, found the third. He pried again, but this time the barrier wouldn't give; he hissed involuntarily when the cold steel bar cut into his abraded hands. "Don't give up your day job," he muttered at Becky. Teeth gritted, he pulled again, hard as he could, and after several seconds the lock finally broke.

The door swung inward on a storeroom with an adjoining lavatory. He crept across the linoleum floor, opened the door in the opposite wall an inch, peeked through. The Redbird Bookstore and Coffee Shop looked much the same as ever. The dim light spilling through the windows revealed a storefront divided into two sections, one filled with bookshelves and the other with wicker tables and chairs. A cash register, a microwave, and several percolators sat atop the counter, and a four-foot refrigerator squatted behind it. Dali prints, original oils and watercolors, most of them surrealistic or abstract, and musical instruments, a cornet, a cello, a flute, and a glockenspiel among them, hung on the walls.

"Nobody here." He flipped on the storeroom light, crossed to the windows, and pulled down the shades.

The others followed him into the larger space. "So why are we?" Miriam demanded.

Tom shrugged. "We need somewhere to rest and plan, and

it wouldn't have been safe to go to your home or Willie's. And this place carries occult books."

"Do you think they have any aspirin?" the boy asked hesitantly. "If they don't, it's okay, but my face really hurts."

"We'll look," Becky said, and led him behind the counter. "I know it hurts, because that's how I got the mark on my face; Steven Vasquez pistol-whipped me too. Maybe we should start a club."

"He's the clown, isn't he? When I saw him tonight, I just sort of knew."

She opened the top drawer, pulled out pens, pencils, paper clips, and notepads. "Yeah, and I'm looking forward to ripping the little fucker a new asshole."

Willie gaped, then grinned.

"Occult books," Miriam said. "That's a great strategy, hunker down and read."

"We might learn something useful," Tom replied.

The willowy redhead sneered. "I thought you already knew how to use evil magic."

Willie frowned. Becky pulled a foil packet out of the bottom drawer.

"Bingo," said Grace. "Go get some water." The gangling boy scurried to the rest room. "Look," she said to Miriam, lowering her voice, "I know you've got good reason to hate this man. But we grown-ups are the only security that child has. If we fight, he's liable to fall apart."

Miriam scowled. "All right," she said after a moment. "I'll try to hold it in."

"Thanks," Tom said wryly. "Thanks for helping us at the church, too. I take it that one of you fired those shots inside."

"Who else?" the redhead replied. She walked around the counter to the refrigerator, removed a tray of plastic-wrapped croissants, then commenced her own exploration of the drawers and cabinets. "Think they've got a bottle stashed anywhere?" She glanced toward the storeroom; the lavatory door was still closed. "If it had been up to me, we wouldn't have done shit. I agreed that people needed to fight, but like that cracker with the cap said, who the hell wanted to do it alongside you? But Grace whipped out her gun and opened up on the audience, so of course I backed her play and did it too."

"Good Lord," he said. "Why didn't you fire at the Vasquezes or Price?"

"People said they were bulletproof," the buxom black woman explained. The gold star on her tooth gleamed in the semidarkness. "I thought it might help you more if I stampeded a wall of people between you and them. I aimed to miss."

He shook his head. "I understand that, but with everyone packed in, shifting around, it's a wonder you didn't hit somebody even so."

"Well, excuse us," Miriam said. "Maybe we should all go back to the church and take it from the top. This time, we dumb, reckless bimbos will keep our pieces safely tucked away in our purses, and marvel as you escape all by yourself without endangering any innocent lives."

Becky grinned. "You might as well drop it, Tom. You'd need the High Priest back to win this argument."

"You're right." He rubbed his eyes. "I'm sorry. I'm so strung out, I don't know what I'm saying. What happened next?"

Miriam shrugged. "Just the obvious. We shoved outside, then waved our guns to motivate some geezer out of his car. I should have just driven away, but by then I'd remembered that Becky risked her life to save a child, and she was in every bit as deep as you. And so we picked you up."

The toilet flushed, then water drummed in a sink. Willie emerged a moment later, still drying his hands on a paper towel.

The redhead smiled. "Everything come out all right?"

The boy ducked his head. "I got sort of sick all of a sudden, but I feel better now. Is there a plan yet?"

"No," Tom said, "and I suppose we'd better get busy. I know from carrying a card myself that its power increases over time. I don't believe Vasquez can command the border beasts yet, or he would have shown up at the church with a few in tow, but he may be able to do it soon. And I don't think he, Steven, and Price are indestructible; I beat Steven up, and Grace blew some holes in the old man, for all that he didn't seem to notice. But they might become invulnerable.

"So we should hit them within the next few hours, give them just enough time to drop their guard. Attack by surprise, when they aren't all together if they give us the chance, ideally when they're asleep, if they still do sleep."

Miriam arched an eyebrow. "That's your whole plan?"

"It sounds okay to me," Becky said. "I just want to be the hunter instead of the huntee."

"It's not exactly Napoleonic," Tom admitted, "but at least it's a start. We'll flesh it out as ideas occur to us. If you've conceived any brilliant suggestions, feel free to mention them now."

The redhead turned from the cupboards, picked up a croissant. "I have one. Vasquez may not be indestructible, but he's getting there, and that armor-plated guy probably isn't easy to hurt either. A lot of big guns will do more damage than three little pistols with only a few bullets left, so before we head out, let's rearm."

"Where can we do it?"

"Lester's a weapons freak, and I can get into his apartment. I did it before."

Grace smiled. "That was you?"

"The bastard was shortchanging us. I had to get the money somehow."

"What if he's there?" Becky asked. "What if he won't let you take the guns?"

Miriam snorted. "If we can't handle a moron like Lester, we sure won't be any use on a devil hunt." She took a bite of the pastry, grimaced, and tossed it on the counter. "Come on, babe, we'll do the real work while the padre and Mrs. Padre study." Grace rose. Willie looked up. "You stay here, kid. Take it easy till the aspirin kicks in."

Becky said, "Be careful."

"Right." The two ex-hookers disappeared through the storeroom door.

Tom, Becky, and the boy carried books on demonology, the black arts, and the Tarot, then two additional chairs, to the storeroom's Formica-topped table. "Should we look for anything in particular?" Becky asked.

Tom opened a thick, glossy-black paperback with a scarlet pentagram embossed on the cover. "Yeah," he said sardonically, "the magic spell we recite to make everything all right. In other words, not that I know of. Just see what you can find out."

For the next few minutes Willie's eyelids drooped. His head nodded, jerked up, nodded again, finally plumped down on his bony chest. He started snoring, a faint buzz.

Becky looked up from her book. "I wish I could do that," she whispered. "My nerves are so frazzled, I'll probably never sleep again. Didn't you tell me that when the cartomancer told your fortune, the Hermit card came out upside down?"

"Yeah," Tom murmured.

"According to this, that didn't really mean good advice. Standing on its head, it signified the opposite."

"Too bad I didn't know that at the time." Tom turned a page, then gasped.

The cartomancer's balding, cherubic countenance beamed up at him.

Becky leaned closer to examine the picture, a black-and-white photo of an oil painting. "Christ, it's him!"

"Sure looks like it." She fidgeted while he skimmed the text.

"Well?" she demanded when he lifted his eyes.

"It's a self-portrait by Russell Cantius Yale, a seventeenth-century artist, rake, gambler, swindler, alchemist, and fortune-teller. He spent his adult life roaming from one European city to another, frequently one step ahead of his creditors and the law, until his disappearance in 1677.

"According to this, a lot of people believed he practiced black magic, or had sold his soul to the Devil. He told fortunes with a Tarot deck he'd drawn himself; supposedly he once boasted that the cards were a sort of prison for seventy-eight demons he'd bound into his service. His predictions usually came true, but unfortunately he often foretold misfortune, and on other occasions prophecies that seemed hopeful were fulfilled in grimly ironic ways.

"When he vanished, the deck vanished with him. It's rumored that someone finds one of the cards from time to time, and generally meets with tragedy shortly thereafter."

"You'd think the son of a bitch could have gotten his fill of destroying people while he was alive," Becky said. "Is there anything in there about the cards devastating whole communities?"

"Doesn't seem to be."

"I wonder why it's happening now. When you drew your card, things got pretty awful for some of us, but for a lot of Corona City, life went on normally. Vasquez draws and suddenly it's the fucking end of the world."

"I think Steven and Price may have drawn too, in which case we're dealing with three cards instead of just one. Or perhaps Vasquez's card is more potent because he has the entire pack in his possession."

She scratched the insect bites on her thigh. "I suppose that could be. And maybe the demons can only exert their full strength when they possess truly evil men."

The light went out.

He groped, found her hand. "Vasquez must have decided he wasn't getting enough respect."

"So much for research. Not that we were learning anything helpful. I mean, it's *interesting* to know the cartomancer's Russell Yale, but what good does it do us?"

"None." He sighed. They sat quietly for a time. After a while she scooted her chair closer, its legs squealing on the linoleum, and he put his arm around her.

"Tom?" she asked.

"Yo."

"Do you think I'm a coward?"

He chuckled. "Absolutely. You seemed particularly gutless when you squared off against the Rattlesnake. What kind of a ridiculous question is that?"

"I'm so scared. I keep thinking about how *godlike* Vasquez is, how he reshapes our world with a wave of his hand. Maybe, *maybe* we could have defeated him with scores of people helping us, but do we really have a snow-ball's chance in hell of doing it now? We *could* hide, and hope for something good to happen. He *might* decide to send Corona City back to earth. His magic could break down. He could drop dead of a coronary. Or someone on earth could notice we're missing and find a way to reach us. You never know."

"No," Tom said, "you never do. But I can't just sit back and wait for some outside force to solve our problem for us. Even if we could be sure something eventually would, what about the victims who'd suffer and die in the interim?

"I have to look out for them, because I own this mess. Okay, not really. I didn't know what I was unleashing when I drew my card; the cartomancer deceived me. And Vasquez is obviously directly responsible for the garbage that's happen-ing now. Still, if I'd been content to grapple with my doubts and difficulties the way everyone else has to, if I hadn't snatched at a quick fix, we wouldn't be sitting here in the dark, would we?"

"What if we wind up killing Vasquez, then find out we're stranded like he said?"

"I truly believe he'll never send us home of his own voli-tion; he and the spirit that possessed him are one entity now. Would you rather be stuck here with him or without him?"

"I know you're right." She sighed. "I'm just in a funk, and it's making me babble."

"I think you're partly right too. We don't *both* have to go, and I don't think you should."

She snorted. "What's this, chivalry?"

"I just remembered something. When Yale told my for-tune, he said I was in danger of losing a loved one. I thought he meant you were going to divorce me, but what if he was really warning me that you're likely to die?"

"Didn't he also say that if you drew from the deck, you'd *change* your fate? And didn't he mislead you, about exactly what would happen if you did draw, and about the signifi-cance of the Hermit when it's inverted?"

"Yeah, but—"

"Then fuck it. If you're going, I'm going. Thanks for telling me, though. It ought to do wonders for my morale."

He swallowed. "I wish I could change your mind."

"Well, you can't, not even if you haul these books out into the moonlight and show me that that part of the reading meant just what he said it did, so please don't. People make the future, not a bunch of dirty old cards."

"Yes, ma'am. I love you, obstinate and foul-mouthed though you are."

"Fuckin' A. The person who's got to stay safe is this little guy."

"No way!" Willie piped. "I'm old enough to help, and you need everybody you can get!" Tom belatedly realized that the boy had stopped snoring a minute or two before.

"I know you could help," Becky said. "You saved my life back in the old factory. But someone has to stay behind to organize a second attack if this first one fails."

"Give me a break," the boy said.

"All right," Tom said, "the truth is that grown-ups aren't supposed to take kids into danger if they can avoid it. It just isn't right."

"You know how I used to be? Scared and sad all the time?"

"Yes," Becky said, "we remember."

"Well, after we escaped from Gary and the clown, I was better. Not just because I was rid of them, but because I'd grabbed the gun and helped rescue myself. All of a sudden I felt stronger and braver, like *nobody* could hurt me anymore.

"Then tonight—or was it last night, even though the sun hasn't come up?—Mom shook me awake, told me we had to run away. Mrs. Farentino from downstairs had come to the door to warn us that crazy men with guns were breaking into everybody's apartment.

"They came out of one stairway just as we were going into the one on the other end of the hall. Some of the lights don't work, and I don't think Steven saw who I was, or I bet he would have chased us. But somehow I recognized him, and as soon as I did I went back to feeling the way I did before.

"I know you're both smart and everything, but you still don't know what that was like. I was scared, but ashamed, too, like I was such a piece of shit that it was okay for people to hurt me. It's awful to feel like that for years, then to think you don't have to anymore, then have it come back.

"And I couldn't take it. When you called people down to the altar, I was afraid to go, but I thought that if I did, I'd stop feeling like I was nothing. I tried to jump up, but Mom held me down.

"Later in the parking lot, I broke away from her. Left her alone in the middle of all this . . . this *stuff*, because she just wants us to hide, and I *have* to fight. So please, don't try to make me stay behind!"

"Much as I hate to admit it," Becky said, "we do need every bit of help we can get. And I'm sure Steven included Willie on the list of 'special enemies.' They'll hunt him down if our attack fails."

"All right," Tom sighed.

"Thanks!" Willie exclaimed. He sounded surprised that the adults had capitulated so easily. "I'll do a good job!"

"I know you will," Tom replied. "Why don't we try to get some sleep, or rest at least."

When the boy spoke again, it was in a softer, younger voice. "Everything's going to be okay, isn't it?"

"I hope so," Tom said.

"I mean, God wouldn't let the bad guys win," Willie persisted. "I prayed for help, and He sent Mrs. Carpenter, so we can count on Him to help us now, right?"

Tom grimaced. He riffled through his armamentarium of platitudes, then abruptly decided that the kid deserved the truth.

"I wish I could tell you I'm sure that's true," he began. "I know a minster's supposed to have the inside story on God, or at least believe he does, but it's been a while since I've even been convinced there *is* a God, much less that He's someone we can count on in a crunch. It's messed me up pretty bad; when I lost faith in Him, I lost faith in everything, particularly myself.

"I suppose I started doubting because Becky and I lost our baby, and because I saw so many other senseless, wasteful misfortunes befalling other people. So, considering all that's happened, I guess I should be despairing even worse now. I mean, just look around. What kind of world is it where a person can go blind squinting for a glimpse of God, but the Devil spray-paints his name across the landscape in letters ten miles high? Where it's easy for him to use the Church itself to work evil? Where sociopaths perform miracles? Where people adored me when I hurt them, and turned from me when I tried to convince them to do what they need to do to survive?

"But you want to hear something weird? Aside from my terror and my guilt—kind of around the edges—I feel better than I have in years. Because I've started noticing some amazingly *good* things happening around me, too.

"For a long time Becky and I couldn't get along. When the demon in the card possessed me, nobody could have blamed her if she'd walked away. Instead, she risked death to save me, and since then we've rediscovered just how much we love each other." He squeezed her forearm.

Becky patted his thigh. "Fortunately," she said, "our differences weren't as irreconcilable as we thought. Nothing a little supernatural cataclysm couldn't put into perspective."

"And despite the horrible things Steven did to crush your spirit," Tom continued, "you defied him to help Becky. Miriam broke the High Priest's spell through sheer willpower, then she and Grace risked their necks to save us at the church. Frail, battered, heartsick Vina Donovan transcended agony to knock Lloyd down before he could knife me.

"I don't know how I forgot how gallant and generous people can be. I still don't know if there's a Bible God sitting up in the sky, some all-powerful Father Who makes everything work out right. But I'm sure there's some glorious spark inside every human being, and that, at least, is worth believing in."

"I guess I understand," Willie said dubiously. "But since I do believe in the Bible God, is it okay if I say another prayer?"

"Sure," Tom said. "If the spirit moves me, I may even join you. Somebody *may* be listening."

28

CORONA CITY WAS silent. Doorways loomed as dark as cave mouths on the deserted streets; no candles or oil lamps shone in the empty windows. Only the breeze stirred, chilling the sweat on Willie's face.

He knew he should be glad the place wasn't swarming with monsters, but the stillness gave him the creeps. "It's like everybody's already dead," he said to the others.

"Don't talk dumb," Miriam told him, shifting her grip on her rifle. "They're just hiding, waiting for us commandos to save the day."

"Maybe they won't have to wait much longer," Reverend Carpenter said. With his scratched face, his cut and bruised hands, his shotgun, the machete sheathed at his belt, and the shoulder bag of Molotov cocktails clinking at his hip, he resembled a soldier of fortune in a movie about the collapse of civilization; his black clerical clothing only accentuated the effect. "Look up and to the right."

Willie raised his eyes. Faint, flickering, multicolored light stained a patch of sky above the roof of a produce wholesaler's abandoned warehouse.

Since they didn't know where their enemies were, they'd decided to head for Vasquez's brownstone. If they managed to pick up their trail on the way, they'd begin stalking them. If not, they'd sneak into the house, attack by surprise if they were home or lie in wait if they weren't.

Now, of course, they would detour to investigate the glow. When they reached the next intersection, the minister led them down the side street.

Willie shivered. "What do you think it is?"

"I don't know," Mrs. Carpenter murmured. "It's so dim, it reminds me of the northern lights. Maybe it's nothing, just something funny about the weather."

But by the time they'd marched three more desolate blocks, and the glimmering had grown a little brighter, Willie was sure it was more than that, because by then he'd surmised where it was coming from.

Reverend Carpenter had obviously guessed as well. As they neared Palm Street, he raised his hand, skulked ahead up to the corner, and peered around the side of the boarded-up shoe repair shop. "It's the church," he said.

His four companions scurried up to see.

Holy Assembly reared black and angular in the darkness. The surrounding trees tossed back and forth like sleepers in the grip of nightmare. A wavering light writhed through the stained glass windows, casting pale, seething clouds of color into the night.

Once the church had reminded Willie of a fairy-tale castle. Now it looked like the fortress of a mad tyrant or a wicked witch.

"They torched it," Mrs. Carpenter said. She squeezed her husband's shoulder.

"I don't think so," he answered. "We left here hours ago. If they set the building alight shortly thereafter, surely we could see smoke and flame from the outside by now. Something else is happening, and I guess we'd better check it out."

Willie's heart thumped harder.

"Hold it," Miriam said. "We damn near got iced getting out of there once already."

"I'm scared too," the Reverend said, "but—"

"I'm *not* chicken," the redhead rasped. "I just believe in following my instincts."

Grace patted her on the arm. "We could watch from out here for a little while, then go on inside if nothing happens."

"All right," said the Reverend, "that makes sense."

Willie tried to relax, but couldn't do it. His own instincts warned him that they were still going to wind up entering the building.

.Five minutes crawled by. No one approached the church or emerged from the double doors. Somewhere far away, almost certainly beyond the border, a drummer started pounding out a monotonous one-two beat on an instrument that sounded like a timpani.

After another five minutes, the pastor drew himself up straight. His back popped. "We can't crouch out here forever. I'm heading in. Anyone who thinks it's a bad idea can stay behind."

Miriam scowled. "Splitting up would be a stupid idea too." She jacked a round into the chamber of her gun.

"Which entrance should we use?" Mrs. Carpenter asked, swiping raven curls away from her eyes.

"Certainly not the front doors," Reverend Carpenter said. "Not the door we ran out the last time, either. How about the side door by my office?"

"Sounds good," she replied. "And since we're sneaking, we shouldn't approach from the street. Let's cut over to Bougainvillea and come in from the rear."

They circled around the block, crept between two dilapidated duplexes, then up to the parsonage. Willie squinted at the church's clear glass windows and the top of the steeple. If there were any lookouts, he couldn't see them.

"Let's move," the Reverend said.

They sprinted across the yard, feet swishing through the grass, red moonlight glinting on their weapons.

"So far, so good," the minister whispered when they stood clustered around their chosen entrance. "Hey, Beck, I know how crazy you are about breaking and entering, but is it okay if I open this with my key?"

She flipped him a bird. "Get on with it," Miriam growled.

The snick of the bolt seemed so loud that Willie flinched. The door swung open on a vacant corridor. Two drinking fountains, a tall one for grown-ups and a short one for little kids, stood against the right-hand wall; a bulletin board with crayon drawings thumbtacked to it hung on the left. The misshapen, strangely colored figures in the pictures looked like demons in the gloom.

They filed down the hall toward the rear entrance to the

nave, peering into offices and meeting rooms as they passed.
All were empty. Once Grace gasped, swiveled, and everybody jumped. She slumped and smiled apologetically when
she realized that she hadn't really seen whatever it was that
she'd thought she had.

The air began to smell smoky. Willie's eyes stung.

They crept the last few feet to the doorway, peeked inside.
Someone had carried a number of trash cans into the sanctuary, then set their contents ablaze. Leaping, crackling flames
sent shadows flitting along the walls.

Corpses littered the floor. The trampled-looking man
sprawled just inside the door had a hole in the back of his
head. Behind him lay a thin, middle-aged Oriental with a
crooked neck, then a woman with a missing arm, and beyond
her, still others, three with most of their flesh stripped away
from their bones. Five more bodies were slumped in the
pews in the middle of the room.

There was no sign of Vasquez, the clown, or the metal
man. Willie felt a guilty pang of relief.

"I guess they camped here for a while, then moved on,"
Mrs. Carpenter said.

The Reverend tried to speak, couldn't, swallowed, tried
again. "Maybe." They stepped into the chamber. Willie's
stomach squirmed at the stench of shit and blood.

One of the women in the pews twitched and moaned. Mr.
and Mrs. Carpenter dodged around the wreckage of the pulpit and trotted down the center aisle to her side. Willie, Miriam, and Grace followed more slowly, still scanning for
someone lying in wait.

The woman was the closemouthed nurse with the wavy
chestnut hair who'd administered first aid before the Reverend called his meeting to order. Like the others sprawled
across the benches, she was naked, and dark, glistening-
moist triangles mottled her pasty body. For a second Willie
thought someone had painted her, then realized that patches
of her skin had been flayed away.

Reverend Carpenter gently gripped her shoulders, supporting her, helping her lift her head. The boy winced. Her

face was almost all raw, her brown, human eyes out of place in an oozing hunk of meat that belonged in a butcher's case.

"It's all right now," the minister said. "They're gone, and we're going to help you."

Clutching his arms, she drew herself up straighter. "Help," she croaked.

"We will, all we can," Mrs. Carpenter said. "But we need information. Can you tell us what happened? It might help us put an end to this, and then we can get you to a hospital."

The nurse's head swayed drunkenly. "Help," she sighed. Someone else moaned.

"Christ," Miriam said. "They're *all* alive."

The four other bodies slumped in the pews whimpered, stirred. The benches creaked, and something rustled, snake-like, at their feet. Willie hastily glanced down, saw nothing, assured himself it had only been the sound of bare soles brushing across the floorboards.

The pudgy, balding, middle-aged man seated in front of the nurse suddenly grasped Willie's right forearm. The boy squawked, almost clenched his finger on the trigger of the Beretta Reverend Carpenter had given him.

Fumbling at their would-be rescuers, seemingly for support, the injured people tottered erect. "Help," they murmured. "Help. Help. Help." Willie tried to pull away and the pudgy man gripped him tighter.

"Get off me!" Miriam snarled, her voice shrill. She tore free of the one holding her, a black teenage girl with a bisected nose and a gaping, bleeding eye socket. Then the torture victims pounced.

Suddenly powerful, agile, like he wasn't hurt at all, the pudgy man twisted Willie's arm. Pain lanced up into his shoulder; the Beretta tumbled from his fingers.

Somehow the boy broke loose, but before he could scramble back, his opponent lunged again, grappled, bore him to the floor. Steely fingers sought his throat.

Willie squirmed, punched, scratched. Jowls quivering, eyes still glazed and piebald face still slack, the pudgy man grabbed at his neck. A pulsing, wriggling ridge ran up his spine to the back of his head. A part of Willie's mind that was still reasoning detached from the fear consuming the rest, inferred that the finger-wide bump had been there under the man's skin all the time; he just hadn't noticed it in the uncertain light.

As they thrashed back and forth, Willie kept writhing over a lashing cord. After a while he realized it was another length of the same thing that had invaded the pudgy man's body.

The man grasped his neck, squeezed. Willie clawed at his arms and fingers, but couldn't break his hold. A pressure built in his chest. His heart hammered. His ears rang and the strangler's face blurred.

Just when Willie was sure he was about to pass out, the pudgy man relaxed his grip, jerked the boy's head up, and whipped it down. The impact smashed the remaining strength out of his body. Dazed, nearly asphyxiated, the man's hands poised to throttle him again, all Willie could do was watch what was happening around him.

Mrs. Carpenter was wrestling a wiry young man with fine, shoulder-length, white-blond hair; his pale mane and her black curls tossed and tangled as they stumbled up and down the aisle. A wriggling tendril hung from the man's anus, ran away into the darkness under the pews. Drying blood caked his ass and the backs of his thighs.

Teeth gritted, eyes blazing, Mrs. Carpenter slowly forced her pistol into line with his stomach. Then hesitated. *Shoot!* Willie silently screamed, but it was already too late. The blond man swept his elbow around to crack it against her temple. As she fell, he knocked the gun out of her hand, then snapped his knee up into her face.

Grace had lost her revolver. Fists raised, mouth working soundlessly, she backed away between two of the benches. A burly Hispanic with an elaborate green, blue, and black tattoo on his left shoulder, the image defaced beyond recognition by his wounds, pursued. A pink worm dangled from his bloody buttocks. Grace feinted with her right hand, kicked at his crotch.

He caught her ankle, yanked and twisted. She fell back onto the seat; he sprang. She snatched inside her denim jacket, jerked something out. The switchblade snapped open just in time for his momentum to ram it into the center of his chest.

The battle had driven Reverend Carpenter and Miriam back down the aisle toward the purple and gold banner and the altar. The minister no longer had his shotgun, but he'd drawn his machete. The heavy-bladed cane knife whistled through the air, repelling the nurse every time she attempted to close. It looked like it would be easy to cut her, if only he'd go on the offensive.

Miriam and the black teenager were both wrenching at the AR-15. Miriam suddenly let go with her right hand, reached behind her back and under her coat, brought out a small pistol Willie hadn't known she had. She thrust it into the girl's mutilated face and bellowed, "Back off!" But instead of obeying, the teenager jabbed stiffened fingers at her eyes.

Miriam shot her, blasting a chunk out of the back of her head. Willie hoped the bullet had struck the serpentine thing inside her.

Suddenly he wasn't quite as afraid. Now that one of his companions was in the clear, with a gun and the will to use it, maybe everything would be all right.

Behind him, midway between the floor and the vaulted ceiling, footsteps thudded. His silvery body humming, Price vaulted over the clerestory railing. He seemed to fall for a ridiculously long time, then, knees flexing, he landed with a report like a crack of thunder.

Shrouded in steam, radiating a chill so intense that Willie felt it even from the center of the chamber, the metal man was even less human than he'd been a few hours before. Frost encrusted his garments and skin. Luminous crimson eyes burned in his mask. His right hand had swelled and fused into a lump studded with spikes, like the head of a mace.

He strode forward. Grace shoved the tattooed man's body off her onto the floor, scrambled up, grabbed her fallen gun, and whirled to face him.

A second figure stepped out of the darkness at the rear of

the choir loft. He raised his left arm, pulled it back, then flipped it forward like a fisherman casting a line.

Strands arced through the air, fell around the black woman's head and shoulders. Two coiled around her neck; the others burrowed at her scalp.

She screamed, began to swing her revolver up at the silhouette in the clerestory, then lowered it again. Shaking, moving stiffly, she turned toward the altar.

Her arm sweeping up and down, Miriam fired alternate shots at Price and the puppeteer. Twice bullets whined, glancing off the metal man's body; if she hit the man in the loft, there was no sign of it. When her pistol was empty, she stooped, reaching for the AR-15.

Price stepped over Willie, his proximity so cold that both the boy and his captor shuddered repeatedly.

Grace started to level her gun at Miriam, then opened her mouth wide and stuck the muzzle inside instead.

"Give up," the puppeteer called in Steven's voice, "or I'll blow her head off, then kill Becky and the boy."

Miriam froze. Still advancing inexorably, Price was three-quarters of the way down the aisle.

Reverend Carpenter ripped open his bag with the Molotov cocktails, then charged, slashing furiously with the machete; he would have split the nurse's head or lopped off one of her arms if she hadn't scrambled back. He smashed down bottles into the space he'd cleared, tumbled one of the burning trash cans into the pool. A wall of flame exploded up, blocking the center aisle.

The one-eyed girl's body lay in the fire. Steven's tendril quickly slipped out of her crotch, slithered away from the blaze.

Price and the nurse pivoted, scuttled between pews. The minister hurled more bottles, extending his barrier.

"We're not bluffing!" Vasquez bellowed from above. "You're *murdering* them!"

The Reverend grabbed Miriam and dragged her through the door behind the altar.

29

As Tom PULLED Miriam out onto the sidewalk, a shot rang out inside the nave. She wailed, attempted to jerk herself out of his grasp. When he resisted, she tried to brain him with her automatic.

He ducked, then slapped her. "Listen to me," he snarled. "You know they meant to kill us all eventually anyway, and captured, we couldn't have done anything about it. Free, we can save Becky and Willie if they let them live a while longer, and at least avenge them if they don't."

Glistening tears slid down her face. The mark of his hand was livid on her cheek. "I hate you," she sobbed. "I told you we shouldn't go in there."

"Fine, hate me, but come on. The fire only bought us a few seconds."

They dashed to the parsonage's tin-roofed carport. As he circled the front end of his Escort, his foot bumped something resting on the ground. He looked down at the vehicle's battery.

Price emerged from the church, the vapor rising from his body blending with the smoke that billowed from the doorway behind him. His stiff-legged stride devouring distance almost as rapidly as an ordinary human being's run, he advanced.

Miriam opened the door on the passenger side. "They disabled the engine," Tom told her. "Get into the house."

They entered through the front door. He locked it, scurried to the back door, swung it open, then led her up the stairs into his bedroom.

A crash sounded below. Footsteps thudded into the house. Then risers groaned.

"Darn!" Tom said.

Miriam slipped a fresh magazine into her pistol. "Did you ever have an idea that worked?"

He pushed the old, scarred pine dresser against the door. She helped him shove the bed behind it. "Out the window," he said.

Floorboards creaked in the hall.

She threw up the sash, climbed out backwards, hung for a moment by her hands. Spikes crunched through the top of the door. She gasped and dropped, landed between two shrubs, and flailed back onto her butt.

Price's fist smashed into the door again, jolting the furniture heaped against it. As soon as Miriam scrambled clear, Tom scurried out the window. Unwilling to trust his barricade to hold for the few extra seconds he'd need to lower himself from the sill, he simply leaped.

He landed hard; his right ankle twisted. He grunted and dropped to one knee.

Miriam pawed at him. "Are you all right?"

"Yeah," he said optimistically. She hauled him to his feet and he hobbled a few steps. "Yeah, it hurts, but I can run. Let's go."

They raced toward Bougainvillea. Price jumped down onto the grass.

When they reached the street, Tom and Miriam veered left, ran past rental houses that were scarcely better than shacks, then empty commercial properties, then the burnt-out shell of an office building. The white faces of refugees stared from the broken windows. Perhaps they had sought shelter inside because they imagined that the structure was so ruined even Vasquez wouldn't bother to drive them out.

Price loped out onto the sidewalk.

For a moment Tom fantasized that the people in the windows would call out, urging him and Miriam to hide inside, but of course no one did. Most of them shrank back into the darkness. The rest just watched, their expressions as inscrutable as the metal man's.

They ran on. The machete slapped his hip and the shoulder bag bumped his butt. Every other step twinged.

He led her down an alley, then south on Twenty-eighth Street, then into an alley again. Breath rasping, they crouched behind a stinking green Dumpster. Back the way they'd come, a tower of smoke reared above the rooftops.

"What now?" Miriam wheezed.

"He was too far back to see us turn down here. If we stay hidden, maybe we'll lose him."

"What if we don't?"

He set his brown imitation leather bag on the ground, removed the last two Molotov cocktails and a red plastic disposable lighter. The gasoline smell stung his nostrils. "Then we'll hit him with these; he didn't like fire back in the church. And if that doesn't work, can you hot-wire a car?"

"No."

"Me neither. So I guess we'll run some more and try to lose him again. Now let's be quiet."

The seconds dragged by. He struggled to breathe softly, sensed her trying to do the same. Once he reached to pat her hand, but she snatched it away.

At last, at the mouth of the alleyway, something hummed. After a moment, when the sound didn't recede, Tom risked a peek. Price was striding forward, his glowing crimson gaze locked on the Dumpster.

Tom sprang up, fumbled with the lighter. On his third try, flame blossomed; he hastily set the rags stuffed in the bottle necks alight.

Their fire-bombs concealed behind the garbage bin, they waited, waited, waited for Price to march into throwing range. Finally Miriam lunged into the clear, lashed her arm around in an arc. Her missile tumbled through the darkness like a meteor, fell short and too far to the right.

As it burst into crackling blue and yellow flame, Tom threw his bottle. It smashed against Price's frozen shirt front. Blazing gas streamed down his abdomen and legs.

Come on, Tom thought, *feel it. You're cold and it's hot, so shatter.*

For a moment, while he beat at the conflagration with his left hand, Price actually seemed to be in distress. Then, evidently realizing that it wasn't hurting him, he resumed his advance.

All right, Tom begged, *then at least burn his clothes off. Burn up his card, if he's carrying one.*

But the icy garments didn't kindle. The flames died or dripped away.

Their lead now eroded to a few paces, Tom and Miriam wheeled and fled toward the other end of the alley. Tom's ankle started hurting worse; perhaps it had swollen during their stop. Almost giddy with fear and fatigue, he reflected that at least it was nice not to have his bag scraping at his shoulder or pounding against his backside anymore.

They spun right, onto the street, then left onto the next cross street. Tom's heart hammered. His lungs burned. Gradually he and Miriam pulled further ahead of their pursuer.

She pawed at his arm. "About to cross . . . border."

He had to slow down, or he wouldn't have had sufficient breath to answer her. "Yeah," he gasped, "Price almost got . . . killed in Hell before. Might . . . not follow us."

Somehow forcing another burst of acceleration from his aching muscles, he led her across Thirtieth Street.

The narrow lanes on the other side were unpaved; they tripped over the ruts in the hardened earth. Patches of phosphorescent mold—orange, umber, and the blue-green variety Tom had encountered before—virtually covered the sagging cottages, obscuring the elaborate designs carved into their lintels, porch columns, and eaves; occasionally motes of purple and viridian light floated past the heart- and diamond-shaped windows.

They turned one corner, then another. Straining to catch whirring, the rustling of bug-things, the clattering of another Rattlesnake, Tom couldn't hear anything but their own gasping and the thud of their own footsteps.

At last, spent, they stumbled up a sandy, weed-infested yard, knelt in the pool of shadow between two of the odd little bungalows. Tom drew his machete and set it on the ground beside him. "Don't touch the fungus," he whispered.

Miriam grimaced. "Don't worry. Do you really think you'll need the knife? With all the intersections we ran through, I don't think he could possibly trail us this time."

"I'd like to believe that, but even if it's true, I can guarantee you, there are other dangers around. Let's hope we haven't been moving through bent space, so we can get back to Corona City fast."

"What the hell's bent space?"

The question made him think of Becky; he almost sobbed. "It's difficult to explain," he said thickly. "I'll tell you if it turns out to be relevant."

"Fine. Be that way."

He massaged his ankle and kept watch. Nothing stirred when he was looking directly at it, but he caught flickers of motion out of the corner of his eye. Shadows shifted, sheets of fungus extruded pseudopods, and leering faces bobbed up in windows. When he snapped his head around, the patches of darkness and phosphorescence froze; the faces burst like bubbles.

Something boomed; he jumped. Off to the north, the timpani player was drumming again.

He wiped his sweaty forehead with his sleeve. "What do you say we wait five more minutes, then head back?"

"Sounds good to me," Miriam said. "This place makes me feel like I'm on acid. I—*What's that?*"

He grabbed the cane knife, listened. The wind sighed and the kettledrum rumbled. "I don't hear it."

"It's Price's guts," she gritted. They rose, weapons in hand. A faint hum murmured through the air.

Tom scuttled toward the front of the cottages, Miriam toward the rear. No one was in the front yards or approaching up the rutted dirt street beyond.

"I don't see him," Miriam said.

"I don't either. Maybe—" Remembering the jelly and the insect-creatures, he whirled and raised his eyes.

The metal man slid down the sloping roof of the left-hand

cottage, his steaming body aimed to drop on the woman. His shoes cut a groove in the particolored carpet of mold.

Tom shouted, sprinted. Miriam spun around, eyes wide, obviously still not perceiving the danger, because she didn't jump out of the way. Glimmering orange and yellowish-brown clods rained down around her, then Tom slammed into her like a lineman. They reeled backward across the sparse, coarse grass, and she fell.

Price landed perfectly balanced, his faceted red eyes glowing through a cloud of vapor and drifting spores. The cold he emanated was almost unbearable; Tom screamed when he lunged at him.

When they'd discussed tactics back at the Redbird, Becky had suggested striking at the metal man's human eyes. The crystalline orbs weren't human anymore, but they still might be more vulnerable than the transformed thug's silvery skin.

So he hacked at them. The mace-hand swept up, blocked. Metal rang and chips of ice flew.

Price counterattacked instantly. Tom expected him to swing his arm like a maul, almost missed the straight punch. He leaped back just in time to keep spikes from driving into his chest.

His mucous membranes crackling with the cold, he darted in again, feinted a cut at his opponent's belly. When Price attempted to parry, he whipped the blade at his face.

The machete shrieked and rebounded, left a thin white scratch across the radiant eye and reflective cheek but didn't breach them. Snatching the blade with his left hand, Price tore it out of his grasp.

Tom scrambled backward. The metal man stalked forward, clubbing. On her feet again, Miriam emptied her pistol at point-blank range. The .22 bullets hammered pockmarks in his forehead, but didn't penetrate; she didn't hit an eye.

But Price recoiled. In that instant, Miriam and Tom wheeled and ran again.

Tom kept shuddering; his teeth chattered. Every other step drove a dagger of agony up his calf, and his stride threatened to degenerate into a stumbling limp.

He now realized that even if they could find the stamina to pull ahead a third time, it would be useless to hide. Price was tireless, and somehow he could track them. If he didn't catch them first, if they didn't simply collapse, they had to find a place and a way to make a stand.

30

"GET THEM!" VASQUEZ called.

The metal man circled the pool of flame, then abruptly pivoted, strode right into it and on through the doorway behind the altar. The nurse didn't follow; Willie hadn't expected her to. Steven's warts could stretch the length of the church, but that didn't mean they could extend forever. Besides, he probably couldn't direct his puppets when they were out of sight.

Grace lowered her smoking revolver, turned, peered up at the choir loft, the weave of tendrils wriggling about her head. Her mouth twitched and drooled, and tears rolled down her gleaming brown cheeks. The boy wondered if she was sorry that Steven had made her shoot at the ceiling instead of into her mouth.

"Let's leave before the fire spreads," the old man said. "Continue this in the parsonage, where Mr. Price won't have any trouble finding us." His heavy footsteps clumped toward the stairway down.

Unable to take that route with his string-warts dangling over the railing, Steven jumped.

The firelight revealed that he was nude like his father; standing straight instead of slouching, he might have been seven feet tall. His forehead was bulbous, with a fat, flopping cone of flesh sprouting from each temple, a wedge of hair stabbing between them in an exaggerated widow's peak. There was a vertical scar in the middle of his narrow chest, and the writhing strands extending from his right hand looped around both forks of his jutting penis before slithering away across the floor.

The pudgy man climbed off Willie, then yanked him to his feet. The nurse and the guy with the pale blond mane did the same to Mrs. Carpenter. Only semiconscious, she lolled in their grasp. Her bruised nose was crooked, flattened, and blood glistened on her chin and upper lip.

Twisting Willie's arm up behind his back, his captor marched him toward the clown. The boy snapped out of his daze, thrashed, couldn't break away. The others moved forward too. Steven's string-warts shortened, taking up slack, like he was an angler reeling in his catch.

He led them out the double doors into the cool night breeze. His father was waiting on the sidewalk. Even huger than before, in the darkness his amorphous bulk was scarcely recognizable as a human form. He no longer had the gym bag; a kangaroo-like pouch bulged among the wriggling horizontal ridges on his thorax. His steam-shovel jaws ground at something that squished and crunched.

By the time they rounded the hedge, he'd gobbled the last of it. Piggy eyes glittering, he turned and reached. Willie yelped, flailed. A warm squirt of pee spat down his thigh.

But Vasquez didn't seize him; he gripped the pudgy man's shoulder instead. "I'm hungry," he said.

"No problem," Steven said. Grace shuffled over, took hold of Willie's collar, and jabbed her revolver into his ribs. The pudgy man stepped back, and the bloody pink worm squirmed out of his ass.

He crumpled, howled as though venting all the agony he'd been forbidden to voice during his hours as a puppet. Supporting and immobilizing him with one hand, Vasquez prodded him with the other, digging his fingertips into his wounds.

Eventually the pudgy man stopped screaming. "Please," he whimpered, "please, please, please."

Vasquez chuckled. "Come now, Doctor, I barely touched you."

"Please. I always did my best to help you."

"Of course you did, and now I want to help you. I'm afraid that from now on your pain will be excruciating unless

you permit me to take the measures necessary to manage it."
His jaws gaped.

The physician shrieked. Lifting him off the ground as
though he were weightless, Vasquez stuffed his entire head
into his mouth. The now-muffled cries ceased abruptly when
massive fangs sheared into his neck, but his body convulsed
for several more seconds. The old man guzzled frantically,
sucking the fountaining gore.

Grace made a choking sound. More tears ran down her
face, a tic plucked at the corner of her eye, but her grip on
Willie's collar didn't relax, and the barrel of her gun never
wavered.

It seemed to take forever for the blood to stop spurting.
When it finally did, Vasquez, his upper body now more red
than pink, chewed up his doctor's skull; it cracked like a
piece of hard candy. Once that was swallowed, he set off for
the house again, biting chunks of meat from the chest and
shoulders of the decapitated thing cradled in his arms. Tittering, the flabby-horned clown herded the rest of them along
behind.

Someone, almost certainly Price, had smashed the front
door off its hinges; apparently the Reverend and Miriam had
fled here. For a moment, knowing it was stupid, Willie
dreamed that they'd destroyed the metal man and were lying
in wait, that they'd leap out and start shooting as soon as
Vasquez and Steven stepped inside.

They didn't, of course. Except for the old man's
chomping, Steven's bursts of giggling, and the scuffing of
their feet and that of their prisoners on the living room floor,
the parsonage was silent.

A triple-branched glass candelabrum sat at either end
of the mantel, bracketing the clock and family photos.
Vasquez dumped the doctor's mangled body on the hearth
rug, found a book of matches, and lit the pale yellow candles. "Well, here's some light. The church will give us
more in a little while."

Mrs. Carpenter groaned, blinked, planted her feet on the
floor to support her own weight.

The clown dropped into the beat-up red recliner, leaned

back. His legs were too long for it; his grimy heels extended far beyond the footrest. "Well," he said, "I suppose you're all wondering why I called you here. Instead of snuffing you in the sanctuary like I promised."

"You want hostages," Mrs. Carpenter said.

Steven smirked. "Nope. We just tried threatening you to force your husband and his other slut to surrender, and, as those of us who were awake discovered, they apparently don't give a damn about you. Pretty smart on their part, I have to admit. Actually, I want *toys*. I want to have that party you so rudely ran out on, only now it'll be a million times better than it could have been before. And when we've had our fun, Papa wants a public execution, to make an example of you."

Mrs. Carpenter spat at him. He giggled.

Vasquez picked up his doctor's corpse, bit another huge mouthful out of its flabby midsection. "People have to see you suffer more than lesser offenders," he said, chewing. "Otherwise, they might think the boss is unfair. Now, I'd like to go upstairs for a while—"

"Going to call again?" Steven asked.

"Don't interrupt," the old man rapped. The ridges on his body wriggled. "But yes. For some reason, it helps to be above ground level, just like it helps to be alone. I'm so *close*! The more I eat, the stronger I grow, the more clearly I can hear their thoughts. I know my 'voice' is sharper too. Soon we'll have *real* communication. Then some will come to serve me, and the other bosses will acknowledge me as one of their own.

"But what I want to know is, have *you* grown strong enough to handle our hostess and her other guests by yourself?"

"My gosh, Papa, of course. You just saw me control five people at once."

"Whom you subjugated one and two at a time."

The clown grinned. "Watch this."

One of his unoccupied warts, stippled with the drying body fluids of a marionette who'd already died, stretched, dropped to the floor, and snaked toward Mrs. Carpenter. She thrashed, twisted and bit, but couldn't break her impassive captors' grips. The tendril, swaying nimbly to avoid her stamps and kicks, slipped up the leg of her jeans.

The black corduroy bulged as the tendril coiled up her calf and thigh. Her rolling eyes glittered in the candlelight. She kept gasping, her teeth clenched, and Willie realized she was struggling not to scream.

The fabric at her crotch fluttered, like Steven was tickling her. After a moment, he laughed.

"It feels wonderful to go in through the ass or the pussy, but I'm not going to do it *yet*. You'd bleed out too fast."

The wart resumed its ascent, wormed past her belt, under her blouse, and out her collar. It looped once around her throat, brushed her lips, then reared like a cobra and nuzzled among her curls, finally stabbing under her scalp to lie a fraction of an inch closer to her brain.

The blond man and the nurse released her. She started to raise her hands, then collapsed to her knees vomiting hunks of croissant.

Another tendril extended, writhed toward Willie, and suddenly Grace's revolver didn't matter anymore. Yammering with terror and revulsion, he punched, clawed, anything to break her hold. Weeping again, she clubbed him over the head.

A blast of pain unhinged his joints, sprawled him limp and helpless on the floor. An instant later, something jabbed behind his ear.

A bit of his strength returning, he tried to yank the tendril loose, just as Mrs. Carpenter had no doubt intended. A tidal wave of fear and sickness crashed over him, an hysterical prescience that if he didn't *obey*, the worst things in the world would happen over and over again forever. It pulverized his will, and when the wart twitched at his nerves, he stood up like it wanted him to.

Another strand crawled up his body and took root. Grace handed her gun to the white-blond guy. Then a pair of her strands dropped away from her head, slithered up the nurse's legs and into her vagina to lodge beside the one that was dangling there already.

"This one's about to kick," Steven said. "I can tell from her pulse and temperature, things like that. So let me show you how *strong* these suckers are getting."

The bump on the nurse's head flattened as the wart beneath her scalp retracted. She wailed and grabbed between her legs.

The strands surged. Shrieking, she fell over backwards, writhed, jolted across the floor as the things inside her rammed up the center of her torso.

Blood gushed from her vagina, rectum, nose, and mouth. After a final, protracted, gurgling scream, her eyes exploded outward.

Willie tried to turn his head, but Steven wouldn't let him look away. Mrs. Carpenter retched.

The tips of the warts, two protruding from the nurse's eye sockets and the other from her right ear, waved for a moment, then withdrew into her skull. The tendrils dragged from her body with chunks of organ wrapped in their coils, the vagina distending, then tearing to pass gobs of brain, heart, lung, intestine, and other things the boy didn't recognize.

Releasing the masses of flesh, the filthy warts snaked across the floor, two toward Mrs. Carpenter and one toward him. She whimpered, and he tried again to rip away the ones that had already attached themselves to him. Another tide of dread and nausea froze him, and a moment later the third stabbed into his head.

"There you go," Steven said. "Three strings on each woman, three on the kid, and one left over to run our friend who's already totally zombified. Three might not control a new puppet completely at first, but they'll definitely keep one out of mischief. And if it takes a little time to break them, that'll just add to the fun." A yellow light started pulsing in the windows, set the shadows of his fleshy horns bobbing on the wall behind him.

"All right," the old man said. "Call me when Mr. Price gets back, and remember, I want them ambulatory." He draped the pudgy man's body over his shoulder, scooped up a handful of the nurse's viscera to munch, and lumbered to the foot of the stairs. There he twisted from side to side, evidently trying to figure out how to ascend without scraping against the banister. Finally he grunted, bashed the bottom section loose, and knocked away the remainder as he climbed. Wood crunched and clattered; the steps groaned.

Willie's eyes throbbed. Unwilling to add to Steven's pleasure, he struggled not to cry.

And, to his surprise, he didn't. Instead he blinked, struck by a sudden sense of familiarity, and after that he wasn't quite as scared.

He realized he'd felt this before.

The paralyzing terror the warts were pumping into him was nothing new, just a souped-up, devil-magic version of the malaise that had afflicted him ever since Gary first sold him to the clown. The malaise he'd shaken off two days ago.

He couldn't expect Grace or Mrs. Carpenter to do the same; surely the feeling would overwhelm anyone who'd never experienced it before. But if God would help him one more time, perhaps he could do it again.

But then what? Even if he did manage to free himself, Steven and his other, stronger puppets could tear him apart. He'd have to do everything the clown commanded, no matter how painful or repellent, until something—please, God, send *something*!—happened to divert his and his white-blond sentinel's attention.

His strings plucked at his muscles; he began to undress. Trembling, their fingers fumbling with belt buckles, buttons, zippers, and snaps, the women stripped too. Scabbed-over cuts covered much of Grace's skin.

Steven chortled. "Very nice. Come over here, Black Beauty." He sat up, folding the footrest back down against the bottom of the recliner.

Grace flailed weakly, mewled, then shuffled over and knelt in front of him. The cords on her head writhed as she slurped at the forks of his penis.

Soon the clown was grimacing and squirming, his flabby horns bouncing up and down. Willie studied the white-blond guy; even when Steven's eyes squinched shut, when he went rigid and whooped, the "zombified" puppet didn't slump.

Grace rose, swallowed, licked at a glistening smear at the corner of her mouth. Steven's branching member stiffened again.

The buxom black woman slowly turned to the mantelpiece. Plucked a candle from its holder. Arm juddering, she drew the long arrowhead of flame toward one of her full, dark nipples.

Mrs. Carpenter gasped, lurched a single step, and fell on her face.

Teeth gritted, every muscle in her body clenched, Grace thrust the candle two inches further away, then jerked it closer again.

Something beat through the air outside, barely audible above the roar of the conflagration consuming the church. When it slammed down on the roof, the whole house shook. *"Yes!"* Vasquez bellowed.

31

PRICE WAS RELIEVED to step from rutted earth to sidewalk, but he recognized that the feeling was as nonsensical as most feelings. He'd been reborn into the dark world and ought to feel at home there; besides, Corona City had become just as much a part of it as the adjacent regions.

The glowing footprints led south, bright red and yellow now, quite warm, Carpenter's limp manifestly hampering his every stride; they couldn't keep ahead of him much longer. Things made of flesh and blood were remarkably feeble.

He marched on in pursuit, past dark, vandalized storefronts and an alley where rats burned like coals. The effortless precision of his movements and the knowledge that he was about to kill, to *win*, afforded him a cold satisfaction deeper than human pleasure.

Carpenter and Miriam had tramped around in front of a steel-gated pawnshop doorway, no doubt because they realized there were probably high-caliber guns inside. Fortunately, they hadn't managed to break in; he could have done it with just a couple sweeps of his right hand.

As he began to turn away, something showcased in the barred window caught his eye—an expensive-looking backgammon set, perhaps an antique, the gleaming black leather case standing open to display its contents. The ivory and ebony stones, the doubling cube, and the dice glimmered with crimson highlights, reflecting the moon or perhaps his own gaze.

Dice. He remembered their cool, hard planes and edges pressing his soft, sweaty palms. Feverish anticipation as they bounced across floorboards, concrete, or green felt. Exulting when he made his point, and his stomach turning over when he needed to but didn't.

For some reason the memories brought the suppressed, hated part of him—the part that feared the dark lands and tried to cringe from flames, blades, and small-arms fire—surging into full consciousness again. His sealed mouth strained to tear itself open, so he could wail at the sight of his altered hands. He shuddered even though he didn't feel a chill.

His machine side reestablished dominance instantly, smashing the useless vestige of human sensibility as easily as his spiked fist could shatter a skull. It hurt to kill these fragmentary ghosts of his former self, but the pain invariably ended in a burst of purgative release, like the pain of squeezing a pimple.

After a moment, he stalked on, once again the efficient, dispassionate instrument he'd always aspired to become.

He caught up with Carpenter and Miriam half a block further on.

Discovering a door they could force, the fugitives had taken refuge in a hardware store on the ground floor of a five-story brick building. One crouched behind the counter with the cash register and the other stood motionless behind a tall shelf. Apparently they still hadn't figured out that he could see the clouds of heat emanating from their bodies.

He wondered if they'd found new weapons. Maybe; the Reverend probably still had his lighter to search through the dark. Not that it mattered. What could they have picked up—hammers, shovels, crowbars? If he could withstand the machete and the bullets from the little automatic, shit like that wouldn't hurt him either.

Killing hand raised, he yanked open the door and advanced on the glow behind the counter.

"Hey!" shouted a hoarse baritone voice. Carpenter gimped out from behind the shelf to intercept him.

Trembling, still panting despite the minutes he'd had to recover, his hair sweat-plastered to his forehead, the minister looked completely exhausted. He had a round, bulky object cradled in his hands, something cold that didn't shine like flesh. Something to hit with, Price supposed.

Then Carpenter's arms jerked, and it sloshed. The detective whipped his arm up, but he was a half second too slow. The flying paint dashed him in the face.

It seemed to solidify on impact. Momentarily disoriented, he started to scrub it away, nearly spiked himself before he remembered he'd better use his off hand. He was still scraping the gunk from his eyes when the preacher hurled a second bucket.

Footsteps pattered across the linoleum. Now completely blind, he pivoted, swung, missed. Something edged and heavy, probably the head of an axe, slammed between his shoulder blades, crunching ice and driving him to one knee.

Miriam chopped him again and again, somehow evading all his counterattacks. The axe didn't penetrate, but stung, sheared away his frozen sheets of clothing.

She had the advantage for only a few seconds. Then he clawed his eyes clean, jerked his head aside when Carpenter tried to splash them again. Now bare to the waist, not angry in any choleric human sense, but displeased that mere animals could throw him on the defensive even for an instant, he sprang to his feet.

Carpenter snatched up another can, then he and Miriam circled, staring. After a second, the preacher's mouth twisted.

Price realized the redhead had cut his jacket and shirt away on purpose. They'd hoped his Tarot card was in a pocket near his heart, the way the Reverend had carried his, and that he'd revert to flesh without it. Nice try, but no cigar. He wondered if they could see well enough to spot the panel in the center of his chest.

Left arm cocked to shield his face, he lunged at the pastor, who ducked between two of the six-foot freestanding shelves. As he pivoted to follow, he heard Miriam scurrying up behind him again. Whirling, he struck, snapped the axe handle in two. The half with the head spun through the air, clanged when it hit the floor. The redhead scrambled back shivering, teeth beginning to chatter.

He strode after her, and more paint splashed him, this time spattering his killing arm and torso. Carpenter must have set open buckets out all over the room.

Price started to wheel again, then checked himself.

If he kept changing targets, the three of them were liable to wind up dancing around for a long time. Since neither was equipped to actually hurt him, it would be smarter to concentrate on one, no matter what the other did to distract him. And since the Reverend had a bum leg, and couldn't get as far if he tried to run again, it would make sense to nail the woman first.

He advanced on her.

Carpenter limped along behind, shouting his name, throwing more paint, finally beating at the back of his head with some kind of club. He made sure more paint didn't cover his eyes, otherwise ignored him.

Miriam grabbed an edger; apparently she had weapons set out all over the store as well. She thrust it like a spear and he knocked it out of her hands.

Eyes wide, shuddering more violently now, she backed between a pair of shelves. Her heel collided with another paint can. It overturned, rolled rattling across the linoleum, and she fell on her butt in a spreading white pool.

He pounced, grabbed a handful of her hair, and swung his arm up for a killing blow.

His spiked fist began to rise smoothly. Then froze for a second before ratcheting up again. His shoulder and elbow burned.

It had to be the paint. Some had splashed into the cracks between his body segments and was gumming up the mechanisms inside.

He struck at the junction of Miriam's neck and torso, but his fist lurched down too slowly. She hurled herself back and tore free of his grasp, leaving behind a tangle of coppery hair. When he tried to seize her ankle, his left arm suddenly flamed and jerked clumsily too; she wrenched her legs out of his reach.

As she jumped up, he kicked; at least his legs, protected by his pants, still worked right. But he missed, and while he was balanced on one foot, Carpenter clubbed him again.

The blow knocked him into the left-hand shelf, which toppled, spraying nails, screws, bolts, and washers across the floor. He landed on his side.

He started to straighten up and Miriam leaped over him, dropped to her knees at his back. Arms reaching around him, she groped at the hatch above his breastbone.

Which was stupid. Maybe there was no way she could know she wasn't anywhere near strong enough to pry it open bare-handed, but she should have understood that her fingers would freeze to his skin.

She screamed. He began bending his elbow. For the moment, the paint had him moving like a spastic, but now that she'd welded her body to his, that wouldn't prevent him from pressing his spikes into her skull.

Miriam went on yowling, her mouth just behind his ear; if he were still made of meat, it would have given him a hell of a headache. Grunting with pain or exertion, Carpenter battered him with a rake. It hurt a little, like flicks from a rolled-up newspaper.

His fist inched backward over his shoulder, surged, froze, jerked, locked, until one of its points indented her skin. With luck, one final push would shut her up.

The rake clattered on the linoleum. Carpenter's hands whipped around him, gripped Miriam's wrists, yanked. She shrieked even louder when her arms ripped free.

Price flopped back, trying to pin her beneath him, slammed down on broken shelving and bits of metal. Rolling over, he bounded up, two white handprints of skin still adhering to his gleaming chest, just as the Reverend dragged the woman to her feet.

Carpenter shoved her toward the back of the room, then stumbled backward himself. Price pursued, gratified to see that at last the weary, half-frozen animals didn't seem capable of moving any faster than he could.

The preacher threw more paint; Price twisted so it would

only splash his left side. The guy was shaking so badly that most of it missed anyway.

Then he started grabbing shelves, tumbling them into the aisle. Price managed to extend his arms. His hands deflected the shelves that would otherwise have crashed down on top of him, and it cost him only an extra second to step over the ones that lay before him on the floor. When the humans staggered through the door in the rear wall, he was only a couple of paces behind them.

Beyond it was another door, probably leading to an alley. The redhead threw herself against it, but it didn't open. Carpenter fumbled at it, evidently couldn't see how to unlock it. Price strode into the vestibule before he figured it out.

He punched at the minister's head. His arm shot out faster than it would have a few moments ago, but still not as quickly as it should have. Carpenter dodged; Price's spikes crunched into the wall. The humans scrambled out of his shroud of vapor and up the staircase to his right.

He climbed after them.

The door on the second-floor landing was locked too. Carpenter wrenched at the knob, kicked twice, the booming impacts echoing down the stairwell. It wouldn't fly open. Then Price set his foot on the landing, and the preacher and Miriam wheeled and blundered upward again. Their breath rasped, and blood from the woman's hands spattered the steps.

They couldn't get through the third-story door either.

As he ascended, Price swung his arms. Maybe his joints were grinding the paint into a dust too fine to hinder him, perhaps they were cleaning themselves in some other way, but at any rate, the heat inside them was dying, and his movements were becoming lithe again. When Carpenter threw a fire extinguisher, he easily batted it away.

Fourth floor locked. Fifth floor locked. His quarries stumbled up the final flight, toward the fire door that must lead to the roof.

To his surprise, that one opened.

Carpenter and Miriam lurched through it, slammed it behind them. Price heard pounding on their side. He pushed the door and it didn't move.

Wedged. They were resourceful animals, he had to give them that.

Not that it mattered. They'd driven the wedges in tight, and the metal door was heavy and solidly mounted, but it only took a few blows to smash it down.

When it crashed off its hinges, Miriam squealed. She and Carpenter stood at the edge of the roof, perhaps looking for another way down. As far as Price could tell, there wasn't any.

He stalked out into the night air, the moon tinting his steam and silvery skin pink. Miriam suddenly sneered, snatched her little automatic out of the back of her pants. He was surprised again when she leveled it at Carpenter.

"Don't kill me!" she croaked. "I'll work for Vasquez! I'll draw a card too!"

Another nice try. But his clients wanted her dead, so that was that. Killing arm cocked, he continued to advance.

"Don't do this," Carpenter pleaded with Miriam.

"Fuck you," she told him. "We're finished, and I'd rather be a live devil than a dead person. Shit, who am I kidding, I'm a devil already anyway. I killed Grace. I killed my baby. I killed somebody else's daughter back there in your stinking church.

"I just want to enjoy one more thing as a human being. I want to blow your ass away, because you murdered Grace too."

Carpenter sprang at her. She fired three shots and he fell.

She hastily set the gun at her feet. Its textured grip glowed with her blood. "See?" she called out to Price. "I'm on your side. Don't you see?"

A final pace brought him into striking range. He thrust his spikes at her eyes, then something scraped behind him.

He whirled, lashing his arm in a horizontal arc. But Carpenter lunged in under the blow, drove his forearm into his midsection. He didn't even feel it, but it cost him what was left of his balance. He reeled backward, the treacherous bitch tripped him, and he plummeted over the edge of the roof.

The lights beyond the borders spun round and round. The black asphalt surface of Thirtieth Street rocketed up at him.

32

PRICE HIT THE pavement with a prodigious crash. His right arm and leg snapped off, bounced, and clattered away. Tom peered down at the flattened, steaming wreckage until he was satisfied it wasn't moving.

At last he turned from the foot-high parapet. Now that they were suddenly safe, he felt dazed; it seemed as if he ought to say something, but he couldn't think what. Oh, well, he was still so cold the words would have gibbered out in an unintelligible stammer anyway.

Miriam shivered, rubbed her chest with her wrists, her hands bent back so she wouldn't scrape their raw inner surfaces. "I wish I could have shot you," she said after a while. "Did you think I was going to?"

"For about half a second. Then I caught on."

"So why'd you jump at me? It startled the shit out of me."

"I was trying to make the act look convincing. Do you feel up to hiking back down the stairs? Not that I do, not really, but we have to keep moving."

"Why?" she sneered. "Do you think that if we hurry, we might still be able to save your wife? She's *dead*, asshole. We murdered her too."

Something twisted inside him. "They'd want us to finish Vasquez and Steven before anyone else gets hurt."

Some of the anger went out of her face. "I know. Look, I shouldn't have said what I did. Maybe Becky is still alive." She stooped, tried to grip the automatic, hissed and snatched her hand away. "Fuck! I don't know if I can make myself do this."

"I'll get it." He picked up the gun, engaged the safety, and dropped it in his pocket, then they slowly tottered to the stairs. His shoe clinked against one of the chisels he'd used to wedge the door.

"For what it's worth," he said as they reached the second-floor landing, "I'm pretty sure that girl had bled too much to survive. And I imagine she was grateful that you put her out of her misery."

"Why don't you tell that to her mother," Miriam growled. "If you have to yak at me, yak about something practical. What do we do now?"

"Hm. Bandage your hands. Search this store thoroughly to find everything useful. Take tools and break into that pawnshop, get more guns. Then try again to sneak in close enough to attack Vasquez and Steven by surprise."

"They aren't idiots, you know. Judging by the way we walked into their trap, they're smarter than we are."

He pushed open the door to the store, flicked on his lighter and limped over to inspect the items in a glass display case. "We'll find some way to nail them." He sounded a lot more confident than he felt.

She shuffled forward through the shadows to crouch beside him. "Well, maybe. We do seem to have our share of luck."

He straightened, moved over to the shelves on the wall, discovered some machetes in a niche at waist level. He pushed one into the cloth scabbard hanging at his side. "If this is luck, I'd hate to see misfortune."

"We're damn lucky Price is dead," she replied. "He jumped out of the choir loft and your bedroom window, and those drops didn't hurt him. Frankly, I never really thought the longer fall would kill him either, even if you had brains enough to realize you were supposed to shove him over the edge. It was just one last thing to try."

Tom shivered. Suddenly he wanted to rush to the door and verify that the metal body still lay shattered and inert in the middle of the street.

Grimacing, he shrugged his trepidation away. Then something hummed, and a chill rose from the darkness at his feet. Cold, hard fingers gripped his ankle.

33

A SICKISH-SWEET BURNT-MEAT odor hung in the air. Gasping and whimpering, her clenched hand encrusted with rivulets of yellow wax, Grace fought the candle. Her quivering arm abruptly yanked it under her scarred, blistered breast, the tip of the golden flame just touching her skin.

Steven tittered, and the tendrils looped at his crotch rustled together. Semen spurted from the heads of his jutting Y-shaped penis.

When the black woman finally managed to jerk the candle away, its fire went out. As she rekindled it against another still burning on the mantelpiece, Willie's strings urged him forward.

Cold wet substances, blood, bits of the nurse's insides, and Mrs. Carpenter's puke, squished under his bare soles. Arriving at Grace's side, he reached toward a candle of his own.

And slipped the tip of his index finger into the luminous teardrop surrounding the wick.

Mrs. Carpenter thrashed till her warts subdued her.

For a second, his finger didn't hurt at all. Then it blazed with an agony more excruciating than he'd ever realized simply physical pain could be.

He couldn't even try to resist the compulsion to hurt himself the way Grace was doing, because if he tried, he might succeed, and if he broke Steven's domination while he or his white-blond puppet was paying attention, it would blow his only chance for freedom.

He just had to take it.

The burning went on forever. He bit his lip bloody to keep

from screaming, certain that if he did scream, he'd lose control.

At last, when the pain had filled the world and his thoughts had all but dissolved into craziness and terror, the pressure in his mind receded. His hand instantly snatched itself out of the fire.

In a way, it almost didn't matter; his blackened, smoking finger hurt like it was still roasting. He tried to pop it into his mouth, but his strings tugged again before he could.

Somehow remaining obedient still, he pulled the candle from its holder. Then his hand slowly dropped toward his genitals.

It was too much. He *had* to resist this time, even though it would destroy their only hope. *I'm sorry, Mrs. Carpenter*, he thought.

The flame dipped past his belly button. He focused his will.

The thing on the roof screeched. Rafters creaked.

Steven turned toward the window, and Willie's tendrils halted his motion. His hand froze in front of his downy pubic hair.

Discovering he could twist his neck, the boy looked out too. He hoped he'd see an army of rescuers charging across the grass.

A half-second later, he sobbed.

Silhouetted against the fiery shell of Holy Assembly, two vapor-shrouded figures advanced toward the house. The tall, slender woman in the lead staggered; the broad-shouldered man behind her shoved her along. He marched stiff-legged, a huge, spiked ball of a right hand swinging at his side.

"All right!" Steven crowed. "Way to go, Price! I didn't expect him to bring one back alive."

Willie glanced at the blond guy. He was still alert, still gazing at his fellow marionettes. Well, what difference did it make? With Miriam captured, and Reverend Carpenter no doubt dead, no rescue or diversion would ever come. His finger still throbbing, the pain impairing his concentration, he struggled to regather his mental strength.

Captor and captive had nearly reached the front steps. The metal man's hair and face glinted.

The boy decided he was as ready as he'd ever be to try to drop the candle and rip the warts out of his scalp. He wondered if he'd succeed, and if he did, what parts of his body the bullets would hit, and how it would feel.

Then he noticed.

Price's eyes were pits of shadow, not glowing at all. His body didn't whir, and his right arm never flexed, simply dangled.

Willie's knees buckled; his stomach felt hollow. He'd almost committed suicide when help was only a few feet away.

He prayed that they could cross the remaining distance before anyone else penetrated the Reverend's disguise.

The beast perched on top of the house shrieked again. Willie flinched, sure it was about to swoop down, but it didn't. Miriam cringed too, but Reverend Carpenter didn't react in any way.

"Is Carpenter dead?" Vasquez called. Without breaking stride or looking up, the impostor nodded stiffly once. Evidently the real Price might have answered in the same way, because the old man said, "Nice work."

The Reverend pushed Miriam up the concrete steps. She stumbled across the stoop and into the doorway.

The clown sat up straighter. His horns bobbed. "Hello, hello. Welcome to—"

The redhead's eyes flicked around the room, locked on Grace. Her features suddenly beamed with incredulous joy, then contorted into a mask of utterly undaunted rage. Even before she fumbled under her jacket, it was obvious to anyone who could see that she wasn't a prisoner at all.

Willie wanted to scream. She'd dropped her act while the clown was looking right at her, when she didn't even have her bloody-bandaged hand on her weapon. What's more, she was blocking the entrance, with Reverend Carpenter still outside.

The pale-blond puppet fired at her; his bullet punched into the jamb. She whipped out her own gun, a huge automatic, not the little one she'd used before, but her hand seemed to spasm and she dropped it.

The thing on the roof cawed, a deeper, even louder sound than before. Huge wings beat.

Grace and Mrs. Carpenter convulsed. Willie strained to act too. Fear and sickness surged through him, washing away the bridge between intent and body. His arms merely twitched, then locked at his sides. His hand clamped down on the candle, sending a fresh pulse of pain shooting up his finger.

And Steven hadn't even glanced in his direction. Apparently the warts had immobilized him automatically, without the clown making any conscious effort at all.

Maybe Willie had been kidding himself. Maybe he wasn't anywhere near strong enough to break free.

Reverend Carpenter drove into Miriam, knocked her stumbling forward onto her knees, then spun aside out of the doorway. The puppet's second shot burned over her head and on out into the night.

A shadowy hulk as big as a limousine plummeted into the yard.

Willie struggled again; dread and nausea blasted his mind apart. He retched, wept, mewled.

Damn it, it wasn't *fair*! He knew the terror and illness were just feelings, that they couldn't really hurt him, so he ought to be able to ignore them. But his fingers still clutched the candle; his arm hadn't even jerked violently enough to snuff its flame.

Price's arm slipped from its sleeve, banged down on the floor, and rolled clanking away. The Reverend's real hand whipped out from under his raincoat grasping a pistol as large as Miriam's, the pinkness of its skin arresting under the silver face.

He fired at the white-blond guy, who fired back; both shots missed. Then Mrs. Carpenter wailed and lurched at him, floundering, hands raised.

At the same instant, Grace blundered at Miriam, kicked her automatic spinning away, and threw herself down on top of her.

The Reverend clubbed his gun at his wife's head. She ducked, then rushed him, moving faster now, the warts in complete control. He struck again. The pistol barrel caught her on the shoulder, jarred her back, but simultaneously a tendril detached itself from her scalp and whizzed through the air to crack across his cheek.

He gasped, stumbled back across the gory hearth rug. Pouncing, she bore him to the floor, grappled his shooting arm, and pummeled.

Meanwhile, Grace straddled Miriam, punching and scratching, ripping at her hands whenever she could. A bloody-tipped string-wart slipped out from behind her ear, swayed, then undulated down toward the redhead's temple.

The white-blond guy stepped toward the couples writhing through the filth on the floor, revolver leveled. Steven laughed.

Willie imagined his mom spending the rest of her life alone in this hell. He remembered all the things the clown had done to him. He *savored* the pain beating in his fingertip, hoping that that agony could somehow overshadow the anguish his strings produced. Then he strained again.

Terror, sickness, *helplessness* crashed over him, sucked him down into chaos. He choked, couldn't breathe; his heart pounded so hard he *knew* it was tearing itself apart. He kept struggling away.

And still only whined and twitched.

The puppet with the revolver crouched, swung his weapon up to hit the Reverend over the head. The pastor tried to point his own gun, but Mrs. Carpenter kept his hand pinned.

The strand jabbed under Miriam's skin. She convulsed, then went limp.

Someone chanted a one-word prayer: "God! God! God! God! God!" Eventually Willie realized it was a voice in his mind.

Then his fingers slowly straightened. The candle slipped from his hand and plopped down on a hunk of ravaged flesh.

No time to yank out his strings; besides, he didn't dare give Steven a second's warning. Shuddering and uncoordi-

nated, still awash in dread and illness, but, for the moment at
least, no longer controlled, he dove.

Miriam's automatic had skidded all the way into the dining room, but Price's limb lay just a few feet away. He
grabbed its forearm with both hands, then wrenched himself
to his knees.

The creature outside the front door shrilled. The clown's
head swiveled, horns flapping.

The boy jerked the chilly length of metal up, hammered
its spikes down at the tendrils winding about the floor.

One split in two, then another. Blood sprayed from the
severed ends, and Steven screamed.

Unfortunately, Willie hadn't broken any of the strings
running to his own head. The cords lashed around him,
jerked him completely off the floor, and slammed him down.
His right leg snapped below the knee, a shard of bone stabbing through the skin. Then the coils shifted, squeezed; in a
second, they were going to mash his skull and chest.

Except that now the other marionettes were flopping like
rag dolls. Reverend Carpenter tumbled his wife off, leaped
up, and knocked the staggering white-blond man aside.
Then, switching his gun to his left hand, he whipped a machete out from under his smoldering coat, and slashed.

The clown shrieked again; red spurted from all five of his
suddenly abbreviated right-hand warts. The coils crushing
Willie relaxed.

Steven surged out of the recliner and hurled himself at the
Reverend, the candles splashing his monstrous shadow up
the wall. His three uncut strings tore loose from their puppets, flailed.

Reverend Carpenter shot twice, then lunged to meet him.
A tendril whipped through his hair, leaving it standing in
stiff silver clumps, and he chopped.

The clown's head sprang backward like the lid of a jack-
in-the-box. Gore showered over the minister's arm.

As the corpse crumpled, the winged beast screeched. His
heart hammering, Willie twisted toward the front of the
house.

But the creature wasn't attacking, just pawing the ground

and bouncing around. Too big to fit through the door, apparently it lacked the intelligence or the inclination to stick just its head or a leg through, or knock down a section of wall.

The young man with the pale blond mane gurgled and collapsed, then sprawled motionless. The caked blood on his inner thighs and the flayed triangles on his arms and torso were as black as onyx in the gloom.

Footsteps thudded. The ridges on his colossal form squirming like maggots, Vasquez lumbered onto the landing at the top of the stairs.

Pistol grasped in both hands, Reverend Carpenter started shooting. Mrs. Carpenter yanked the tendrils out of her raven curls, scrambled for the gun in the dining room. Grace snatched up her fallen revolver. The tatters of her bandages sopping red, Miriam attempted to fumble a second automatic out of her jacket, but her fingers would hardly bend, and she dropped it. Willie's leg began to throb as fiercely as his finger, but for the moment, he was too excited to care. He rolled toward the redhead, grabbed her weapon, aimed the way she and the Reverend had taught him, and fired.

A hole burst open above the old man's gaping navel. He blinked; then, evidently concerned primarily about his ability to keep his balance on a staircase that was too narrow for his bulk, he carefully set his foot on the top riser.

More wounds exploded, in arms, thighs, around the pouch in the middle of his white-haired chest and across his immense, sagging belly. Still undeterred, his chisel-fanged, impossibly wide mouth sneering, he continued his deliberate descent.

By the time he was halfway down, Willie was all but sure they couldn't hurt him. If he'd had two good legs, he might have run.

Then a bullet ripped away the top of Vasquez's left ear, and at the same moment Mrs. Carpenter darted to the side of the staircase, crouched, and fired.

Vasquez grunted and doubled partway over, clapped one hand to the side of his head and the other to the injury beneath his wobbling overhang of stomach. Another shot splashed his right eye out of its socket.

He squealed, grimaced, and retreated up the stairs far faster than Willie would have imagined he could. Reverend Carpenter hesitated an instant, then charged after him, Mrs. Carpenter, Grace, and Miriam at his heels. Out in the yard, wings thrashed.

The pursuers sprang to the top of the steps, disappeared down the bedroom hall. More shots rang out, and something crashed.

When they stalked back into view, glaring, mouths twisted, muscles still tight, Willie knew that the flying thing had carried Vasquez away.

34

TOM SUCKED IN a deep breath, let it out slowly. Gradually his body unclenched, and his frustration loosened its grip. All right, the war wasn't over, but at least Steven was dead, and, miraculously, Becky, Willie, and even Grace were still alive. He ought to count his blessings.

Sticking his Auto-Mag back in its shoulder holster, he turned toward his wife. Her misshapen nose, the rusty stain beneath it, and the fresh red trickle dripping down from her temple raised a lump in his throat. He took her in his arms.

She hugged him tight. "I was never so glad to see anyone, but you're freezing my ass off," she murmured after a while. Her words came out too nasal.

He tried to match her jesting tone, but his voice sounded choked. "Anyone ever tell you you talk like a cartoon character? Actually, now that you mention it, I'm freezing myself too. We stuffed the coat with dry ice from that ice company on Twenty-ninth." He shrugged the fuming garment off and dropped it on the floor.

"And padded the shoulders and painted yourself silver. Nice disguise." She embraced him again. "I was so afraid you wouldn't be able to kill him!"

"Well, it wasn't easy. We had to knock him off a five-story building, and even after that, he sneaked up on us again. Fortunately, he finally died before he could do any more damage.

Miriam hugged Grace as best she could without using her hands or touching the other woman's breasts. Grace kept shuddering, started to cry.

"It'll be okay," Miriam said. "I know it hurts like hell, but we'll fix you up."

"It *does* hurt, but that's not—I did terrible things. I *betrayed* you."

"Nobody cares about that. We know you couldn't help it."

"He was *dirty* and he was in my *mind.* Every time I tried to push him out, he—" She crumpled. Sobbed.

Miriam rounded on the Carpenters. "You can grope each other later. We've got injured people here."

Becky nodded, turned toward the bathroom. "I'll dig out the first-aid stuff. Tom, you go on downstairs."

He did, though it was hard to leave her side. She probably felt nearly as violated as Grace; she was just hiding it. He realized he was *glad* he'd had to kill Steven and Price, and glad it would almost certainly be necessary to kill Vasquez too.

The white-blond man sprawled near the foot of the stairs. Tom stooped, held his hand before the puppet's mouth and nose, then pressed the side of his neck. As he'd expected, there was no respiration or pulse; perhaps it was his imagination, but the body already felt cooler than living flesh.

Willie lay bloody, bruised, and shivering in the center of the filthy living room floor. "How is he?" the boy asked.

"Gone," Tom replied. "How are you? Hurt anyplace I can't see? Does it feel like anything's broken inside?"

"I don't think so."

"Then you'll be as good as new." He overturned a dining room chair, stamped it till a leg snapped off. "But you'll need a splint."

"We never got a good look at the flying thing. Was it . . . bad?"

He tore strips from the old baby-blue blanket Becky kept folded over the back of the couch. His hands left red and silver smutches. "Pretty bad. It was big, and, as near as I could tell in the dark, part dragon, part hornet, and all decayed." The long walk across the grass, under Vasquez's eyes and the creature's four glimmering, faceted orbs, had frayed his nerves to shreds.

Willie's mouth twisted. Tears, shining bronze in the fire-light, oozed down his cheeks.

Tom dropped to his knees beside him, flicked a length of tendril away from his leg. "Hey, hey. The worst is over."

The boy shook his head. "We blew it."

"No, we didn't. Thanks to you, we won one heck of a battle."

"It doesn't matter. Vasquez got away, and from now on he'll have an *army* of devils protecting him. You'll only have Mrs. Carpenter fighting on your side; the rest of us are hurt too bad. And just two people haven't got a chance."

"You're probably right." Tom bent to inspect the broken leg. "But I intend to find some reinforcements."

35

AN HOUR LATER, washed, dressed, and bandaged, they headed down Bougainvillea. The drummer thumped out his monotonous cadence, and, somewhere behind them, a creature howled. A pair of shadows darted across an intersection a couple blocks ahead.

Tom limped along carrying his grubby old duffel bag in his left hand and the Auto-Mag in his right. Despite two scrubbings with turpentine, silver still tinged his face and streaked his hair.

Willie hobbled awkwardly on an adult-sized crutch. Grace and Miriam shuffled glassy-eyed with pain, fatigue, a triple dose of Extra-Strength Tylenol, and the Mateus the redhead had discovered in the kitchen cupboard.

Becky brought up the rear, poised to catch the black boy if he fell. It grieved her to watch the three invalids exert themselves, but they'd insisted on coming along.

Actually, she felt like an emotional invalid herself. Waves of fear and sickness kept sweeping through her mind without any warning whatsoever, as if Steven still had tendrils stabbed into her scalp.

In a sense, he'd raped her, and it would take time and work to recover, but she couldn't afford to think about it now. For the moment, she had to put it out of her mind, try to rejoice that at least she and Tom were alive, and concentrate on killing Vasquez.

Tom turned in toward the burnt-out building he'd told her about. Movement flickered in some of the shadowy windows. Then something flashed and popped on the second floor; the bullet cracked against the sidewalk several feet in front of them.

"Isn't that lucky," Miriam said sardonically. "Some of them already have guns."

"Go away!" a male voice quavered.

"Hello, Alan," Tom called back. "Is your girlfriend safe? Is she in there with you?"

After several seconds, the skinhead answered, "Yes."

"Glad to hear it. We—"

"Go away! You know what Vasquez would do if we took you in."

"We don't want to be taken in. But I have something to say, and unless you shoot me down in cold blood, I'm going to say it. I'd appreciate it if you'd show yourselves, so I won't feel like I'm talking to the air."

Becky fancied she heard them muttering, a sound like vermin rustling in the walls. Eventually heads slipped into view, and a moment later, three males came through the doorway, scraps of broken wood crackling under their feet. Alan gripped a board with rusty nails sticking through one end; the rangy, ponytailed teenager in the cobra-patch vest had a pistol; and the chunky, fortyish black man in a filthy white suit and matching tasseled loafers was carrying an empty fifth. The latter pulled back his sleeve, exposing his watch. "You've got two minutes," he said.

"Fine," Tom replied, pitching his voice so the people in the windows would hear him too. "I'll begin by reminding you of what you already know. Howard Vasquez promised that if you stood aside while he tortured and murdered his 'special enemies,' he'd let you live, leave the power and water on, keep the creatures beyond the borders, and ultimately return you to earth. And so you did.

"But Vasquez isn't holding to his end of the bargain. The electricity's gone. He's killed a lot of people who never had anything to do with the Corona Coalition, his own doctor among them. And you must have seen demons flying, loping, and crawling in from the south and east, all headed in the general direction of his house."

"Not everybody did what Vasquez ordered," the black man said. "*They* helped you."

"True enough. *Three people*, one of them a child, dared to defy him. That, such as it is, is his sole justification for breaking his word and committing further atrocities against an entire community, not that I think he actually felt he needed any excuse at all.

"Surely now you see that he'll never send you home of his own free will. He *is* home, and you're his playthings and his cattle, to torment and devour for as long as you last."

"And even if you managed to avoid him," Becky added, "how long do you think you could survive here?"

The gang member scratched his chin, rasping stubble. "You have to admit, she's got a point. Without power, the food in all the refrigerators will spoil." His lips twitched into a momentary smile. "Not that we were all that crazy about the idea of walking the streets to get to the refrigerators in the first place. And if—hell, *when*—the pipes go dry, we'll have to get our water from the river. Let me tell you, I saw the shit in the river, and you *don't* want to mess with it."

"I don't want to mess with Vasquez either," the black man said. "In case you've forgotten, some dead friends of yours already tried it."

Tom said, "We tried it too."

He unzipped the duffel bag, lifted out Price's arm, and brandished it over his head. People gasped, and the silvery skin flashed crimson in the moonlight. "We killed the metal man." He dropped the limb to clatter on the sidewalk, then hauled out Steven's head by one of its horns. "We killed Steven." He tossed the head away, held up two Tarot cards. "Here are the demons that possessed them, caged and helpless." Slipping the grubby pasteboards into his jacket pocket, he displayed a ragged-edged chunk of cartilage. "Finally, here's a piece of Howard Vasquez's ear. As you can see, he's not indestructible either."

"Okay," the black man said, "it's good they're dead. And it's interesting to know that *maybe* the old man can die too. But it doesn't mean we'd have a chance in hell if we attacked dozens—fuck, maybe *hundreds*—of monsters. How do you know that all of *them* can die? You don't, just like you don't *know* that Vasquez won't send us home eventually, or that the government or somebody won't rescue us if we just sit tight."

"You gutless cunthead—" Miriam began.

Tom raised his hand and she subsided. "You're right," he said, "I can't guarantee that if you fight, we'll win, although I think the five of us have demonstrated that it's possible. And I can't see the future, so I'm not certain that some miracle won't deliver you even if you won't lift a finger to help yourselves, although any reasonable person would agree that it's unlikely.

"But let me ask you this: how did you *feel* when evil threatened you and you knuckled under? When you agreed that if only it would spare you, it could destroy any other human it cared to molest."

Alan frowned. "We never said—"

"Your actions spoke for themselves. Were you pleased with yourselves afterwards, smug that you'd closed a deal that would keep you safe while others suffered?

"I doubt it. I suspect that each and every one of you was ashamed that he'd given in to fear. And that you still despise yourselves right now.

"So here's a second chance to do the right thing. If you don't take it, you might live a few days, even a few weeks or months longer. Who knows, maybe you'll even get back to earth and live to be two hundred. But it won't be a lot of fun, if you flinch every time you look in a mirror.

"The Bible's got it right, folks. Life's precious, but someday you're going to lose it no matter what. It's more important to hang on to your soul."

"Fuck it," said the teenager. "If we *can* kill 'em, what else do we need to hear? I got me some brothers to revenge."

"I'll help!" a woman shouted from above.

"It's crazy!" the black man said. "We're not soldiers!"

"I'm scared too," Alan told him, "scared shitless. But everything the Reverend said is right."

The black man grimaced, slumped. "Okay, fine. If everybody else is going too jump off the cliff, I might as well do it too."

The teenager slapped him on the shoulder, then turned back toward Tom. "What do we do first?"

"Form squads to collect weapons, cars, and recruits; send scouts to watch Vasquez's house."

The kid nodded. "I'm on it."

36

THE WALL AND the three-story mansion inside it shown dull yellow and bloody orange, phosphorescent fungus burgeoning on the brick. Gargoyles and chimeras, no two alike, swarmed along the top of the enclosure, the roof, and the gables. They sent up a hissing, shrieking, bellowing clamor, audible even above the roar of the engine, as soon as the lead vehicles rounded the corner.

Tony, the Cobra who'd accompanied Alan and Laurence, the black man, onto the stoop of the burnt-out building, had insisted on driving the school bus. He jerked the gearshift, grinning mirthlessly. "They're almost as hard on the ears as they are on the eyes."

Tom and Becky sat on the first seat to his right. Tom wanted to answer, but couldn't think of anything to say.

"Bet they smell like shit, too," Becky said. She studied her assault rifle one last time, no doubt reminding herself exactly how it worked.

Two flying creatures, one with iridescent feathers, the other with shredded, useless-looking monarch wings, leaped off the wall. Some of the other Cobras leaned out their windows, fired wildly. The fliers swooped over and vanished.

The Peterbilt tractor pulled ahead as planned; its job was to ram down the nearer gate. Bimanual beasts pelted it with missiles, a couple discharged flare-muzzled weapons resembling blunderbusses, and one breathed a jet of blue flame. The truck hurtled on regardless, and slammed into the center of the wrought-iron grille.

The gate ripped away from its mooring. The Peterbilt rolled over it, came to a stop twenty feet up the semicircular drive. Devils raced across the grass, poured over it. Tore at the doors and battered the windshield.

A blue Ford pickup, its cargo bay full of men who claimed to be good shots, sped through the opening next. The sharpshooters were supposed to concentrate on bringing down fliers, but they didn't get the chance. Nimble as gibbons, apparently indifferent to the spray of bullets, a pair of demons, one long-armed and hunchbacked, the other tailed and crested, pounced off the wall down into their midst.

The bus raced toward the gate, another stream of azure fire licking across its hood. Everyone but Tony fired out the windows. The flame-breather toppled backward, and Tom wondered if he was the one who'd hit it.

As they flew through the breach, the roof thudded. A beast with an amorphous, black-furred body and a simpering Kewpie-doll head swung itself down into Tom's window, pinning his shotgun barrel against the frame. Segmented, saw-toothed tentacles stabbed in.

Becky's rifle barked beside his ear. The creature squeaked and fell away.

The next vehicle in their convoy, a rusty Buick Regal flying the Cuban flag and the Stars and Bars from its antenna, plunged through behind them.

All the gunners on the bus shot at the beasts clambering over the tractor, but they didn't stop to find out if the driver and his partner were alive. Their job was to penetrate the house.

Since the Peterbilt was blocking the drive, Tony swerved between two palms onto the grass, then careered on toward the brownstone's front entrance. The bus jolted, running over demons. Struggling to hold his gun steady, Tom drew a bead on the centaur-thing galloping along beside them smashing at the door.

He fired, and it dropped beneath their wheels; a colossal shadow swept across the yard. Slimy bat-wings beating, putrescence oozing from its thorax and six spindly legs, the flier that had borne Vasquez away from the parsonage landed in front of them.

"Eat shit," Tony rapped. The engine growled louder.

The creature crouched motionless, eyes gleaming, stinger cocked to whip forward like a scorpion's. Tom squeezed off two rounds, then hauled his upper body back inside and braced himself.

Becky sat back down beside him, touched his thigh, gripped the square of sheet metal that separated their seat from the steps. "Move, motherfucker!" Tony said.

It didn't; either it didn't understand how hard the bus would hit it or it was so determined to block their approach that it didn't care. Tony finally wrenched the wheel, too late.

Metal crashed, then glass. As the windshield exploded inward, Tom and Becky slammed against the barrier.

He must have been stunned, because suddenly she was shaking him. He raised his head to see a heaving mass of decay jammed into the space where the glass had been; its thrashing rocked the carriage and its stench was nearly enough to choke him. Its barbed stinger was still impaled in Tony's chest, sticking out the back of his seat; apparently it couldn't pull it out. But its two remaining eyes blazed, and its mandibles clacked open and shut above the dashboard.

Tom glanced out his window. Demons were rushing toward the bus. If the humans didn't get out fast, they'd have to stay bottled up inside.

He raised his shotgun, pulled the trigger, found that it was empty. He dropped it, drew his pistol, and fired twice. The faceted orbs burst into jelly and tatters; the struggling subsided to quivers and twitches.

He tiptoed forward, reached for the door control. The beast's head jerked, spattering him with rot; the serrated mandibles snapped at his skull. He ducked, yanked the lever, scrambled back.

The creature started thrashing even more violently. Afraid it would wriggle further inside, they retreated. "Everyone out the back door!" Becky yelled.

The other humans groaned, cursed, stumbled to their feet. Bubba pressed his hand to the gash in his forehead. Laurence hoisted up a Cobra who was too dazed to walk.

When everyone was off, they dashed for the brownstone, those who were still more or less intact dragging the more seriously injured ones along. Devils charged with kamikaze ferocity; the humans shot and shot and shot until they fell.

The first-floor windows were shuttered, the heavy oak door undoubtedly locked. A Cobra who was probably only a year or two older than Willie produced a hand grenade, pulled the pin, and threw.

The blast shattered the door, blew chunks out of the pillars at the corners of the porch; splinters flew through the air. Tom and his companions ran on, and six more demons surged in pursuit.

The Regal roared up the drive and cut the demons off, ground the two in front beneath its tires. A hail of machine-gun fire dropped the rest.

Nothing seemed to be waiting, but Laurence and Bubba discharged a few rounds into the foyer anyway. Then, gasping, they all staggered inside. Tom was pleased to see that more patches of luminous mold encrusted the wallpaper, carpet, and ceiling; if it was flourishing throughout the house, they might not have to bother with the flashlights.

Two Cobras positioned themselves at the end of the vestibule, where they'd see anything approaching from further inside the building. Everyone else reloaded.

As he fumbled with the Auto-Mag, Tom peered back out the doorway. The Buick, still guarding their rear, obstructed his view, but as near as he could tell, the rest of the convoy was holding its own. A couple of vehicles were burning, and a few others sat inert, overrun, but most were still fighting. The majority of the devils couldn't attack at range, so gunners ensconced in moving cars were difficult for them to contend with.

Too bad he and his squad couldn't drive through the mansion.

"It sure was a bitch getting in here," Bubba said. "I hope the old bastard isn't really out there running around on the lawn somewhere."

"No, he's in here," Tom replied. "He isn't especially afraid of bullets, but he's not inclined to get seriously shot up when his slave-creatures can do it for him; otherwise, he wouldn't have fled from the parsonage. He's probably directing them from a third-story window, where he can see well and communicate easily. So if everybody's ready, let's hit the stairs."

"A few of us aren't in good enough shape to continue," Becky said.

He grimaced, a bit ashamed that he hadn't realized that himself. His nerves were crawling; suddenly he was feverish to press on, to win or lose, live or die, but have the fear and pressure over. "You're right," he told her. "I'm sorry. Kate and . . . Greg? Greg. You stay with them. Everyone else, come on."

An expensive-looking porcelain vase sat by the foot of the staircase; a Cobra casually swatted it off its stand. Bubba took his hand from his forehead and wiped it on his jeans, swore when the wound started bleeding again.

They climbed three abreast. When they were halfway up the first flight, something trilled, then crooned. A moment later, several huge, plump, eyeless worms rather resembling someone's intestines oozed off the second-floor landing.

Tom tried to aim at them. His pistol barrel seemed to wink in and out of existence, as though it were swinging in strobe light.

The effect was so fascinating that he goggled. By the time he wrenched his eyes away, the worms had wriggled down the top three risers.

As he sighted, he noticed the way the scarlet and golden fungus-light rippled along their bodies, seeming to pulse in time to their song. The sheen and the music were so lovely that he was almost sorry he had to shoot them.

But he did, so he tried, and almost pulled the trigger before he realized his arm had fallen to his side. It tingled as if the circulation had been cut off, and when he attempted to lift it, it rose in slow motion.

The lead worm plopped onto the step just above his feet. Since he couldn't quite manage to point the Auto-Mag at it, he decided he ought to jump back. But now his legs were numb and balky too.

The creature reared and nuzzled at his shin.

Then several guns cracked. The worms splattered into mush, emitting a fecal smell.

Tom snapped fully awake. Shuddered. "Whoever shot them, particularly the one that was about to eat my leg, nice going."

Becky smiled. "You're welcome."

"How'd you guys break free? I was as good as paralyzed."

"You forget, some of us have had experience with hypnotic voices." She gestured toward the top of the stairs. "Shall we?"

They reached the third floor without anything else molesting them. A row of mold-blotched doors, all closed, cut-glass knobs glinting ruby and topaz, ran along each side of the railed central stairwell. Gun-blasts, inhuman cries, and the rumble of engines, the sounds of the battle outside, murmured through the hall, strangely muted. A textured miasma, seemingly compounded of a number of simpler stenches, fouled the air.

"What now?" Laurence asked.

Tom led them to the right of the stairwell. "The fight's in the front yard, so Vasquez has to watch from a window on this side of the house. Start checking rooms, but be careful. I'm sure he kept some demons on guard up here."

A swarthy Cobra with a wispy goatee reached for a doorknob. Before he touched it, the door snapped inward, and a yammering beast like a gaunt, furless bear flailed out at him. A burst from his Uzi cut it nearly in two, but as it collapsed, a spider the size of a cat leaped over it onto his face. He reeled back, struck the banister, and flipped over.

A second later, all the doors were jerking open. More demons, deformed shadows in the dim red and yellow light, lurched out.

The ensuing fight was a deafening cacophony of gunfire, shouts, and screams, a maelstrom that bashed the combatants back and forth. Tom barely had time to snatch out his machete before a semihuman thing with a snake growing out of its sternum tried to grab him.

He sidestepped, hacked a chunk from the side of its neck.

It didn't bleed or seem to notice, so when it lunged again, he chopped at the writhing serpent. When that neck broke, it went down.

Another manlike creature, this one squat and bandy-legged, with yellow, six-inch claws and a hide of leathery-looking plates, sprang in to take its place. He slashed at its arm, connected, but the blade glanced off.

It dodged to his right, so he turned with it. Saw Becky.

She was a few feet ahead, at the periphery of the battle. Eyes shining, raven curls flying, blood from a shoulder wound staining a dark circle on her shirt, she shot a beast with quills, clubbed a gauzy-winged monkey-thing out of the air. A huge hand with a squirming pink ridge in the center of its palm stretched out of the doorway behind her.

When Tom opened his mouth to yell, the clawed beast spat green liquid in his face.

Suddenly gagging, blind, his eyes on fire, he snapped off three shots. Then the creature slammed into him and carried him down to the floor.

A moment later, when it didn't rend him, he knew that at least one of the shots had hit it. After a second, his vision began to return.

Trying to roll the demon's carcass off his chest, he found himself tightly surrounded by kicking, stamping legs. He killed a spurred thing to make room to stand.

By the time he struggled to his feet, Becky was nowhere in sight.

The world still a blur, tears streaming down his cheeks, he fought his way forward. Something with talons raked him across the ribs before he cut it down.

Beyond the doorway, plastic airplanes hung from the ceiling. Model sports cars, toy soldiers, a baseball, and an out-fielder's glove perched among the volumes on the bookshelves, and an elaborately landscaped electric train setup adorned the long table on the right-hand wall. Once, no doubt, the room had been Steven's playroom.

Now, sheets and blobs of fungus sprouted everywhere; bloody, broken skeletons and partially eaten corpses littered the floor. Vasquez gazed out the gabled window, chewing noisily, Becky squirming helplessly in his grasp.

He turned when Tom entered. His ear was still torn, but he'd grown a new eye, larger than the old one, crimson with a diamond-shaped pupil. "Nice to see you again, Reverend. I was hoping we could finish this face to face."

Tom gripped his gun in both hands, aimed. "Our side's winning. Even if your demons clear the hall, more of our friends will charge into the house any second. Let Becky go and send us back to earth."

Vasquez chuckled. "For a moment, I thought you'd lost your mind. Then I realized you can't see past me." He stepped away from the glass.

Tom stared, stricken.

A long column marched up the street, scores of armored lancers astride hideous mounts at the fore. Behind them loped hundreds of beasts afoot and at least a dozen vehicles like huge, artillery-bearing beetles.

"The boss of the land across the river has come to help me," the old man continued. "Your rabble hasn't any chance at all."

Tom sighted down his pistol barrel again. "Could be he's arrived too late to do you any good," he said.

Vasquez shrugged. His cicatrices wriggled. "I doubt it. As you've discovered, I'm difficult to kill. I really do think I'm the one in a position to dictate terms, so here they are.

"If you surrender, we'll spare anyone else with brains enough to do the same. Becky too.

"If you don't, we'll slaughter each and every idiot who followed you, in the most excruciating manner possible. I'll kill your wife this instant, while you stand there plinking away with your popgun."

"Shoot him!" Becky screamed.

He knew he had to, and so she was going to die, just as the cards had foretold. He sobbed and squeezed the trigger.

All four remaining bullets hit their mark, annihilated Vasquez's other, human eye, shattered his brow, and blew brain out the back of his skull.

The old man roared, dinosaur jaws gaping, and hurled his hostage aside. Her head cracked against the edge of a shelf.

As she fell, he strode forward, arms outstretched. Tom dropped his empty gun and lunged.

Vasquez grabbed his shoulder; pain sheared into his flesh. When he wrenched free, he saw that the ridge in his enemy's palm had opened into a maw, the ruddy lips and massive incisors speckled with his blood.

Vasquez swung his other arm. Tom dove in underneath.

All the old man's scars ripped open. He toppled, and as he did, his body melted. Suddenly there was nothing like a human form to grapple, just an onrushing avalanche of meat.

It smashed over Tom and engulfed him, squeezed him like a giant fist. Countless mouths worried at his flesh. Sightless and suffocating, nearly delirious with agony and terror, he wormed his hands through churning folds of protoplasm.

Centuries of anguish later, he found a sac that might be Vasquez's chest pouch. Dug his fingers inside.

Whatever else it was, it was another maw, a biting weapon nearly as formidable as Vasquez's original set of dragon jaws. Rows of jagged fangs gouged into Tom's wrists.

He screamed, gasped for air, gulped in a mass of flab instead. A mouse-sized set of teeth chewed at his tongue.

He groped once more, extending his arms, exposing fresh expanses of skin to the gnashing tusks. Eventually he encountered something that felt like a rectangle of slimy pasteboard.

He snatched, and it slipped away. It took several fumbling seconds to locate it again.

When he attempted to tear it, it seemed to thicken and stiffen, till it felt like a sheet of plywood. The mouths bit even more savagely.

Tom tried to shriek once more. Choked. Knew he could have only moments of consciousness left. He *pulled*.

The Tarot ripped in two.

His cocoon clamped down in spasms, then its crushing pressure eased. The mouths stopped snapping, screeched, fell silent.

He thrashed feebly, certain he was too weak to burrow

free. But Vasquez's bulk was already decomposing into slime and lace, and it only required an instant to drag himself clear.

He retched out deliquescence, gasped in air. Blinked and peered about.

Blood gushed from his myriad bites, spurted from his ravaged forearms. Becky lay twisted and motionless, her face in a crimson pool.

Gunfire, screams, and caterwauling still echoed in the hall. Outside, the first lancers cantered into the yard.

Tom had prayed that killing Vasquez would return Corona City to earth, banishing the demons in the process. But it hadn't.

So he turned back to the old man's body, rooted to find the pouch again. He was dizzy, freezing, his extremities numb. The stink of corruption and the reek of a destroyed Tarot hung around him, so sickening it was a torment just to breathe.

Black spots swam at the corners of his vision. The room spun; then suddenly he was sprawled across the corpse.

Somehow he managed to sit back up, dug again. Scooped away another handful of pink sludge. Uncovered the Tarot box and a folded piece of paper.

Intuition prompted him to examine the paper first. It turned out to be a map of the district with a line drawn around the border. Giggling crazily, he ripped it in two.

The world blazed white. For a moment, he thought lightning had struck the window. Then, when no thunder boomed and his eyes began to adjust, he saw that the sky was a radiant blue.

In the hall, the sounds of conflict waned and died; shouts of triumph and amazement took their place. Outside the mansion, fliers crashed to the ground. Some demons collapsed, some burst into flame, and others froze till the humans shot them or ran them down. Most of the army from beyond the river simply faded away, dissolving or retreating into their own realm.

Tom fell supine; it occurred to him that he was about to bleed to death. Not that he hadn't realized before, but then he'd been struggling so frantically that he'd more or less forgotten again.

He didn't mind. If Becky was gone, he'd be glad to follow.

A woman with a bruised, crooked nose and tousléd black curls bent over him. Heedless of the blood streaming down from her hairline, she yanked off her belt and looped it around his arm.

"Beck?" he whispered.

"I told you not to believe in that fortune-telling shit."

37

WHEN THE DOCTOR made rounds he told them they could have visitors. Bubba rolled through the doorway shortly thereafter, growling when his wheelchair caught on the jamb.

Tom wanted to sit up straighter, but he still felt so tired, sore, and feeble that he just couldn't bring himself to make the effort. "Hi. How are you?" he wheezed.

"I'll be a lot better when I can walk out of here," Bubba replied. "I never broke a leg or had to be in a hospital before. I hate it. How are you doing?"

"All right. They saved my right hand."

"And—?" Bubba nodded toward the blanked-shrouded form on the other bed.

"She'll be fine too. The medication just makes her sleep a lot of the time."

"Should I take off? I don't want to wake her."

"Unless you're planning to set off some high explosives, I wouldn't worry about it. Look, nobody's told me anything. Do you know how many we lost?"

"Twenty-three in the attack. The cops and rescue people're still finding bodies, but they estimate that maybe another fifty died around the district, murdered by the Vasquezes, mauled by devils, burnt in fires, whatever."

Tom closed his eyes and shook his head. "Dear Lord. So many."

"It's pretty bad," Bubba agreed, "but it would have been a lot worse if not for you. I talked to a bunch of people from church, and we still want you to be our pastor. We'll tell the Regional Council the same thing if they give you any crap."

"Are you kidding? I caused all this."

"It was an accident, wasn't it?"

"Sure, but—"

"The way we see it, you did wrong when you messed with magic, but we did just as wrong when we caved in to Vasquez. We can forgive you if you can forgive us."

"Of course I forgive you. But I didn't expect this, and I'll have to think about it before I'll know what to say."

"Just say yes."

"You can tell I want to, can't you? But I have to finish sorting out my feelings about God. About myself, too. I killed people. It was necessary, but that didn't make it right.

"For what it's worth," Tom went on, "I can tell you that Becky and I have talked, and even if I decide I don't belong in the ministry, we plan to stay in Corona City, to help rebuild Holy Assembly, take care of the people Vasquez hurt, and revitalize the area the way our Coalition originally intended.

"Once a bleeding heart, always a bleeding heart, I suppose. I have a feeling I'm actually going to start enjoying the work again."

Miriam appeared in the doorway, an orange-juice stain on the front of her hospital gown and her hands encased in inflated plastic balloons. "Don't be an asshole," she said. "Stay in the clergy. Not only do you belong there, you'll have serious job security. No matter how bad you fuck up, you'll look good compared to the way you performed before."

Tom grinned. "Gosh, Red, encouragement—of a sort— from you? You must have been injured worse than I thought."

She looked down at her slippers; for a second, he half suspected she was blushing. "No, I wasn't. Things just seem . . . different."

"Oh, yeah? How so?"

"Well . . . you Holy Rollers talk about being born again, and I guess a lot of people would like to be. Maybe if you fight your way through Hell and make it out the other side, you *can* be. When I woke up this morning, I realized I felt a little, I don't know, *cleaner*, like I'd proved myself or paid a debt. Of course, I am doped up. But maybe I can finally say goodbye to my daughter, and stop being so goddamn angry all the time. Stay out of the life, finish school, and go on to business college or something.

"Look, I'm going to run. The dermatologist is supposed to see me in twenty minutes, and I'd like to visit Willie before he comes. I tried before, but he was talking real serious to his mom and dad, and I didn't want to interrupt. Tell Becky I said she snores like a rhino." She vanished down the hall.

Bubba shook his head. " 'Finish school'; it sounds strange to hear somebody talk about normal life. But I guess it shows the weird shit's really over."

"I guess," Tom agreed, but he knew it wasn't. Not for him.

38

TOM'S PINKIE AND ring finger crawled, the maddening itch he could never scratch. The doctors called it a phantom-limb sensation, and promised it would go away eventually.

Becky took a deep breath, put her hand in her coat pocket with her pistol. Green light glinted in her shiny hair. "Ready?"

"No." He kissed her. "I love you. And now I'm still not ready, but I'm as good as I'm likely to get." He gripped the brass handle, pulled open the door.

The curtain hung there once more. They listened, heard nothing, pushed warily through.

Overloaded, rickety bookshelves; candlelight; shadows; floating dust tickling his nose. No lingering odor of burnt flesh, and no blackened cadaver crumbling on the floor. The *bontanica* looked just as it had the first night he'd seen it. He jumped, but wasn't truly surprised when the cartomancer stepped out of nowhere.

"Good evening, Mr. Yale," Becky said.

The little man beamed. "My goodness, no one's used that name in ages. But I daresay it's still appropriate. What's left of him does comprise a significant portion of myself."

Tom swallowed. It would seem strange, almost surreal, to talk affably with the creature who'd cursed him and his entire community, but it would be a lot better than provoking him. "It's been months," he said. "We were afraid we wouldn't be able to find our way back."

The cartomancer smiled. "Even if I hadn't cared to see you, the deck would have opened the path. I must confess, I'm surprised the authorities let you have it back."

"The first people who were debriefed said a lot more about devils and endless night than they did about Tarot cards. When they got to me, I claimed that when I talked about Tarots, I was only using them as a metaphor, whatever the heck they thought that meant.

"We found out pretty quickly that public officials hate things they can't explain. Force them to deal with a mystery like a community that, from an outsider's point of view, is perfectly normal one instant and a disaster area the next, and their primary concern will be to hush it up and pretend it never happened. After their scientists tested the cards and didn't find anything, they were glad to give them back. It put them one step closer to closing the book on the whole affair."

"Do you know *why* we came back?" Becky asked.

"I can surmise," the little man said wryly. "Because I hinted that this is the only place in all the worlds where the deck can actually be destroyed."

Tom slipped his hand in his coat, making sure the cards hadn't somehow vanished. "Are you going to let us?"

"Now, that's a good question. Perhaps I should hurl fire at you, as I did at that greedy lout who accompanied you last time. Ah, but you soaked the pack in kerosene or something similar, didn't you? If I burned you, I'd kindle it as well."

Tom shook his head. "Do you know everything?"

The cartomancer chuckled. "Alas, no. But I have a keen sense of smell, and I caught a whiff of the fumes.

"I'll tell you the truth," he continued. "I can't even *attempt* to stop you. Even the dark kingdom observes rules of engagement, a system of sanctions and strictures, bizarre and haphazard though they are. Having vanquished its agents and returned of your own free will, in this place, at this moment, you're dominant.

"But are you *sure* you want to destroy the cards? What if I could teach you to control them completely, the way I did when I walked the earth? Think of all the good you could do, if you recovered the High Priest's gifts of healing and persuasion without the side effects."

Tom snorted. " 'Get thee behind me.' "

"Don't be too hasty. You thirsted for the miraculous. Discard it now, and I doubt that you'll find it again."

Tom squeezed Becky's forearm. "I bet I'll find it every day."

"Well, then, consider this. If you destroy the source of my magic, you might destroy the bridge that links my home to yours. I don't imagine you want to stay here forever."

"*Is* that what will happen?" Becky asked.

"Frankly, I don't know."

"I guess we'll just have to risk it."

The cartomancer grimaced. "Drat. I must say, it makes my predicament even more galling, understanding full well that I have only myself to blame. If I hadn't released more than one or two cards at a time, we never could have seen such a fundamental shift in the balance of powers. But you can't play the same game for centuries without growing bored. Then you raise the stakes, change the rules."

Becky brushed a curl away from her eye. "What's going to happen to you?"

"I compelled seventy-eight spirits to serve me. Now it will be my turn to serve them. Much of my bondage is likely to be painful; some of it, I hope, will at least be interesting." He laughed. "Dear lady, the concern in your face! You mustn't feel sorry for me. I certainly never felt sorry for you."

Tom said, "I don't understand you at all."

"Good. Every intelligent man needs enigmas to ponder." He swept a stack of books off the top of a shelf, raising a cloud of dust and clearing a space. "Spread them out here if you like; then I'll do the honors."

Tom took out the wooden box, dumped the pasteboards, fanned them. The Nine of Cups was in one piece again.

He and Becky kept their eyes on Yale, alert for an attack or an attempt to whisk the cards away. But the avuncular little man just stood there smiling.

When Tom put the can away, he glanced at a candle. A blob of flame floated up from the wick, drifted through the air. "I'd step back, if I were you."

The instant the spark touched down, the deck exploded, a

dazzling burst of heat and stench that nearly blasted Tom and Becky off their feet. The fire spread with ghastly, unnatural speed, consuming much of the shop in the first few seconds, books, shelves, display cases, jewelry, jars, bottles, flooring, walls, and ceiling all burning as eagerly as the cards. The cartomancer remained in place, chortling as tongues of flame licked up his suit, seared his cheek, and set his hair ablaze.

Becky stared, fascinated. Tom grabbed her and spun her around. They scrambled through the drape, the door, out into the middle of the street. Stopped and looked back.

Tom expected the building to contain the fire, at least for a little while. But the moment he turned, it flared like a flash-bulb, ceasing to be a structure anymore. A crackling wall of blue and yellow flame swept toward them, feeding on the pavement as readily as it devoured everything else.

They wheeled again, sprinted toward Aragon Street, gasped for air, and sucked in smoke and embers. The conflagration roared at their heels, blistered their backs, lit the night bright as day. Buildings on either side blazed up, then crumbled.

Tom was aghast. A firestorm like this could incinerate the entire city. He was terrified that he'd saved his parishioners from Vasquez only to massacre them himself.

He tripped over a bump, fell headlong. Flame surged up his soles. Becky whirled, yanked him up, hurled him forward; he staggered the last few steps onto Aragon.

And suddenly the world was cool and dark. By the time he turned, the storefronts had shifted; the *botanica*'s street was gone.

Becky panted, finally caught her breath. "Some people never learn," she said. "For a while, when the three of us were chatting like best buddies, I thought we might make it through the end of this without having to run our butts off. Do you think we really destroyed the cards, or did he trick us somehow?"

Tom pulled off his smoking shoes. Considered. Smiled. "I think they're toast."

EPILOGUE

He believed it, and nothing ever happened that convinced him otherwise. But in his dreams, that night and many a night thereafter, he wandered through a city, sometimes New York, Miami, London, Paris, or some other place he recognized, more often one he didn't. Wherever he found himself, eventually he turned down the same narrow street, entered a shop with a green light over the door.

Inside, a jolly little man greeted him cordially, proffered a pack of filthy, malodorous cards. He didn't want to draw, but did it anyway.

Just as he touched them, he always jolted awake, then lay sleepless, his stump and scars aching, till dawn.